SHAMELESS

SHAMELESS

A Novel

Taslima Nasreen

Translated from the Bengali by
Arunava Sinha

HarperCollins *Publishers* India

First published in India in 2020 by
HarperCollins *Publishers*
A-75, Sector 57, Noida, Uttar Pradesh 201301, India
www.harpercollins.co.in

2 4 6 8 10 9 7 5 3 1

P-ISBN: 978-93-5357-799-5
E-ISBN: 978-93-5357-800-8

This is a work of fiction and all characters and incidents described in this book
are the product of the author's imagination. Any resemblance to actual persons,
living or dead, is entirely coincidental.

Taslima Nasreen asserts the moral right
to be identified as the author of this work.

Typeset in 11.5/15 Adobe Garamond at
Manipal Technology Ltd, Manipal

Printed and bound at
Thomson Press (India) Ltd

MIX
Paper
FSC FSC® C010615

This book is produced from independently certified FSC® paper to ensure
responsible forest management.

To women – who are not only unashamed of showing their faces,
but also have no fear of what others might say

Author's Note

I wrote *Besharam* or *Shameless* in Bangla in 2017, when I was living in a flat in 7 Rawdon Street, Kolkata under police protection. The state government was putting pressure on me to leave West Bengal. The police would keep coming and telling me that an Islamic terrorist outfit was going to make an attempt on my life, and that the state government would not be able to give me protection. It would be best if I were to leave the city, the state – indeed the country.

I had lived in Europe for over a decade after I had to leave Bangladesh, and was now settled in Kolkata. I would roam about freely around Kolkata, in the Muslim areas and elsewhere; not only had there never been an attempt to assault me, but I don't remember anyone even speaking a rude word to me. I did not believe that there was any plot hatched by Islamic fundamentalists to murder me; this seemed to me to be the state government's ploy to get rid of me.

Where would I go leaving my home in Kolkata behind? Which country could I call my own? The carpet had been snatched from under my feet quite a few times in my life, but I don't think I've ever known despair like I felt then, when I thought I would have to leave Kolkata and go away – for Kolkata and West Bengal were my last refuge.

I turned a deaf ear to the advice of the state government, and dug my heels in. It was then that I started thinking of Suranjan, the central character in *Lajja*. How different was his plight from mine? Suranjan had had to leave his native Bangladesh, just like me. And now, separated from near and dear ones, with no country to call my own, would I have to leave Kolkata and Bengal, the city and the state I had come to love? Did Suranjan feel the same way when he was driven to exile? How was he these days? He too was now in Kolkata, wasn't he? I imagined what Suranjan's life today would be like. He wasn't well, I thought. Like me, he was in exile; perhaps our hurts and heartaches were alike as well.

That was when I decided to write a new novel about Suranjan and his family, whom I had written about in *Lajja*. In the new novel, alongside my fictional creations, I too would be a character, in my real self.

Lajja was a political novel; *Shameless*, its sequel, is not, and deliberately so. It is a novel about society, about the interplay of religion, caste, class, gender, and about human relationships. It is a story based on complex psychological currents, but told in a simple way. I wrote it in one inspired burst. The walls were closing in around me then, there was a threat looming around every corner. A political conspiracy was afoot to kick me out of Kolkata. And in my room, all alone, I was writing – to the terrible sound of solitude broken only by long-drawn sighs.

I did eventually have to leave Kolkata and Bengal, and I had to leave empty-handed. The draft of *Shameless* was left behind in the Rawdon Street flat with all my other belongings. I was able to retrieve some of these belongings a few years later. By then I had forgotten all about the novel I had written – the sequel to *Lajja*. Quite recently the PDF of the novel surfaced among my papers. It has been published now in Hindi as well as Bangla – and HarperCollins is now publishing it in English, translated by Arunava Sinha.

I was distraught when I wrote *Shameless*; my characters in *Shameless* are quite distraught too. But even as I was being targeted by the dirty politics of the subcontinent, I tried to keep my characters away, as much as possible, from the effects of that politics. Thus Suranjan, who was so politically aware in *Lajja*, has grown completely indifferent to politics in *Shameless*. In fact, he has developed a deep hatred for politics – the politics of religion and divisiveness that takes away those close to us, makes us homeless, and destroys our peace of mind.

My heartfelt gratitude to HarperCollins Publishers for bringing *Shameless* to a wider English readership.

New Delhi, April 2020   Taslima Nasreen

One

I met Suranjan quite unexpectedly. He rang the bell one day at my Rawdon Street flat, and I opened the door to find an unknown young man. 'Whom do you want?'

'You.'

'Me? Why?'

'It's urgent.'

'That's not good enough. Why are you here, where have you come from?'

He scratched his head, or maybe his hand, I don't remember, but he did scratch something. He didn't seem particularly confident.

'You can't just turn up out of the blue to meet me. Make an appointment on the phone.'

I shut the door in his face. From the other side, I could hear him say, 'I'm Suranjan, Suranjan Dutta. Open the door, I need to talk to you.'

Suranjan Dutta. The name seemed familiar, but not the face. Maybe I would recognize him if I took another look at his face – it was with this thought that I opened the door and surveyed him from head to toe. One moment it was like I had seen him before, and the very next, no, this was the first time.

Smiling awkwardly, he said, 'I'm Suranjan. Don't you recognize me? You wrote a novel about me.'

'A novel?'

'Yes, a novel. You called it *Lajja*. Don't you remember?'

I trembled. This was probably how it would feel if I found someone I knew to be dead walking up to me. I'd just stand there like a fool, rooted to the spot, frozen. As I was doing now, gazing at Suranjan, who alternated between looking at me and lowering his eyes and scratching his cheek. Yes, scratching his cheek. I remember, because he had a large mole, and every time his nails grazed it, I felt the mole would come off. Thinking of the mole made me stop trembling. I had been apprehensive about moles for several years now. A friend of mine, a Frenchwoman, had a tiny, innocuous mole on her hand which spread everywhere, I don't know how, to become cancerous. When I was young, I used to yearn for a mole on my face, no matter how small; I would even draw one just above my lips, a little to the right, with a kohl pencil. But now the sight of a mole anywhere terrified me. It was Suranjan's mole that unfroze me. I opened the door fully, inviting the stranger in.

The two policemen sitting outside the door with guns were not exactly asleep, but they didn't bother to frisk the person I was ushering in for hidden bombs or bad intentions. I didn't actually know why policemen were stationed outside my home, for they didn't question any of the numerous people who visited me. I had opened the door myself today, but usually it was Sujata who did it. Although she had been told not to open the door to strangers, she didn't always remember, brought up as she had been in a village where houses weren't locked. My intercom hadn't worked in two years. The maintenance committee of the building couldn't care less, no matter how much I complained. Completely unknown people had often marched past the policemen into the house while they napped, their guns on the floor.

Did Suranjan seem jittery at the sight of the policemen? So it seemed. His face was pale. I asked him to come in, which meant passing between the sitting policemen and me. This made him hesitate, and led to some additional scratching of the mole. His second step was more hesitant than his first, and the third, even more so. The fourth, however, brought him to the door, from where he shot inside.

The door closed behind Suranjan, and he sat down on the sofa. Asking Sujata for some tea, I sat down opposite him, in response to which he lowered his eyes again. It occurred to me that the heart is a strange thing, and it appeared to me that I had heard Suranjan say this. What if it was someone else claiming to be Suranjan, here with nefarious motives?

It was time to exchange how-are-yous. But I jumped to my feet before we could get there and opened the front door again – not wide – and left it ajar. If the person claiming to be Suranjan had evil intentions, this would remind him that a pair of policemen was stationed outside and would rush in to rescue me from an assassin if I so much as whimpered. It would also give him the opportunity to reflect on the usually macabre outcome for a terrorist or a criminal in such circumstances.

'So, how are you?' I asked.

Suranjan took his time to speak, and his head seemed to droop even further. He had greyed – how old was he now? I calculated in my head. He was younger than me, though not a great deal younger. I had greyed too. The years disappear in a flash from one's life; nothing else vanishes quite the same way. How had mine gone away from me? One day I suddenly found a bunch of grey strands when I looked at myself in the mirror. I didn't even recognize myself, was it really me? Even the other day I had considered myself a girl.

'How do you suppose?'

When our eyes met, he looked familiar. Had I met him before? Suranjan had nothing to tell me about how he was. What was there to say anyway? It would make more sense if I told him instead how I was, and so on. And I continued wondering when and where I had met him.

'Tell me, have I ever...'

'No, you've never met me.'

'Is that possible? We must have met. How could I have written the novel otherwise?'

'You heard the story. Kajal Debnath is my friend; you knew him too. He told you my story.'

'But I went to the house in Tantibajar where your family lives. Didn't I meet you there?'

'No, not me. You met my mother. I got home exactly seven minutes after you left.'

Seven minutes. I laughed.

'Such a precise memory.'

Suranjan smiled and nodded. 'Do I have a choice?'

Every time our eyes met, I felt I had set my eyes on his before, though I couldn't remember where or when. But Suranjan was denying it; we hadn't met, he kept insisting. If he remembered that he made an entry seven minutes after I had left, he would certainly have remembered if we'd actually met.

He didn't seem particularly enthusiastic about telling me how he was.

Sujata brought the tea, with crackers on the side. It's an old practice in my family to serve crackers with tea, but I've noticed no one eats them – all they do is drink their tea. Suranjan dunked a cracker into the tea and bit into it. These crackers reminded me of home. Baba would bring something or the other home for us every night, and crackers would always be a part of it. As a child, I never saw Baba at night without crackers. He brought them without fail, wrapped in brown paper. I was so sick of eating those crackers that I'd be depressed every time he came home with them; I'd be furious with him too. I wanted other kinds of biscuits – sweet ones, cream biscuits, anything other than crackers. And now, caught in an existence thousands of miles away from that life, it is the cracker than I lovingly pick out from among all kinds of delicious biscuits. I don't know what it's called, this act of picking it.

I was consciously addressing Suranjan with the informal 'tumi' instead of the formal 'aapni'. I think that was how I had addressed him when I met him. I have forgotten many things over these past years, including everything to do with meeting a young man named Suranjan. Not even a remote memory about the date or time of the meeting has remained.

'So you came to this country in '93. That's a long time.'

Suranjan nodded.

'Yes, a long time.'

'My exile has lasted thirteen years and yours has lasted fourteen.'

I realized I'd made a small mistake. I corrected myself quickly.

'Actually, I'm the one in exile, not you.'

Suranjan smiled. An enigmatic smile.

I was keen to find out what kind of life he led now. He was an honest, sincere, idealistic young man who had been led astray; that was as far as I knew. I felt nothing but pity and sadness for him, just as I do for the Taliban. The difference between them and Suranjan was that they had been offered no alternative to fundamentalism. And, while Suranjan had indeed turned communal, he had had the option of taking a different route. In fact, he now looked like the idealistic young man he once used to be. It hadn't occurred to me all this time that he had changed, that he had become small-minded. Now that I remembered, I felt compassion for him, what we call maya. And that reminded me of Maya. She wasn't here any more, she had been murdered and her body flung into the lake. Suranjan must have suffered very much, and his mother, even more so. Kiranmayee. I wanted to ask if his father Sudhamay Dutta was alive, but I didn't. Instead, I asked where he lived.

A faint reply.

'Park Circus.'

'That's not far.'

'Yes, it's quite near.'

'Who else lives with you?'

This was how I posed the question instead of asking directly whether Sudhamay was alive. I've noticed in my own life that I am caught on the wrong foot whenever I'm asked, your father is alive, isn't he? Most of the time I change the subject without answering the question, as though I never heard it. And if I'm forced to answer, I change the subject after saying something along the lines of yes.

Suranjan answered.

'It's just my mother and I.'

'Your mother and you?'

I echoed him, knowing that I was doing it. In fact, I repeated what he had said just to absorb the fact that his father was dead. And that Suranjan himself had not married, for there would have been a wife in that case. Or perhaps he had married and they had separated.

'How's your mother?'

This was probably a better question than the previous ones.

Is your father dead? How did he die? You must be in trouble now that he's gone. What about money?

I realized that thinking about the questions I had wanted to ask, but didn't, inevitably led to the question of money, at which point I no longer suppressed it. It emerged like a sparrow slipping in through a crack in the door.

'What do you do? Do you have a job? Or a business or something? What do you do for a living, I mean.'

Wringing his hands defensively, Suranjan said, 'Nothing much at the moment. I coach students.'

This was undoubtedly bad news. I could not imagine how he was surviving without a job. I realized I couldn't be spontaneous with Suranjan, possibly because I simply hadn't been able to accept the fact of his shift towards communalism. I wouldn't have had a problem if a security threat had driven him out of his country. But the hatred that he had flung at everyone when leaving had shaken me. It's quite possible to be full of hatred for fundamentalists or even the government; all kinds of reasons can be cited. But I have grave objections if it is aimed at ordinary people, for any and every person simply because they're Muslim. I believe that an individual can be honest and generous irrespective of whether they're a Hindu or a Muslim.

'Have you been staying here for long?'

It was Suranjan who asked the question this time. It relieved me in a way. Sometimes, entertaining a guest means firing a barrage of questions just to keep the conversation going. Here, it was the guest who had rescued me from this awkwardness.

Leaning back in my sofa and gathering a cushion in my lap, I answered, 'Yes, quite a while now, nearly two and a half years.'

'You had a visa problem; has it been sorted?'

'I'm getting a residence permit. They renew permission every six months.'

'No progress on citizenship?'

'None.' Whenever I say this, I've noticed, I add a sigh. Since there was nothing else to say, I said the inevitable: 'You seem to know everything.'

'I read the papers.'

'Why did you suddenly want to meet me?'

'I've been meaning to for several years. You used to visit Calcutta sometimes from the foreign countries you lived in then. You stayed at the Taj Bengal each time. It wasn't as though I didn't have the courage to meet you. It was more a matter of being unsure.'

'Unsure? Why?'

Instead of answering, Suranjan said, 'So you'll be here for some time now.'

My reply was measured. 'Yes, that's right. This is where I live. I'll be here as long as I have permission.'

'But you do travel?'

'Yes, I go to Europe or America for various programmes, but I always return to Calcutta.'

I didn't particularly want to talk about myself. I'd rather listen to what Suranjan had to say. He lived in Park Circus – an area that, so far as I knew, was populated largely by Muslims. And Suranjan, who was a staunch Hindu, had chosen to live there. I couldn't reconcile these facts.

'Why don't you come over one of these days? Ma talks of you often. She feels bad for you.'

'Feels bad for me? Why?'

'She says your plight is because you wrote about us. That's why you were expelled from your own country.'

Asking Sujata for two more cups of tea, I replied, 'I wasn't sent into exile because I wrote *Lajja*. The government had banned the book anyway. The religious fanatics were furious with me because I criticized Islam. All religions are a roadblock to women's freedom – the fanatics and the religious-minded couldn't accept this.'

I had brought up religion intentionally. Since Suranjan had been converted to religious fanaticism himself, he needed to know that my views about religion had not changed. Let him grasp the fact that I wouldn't sway from my ideals just because I had become a victim of political persecution.

The balcony was flooded with sunlight now. My cat Minu was asleep on her back in the rocking chair. The potted plants were shooting up. I usually left the glass doors leading to the balcony open; it made the drawing room seem larger. If only there was a view of the sea from the balcony, or perhaps a mountain. I've seen many maddeningly lovely scenes in nature; I've been face to face with much that is beautiful in the world. But nature alone cannot be fulfilling, I need people, people.

Should I have counted Suranjan among those people? Would I feel the urge to see him again? When I looked at him, though, I felt sympathy instead of anger. What a devastating storm he had been through! I had barely managed to write about any of it.

'The fact is that I didn't want to make up things about you or your family in particular. I relied more on factual information, because I wanted to write a book based on facts.'

Suranjan offered me that smile of his again.

Remembering suddenly, I told him, 'Many people got asylum abroad because they were named in *Lajja*. Many Muslims adopted Hindu names so that it would be easier to get asylum. I'm certain more than one person named Suranjan Dutta has got asylum. You could have, too. But then you probably wanted to come to India…'

His eyes were locked on mine. He may have realized that I was trying to say that he had considered India and not any other country for refuge because he was a Hindu, that all fundamentalists believe that India is the land of Hindus. And Suranjan wasn't too far from becoming a fundamentalist himself.

'I'll bring Ma over one of these days to see you.'

His shabby shirt, the torn jeans, the worn-out shoes that he had taken off, all told me that his financial situation was shaky. Was he here to ask me for money? Or a job? Even though I have no power in this regard, many people insist I find jobs for them. A number of them think I am extremely resourceful. Nor is there a lack of people who think I have so much money that I will never run out of it.

Sipping the fresh cup of tea, Suranjan looked around my room, observing the paintings on the walls with great attention, and spending a lot of time surveying my bookshelves and the fridge sticker that said 'Beware of Dogma'. The room was decorated mainly with local artefacts. Had he realized that there were no signs in the room of the many years I had spent abroad?

'Should I bring Ma?'

'Yes, of course you must.'

Placing the cup he had emptied long ago back in the tray, Suranjan suddenly said, 'I have to go now.' And at once he walked towards the door.

Helping him open it, I said, 'Are you in a great hurry?'

Suranjan both nodded a yes and shook his head to indicate a no. I didn't normally walk my visitors to the door, but for some reason I was feeling great compassion for Suranjan. Was it because he was the hero of one of my novels, or because I had been witness to his genteel poverty?

Entering the lift, he said, 'Maya wants very much to come too. Should I...?'

'Maya?'

I realized he could see the astonishment in my eyes.

'Yes, Maya.'

'Maya?'

'Yes, Maya.'

'I see.'

I felt an agonizing weight being lifted off my shoulders after a long time.

The lift went downstairs. I sat in the chair that Suranjan had occupied, leaning back and closing my eyes.

It was difficult to believe what had happened. Suranjan Dutta had been sitting in this very chair; he had said Maya was alive. I remained sitting there for a long time. It seemed to me that reality had just met fiction. Suranjan was not exactly the way I had imagined him to be while writing the novel. His appearance, his manner of speaking, the way he looked at you, even his dimensions, did not match those of the Suranjan of my novel. Although he had denied it, I felt now that I had in fact met him somewhere. He had been to my house in Shanti Bagh not once but twice. I had no idea why he didn't remember. Can anyone explain why they remember certain things but not others? We forget a great many things about ourselves that others remember, but is it their responsibility alone or should we also take some of the responsibility of remembering?

The truth was that I had spent more years gazing at the Suranjan I had modelled on the real-life person than at Suranjan himself. With the actual man having faded, the Suranjan of my imagination was the more real figure. Even though I'd met him twice, what I had come to know about him directly was far less than what I had come to know through my imagination. I had in fact conjured up a great many things about him in my head. I may not have imagined the main events, but I certainly made up the parts branching out from those incidents. For instance, when he asked Pulak for some money, it was not at Pulak's house, but in front of a shop nearby, after which they went to Pulak's place together. But in my book, I had directed Suranjan to Pulak's house first, for I had not known at the time of writing that they had met earlier on the street. In the course of my subsequent writing, I had had to reread what I had written in *Lajja*, so much so that what had happened in the book seemed to me to be truer than what had taken place in reality. For I had repeatedly thought only about what had happened in the book, not outside it.

I knew about Suranjan and Pulak meeting on the street, but because I didn't talk about it or think about it, the meeting grew blurred in my mind, and forgetfulness swept it away altogether. Maya, I had thought, had died. Who would imagine that a woman who had been found floating in a lake had in fact survived? And so two Mayas stood in front of me – one dead, her body bloated after drowning in the lake, while the other was in Calcutta, alive, sparkling. Both of them pinned me to the wall, so that I spent the rest of the day in a daze. I didn't tell anyone I had met Suranjan. The encounter remained with me as my personal possession. I didn't tell anyone that somewhere in this city was a woman named Maya who was supposed to have died but who was alive nevertheless.

Two

Suranjan didn't go towards Park Circus from Rawdon Street although he had meant to; he didn't take the metro on Park Street either although he had meant to. Walking past the planetarium, he had considered going to the Academy of Fine Arts, maybe visit an art exhibition in case there was one; but no, he didn't feel inclined. Still walking absently, he entered the maidan, settling his fatigued body in the shade of a tree with a shaggy top, the leaves swaying gently, the breeze caressing them. Taking off his shirt, which was soaked with perspiration under the strong sun and sticking to his chest and back, he lay down on the grass dressed in his undershirt. Not many people knew him in this city; it wasn't where he had been born or grown up. He was wearing a cheap watch, and had thirty rupees in his pocket. With such meagre possessions, there was nothing to fear if he fell asleep. Even a thief had more money in his pocket, a better watch too. Suranjan had been wondering if he needed a watch at all. His own answer was, no, he didn't. Time only went by, it never returned. The past would not come back even if he worshipped his watch devoutly. What was the point of wrapping it lovingly around his wrist then, considering it only went in one direction, taking him

13

along, towards a dark ravine, towards uncertainty, towards death? Suranjan felt an urge to take off his watch and toss it into a lake.

He wanted to sleep, but could not. It could have been a memorable day. Today in Calcutta, Suranjan Dutta, the hero of *Lajja*, had met Taslima Nasreen, who had become famous for her novel about him. But no one had got to know they had met today. The room in which they had conversed could have been filled with journalists. Did he want to be part of something so grand? He sensed that he did not; he knew he would be a misfit, he was a 'nobody at all' now. Those who had expectations from Suranjan Dutta, who had once imagined him to be a revolutionary, would be deeply disappointed if they saw him now. This was better, his present condition, far from everyone's eyes.

Those older days, the ones Suranjan wanted to forget, kept coming back to him from the distance to which they had retreated. He was the subject of much excitement in the beginning, soon after leaving Bangladesh, although it was limited to his neighbourhood, without attracting journalists. Only when Sudhamay died did some journalists appear from nowhere with questions. Suranjan hadn't remotely cared for their stony faces, and the flashes on their cameras had made his eyes water. He didn't know whether the news of Sudhamay's death had been published anywhere; he hadn't checked.

The newspapers were full of articles about *Lajja* those days. On his way back and forth between Calcutta and Sonarpur, Suranjan would see the book being sold every day on the train. The hawkers screamed out its name. They had only just moved to Calcutta then, and were staying with some distant relatives in Belgharia. Suranjan would go to Sonarpur often those days – a relative of a distant relative there had promised him a job. Suranjan had lived in hope for a long time. Confessing that he was the Suranjan of *Lajja* had earned him taunts in many places. He had even been beaten up once. Punched in the face, he had sported an under-eye bruise for two months.

Eventually, he had stopped talking about the book. Many had looked askance at his accented Bangla after learning that his name was Suranjan Dutta, saying that if he came from Bangladesh after Babri Masjid, he must be the Suranjan of *Lajja*. He had denied it vehemently. Who knew what might happen if he admitted it?

It was true that no one had believed him at first, but after a year or so, for reasons he himself didn't know, a few people had actually accepted that he was the Suranjan of *Lajja*. He had been called on stage at local events and felicitated. Some had even tried to find him a job. But not everyone had come to know that the Suranjan who was eking out an existence with his parents and sister in a single room in the house of a distant relative in Prafulla Nagar in a suburb of Belgharia was the Suranjan of *Lajja*. What if they had, though? Perhaps some of them would have come forward to help, or perhaps not. It wasn't as though anyone was waiting eagerly to come to the aid of destitute refugees and lift them out of their penury. As he gazed at the sky, its blue agony pricked Suranjan in his eyes like needles. He closed them.

In the afternoon, Suranjan went back home and took a nap. Two boys came for coaching in the late afternoon, and two in the evening. Twice a week, he also tutored two students separately in their homes. Suranjan was living proof of the fact that effort did not necessarily bring rewards. The family could not survive on what he earned from his coaching. Kiranmayee had managed to bridge the gap to some extent by selling saris. She embroidered designs on saris at home and made some money by selling them. She hadn't been doing it very long – it had all begun thanks to the encouragement of another woman in the same line of business. Motivated by the prospect of augmenting the meagre income of the household, she had been quite successful in her venture, and was once again able to provide her son with properly cooked meals. She waited eagerly every day for him to come back home.

As he ate, Suranjan told her: 'Ma, I met Taslima Nasreen this morning.'

Kiranmayee was flabbergasted, and then too excited to talk. Drinking a glass of water to calm herself, she finally said, 'How did you find out about her? Who told you where she lives?'

'A friend of mine who's a journalist told me. About a year ago. But I didn't go all this time. I was passing that way today; so on a whim I decided to find out what she's like face to face.'

'What did she say? Did she ask about me?'

'Of course. About you, about Baba too.'

'She doesn't know about your father, does she? How will she know.' After a pause, she continued, 'So is she going to live here alone? What do you think, will the government let her stay?'

Suranjan shrugged. 'I don't know.'

'I'm glad you got in touch with her. But I wonder what she'll think if she sees our hand-to-mouth existence. Maybe she'll say we weren't right to leave our country.'

'She didn't know Maya is alive. She was quite surprised to find out.'

'Entirely possible. She probably didn't keep track; she had to leave the country after all, poor thing.' Kiranmayee sighed. Both of them were silent after this.

Suranjan finished his meal of pui shaak and fish with rice, drinking up the dal straight from the bowl in the end. People in this neighbourhood ate their rice with dal as the first course, but Suranjan and his family stuck to their old habits. The flavour of paanch phoron stayed if you had the dal at the end of the meal.

He hadn't been born with a silver spoon in his mouth, but in a middle-class home. He had seen poor people, but had never had to share their experience personally, for he had always had a house to live in, food on the table, an environment where he could be educated. After leaving his country, though, the fangs of poverty had sunk into his skin. The relative whose house in Prafulla Nagar they had put up in was a distant cousin of Kiranmayee's: Shankar Ghosh. The arrangement was that the entire family would stay there till they found a place they could rent. Meanwhile, Sudhamay would start his medical practice; Suranjan would find a job; Maya would tutor students till she got a good job too. But although he gave them shelter, Kiranmayee's cousin had a permanent frown on his face, and lost no opportunity to inform them of the difficult times he and his family were facing. They had been given a twelve-foot-by-twelve-foot room in the yard, and they had to make their own arrangements for cooking on a makeshift stove. Shankar Ghosh's family made meat and fish for themselves in their kitchen, while the refugees had to make do with ruti and potato curry.

The very self-respect that Sudhamay had wanted to preserve when he decided to migrate out of his country began to disintegrate with every passing day after moving into Shankar Ghosh's house. Still, he refused to crumble, setting himself up instead in Shankar Ghosh's narrow front veranda with a small table and a stool to examine patients. Because he had come from Bangladesh to start his practice here, nobody quite believed he was a good doctor, or even that he was a doctor at all. Sudhamay didn't know the brand names of medicines here, so he would prescribe the generic forms of drugs and tell his patients to ask for the corresponding local brand at the pharmacy. The patients couldn't make sense of the generic names, and would ask why he didn't know the brand names if he was a doctor. He hardly had any patients – maybe five or six a day – with a fee of five rupees each, all of which he had to turn over to Shankar Ghosh as payment for board and food. Sudhamay had no savings; he had taken very little money on the journey out of his country for fear of being robbed. He was desperate to take a place on rent, but realized that working as a doctor would not earn him enough for even a small house for his family. And because he had no money, he had to depend on his practice. But the question was, why didn't he have any money? What was the point of liquidating his four-lakh-taka fixed deposit before leaving? He could neither carry so much money himself, nor transfer it through a bank. People advised him to use the hand-note system, but he had no idea whom to ask or how it was done. During telephone conversations about moving to Calcutta, Shankar Ghosh advised Sudhamay to give the four lakh taka to Gautam Saha of Narayanganj, who travelled regularly to Calcutta, where he owned a garments business. Sudhamay would get his money, with a little commission deducted, once he reached India, from Shankar Ghosh. Relying on this advice, he had handed over his savings to Gautam Saha, but Shankar Ghosh had not kept his word. He had told Sudhamay that the payment would be made not by him but by Pratap Mandal, who ran a business in Bangladesh, but was currently in Bhopal, from where he would return shortly. Waiting for his imminent return, Sudhamay developed breathing difficulties. Kiranmayee brought up the subject of the money with Shankar Ghosh, who was actually her cousin's wife's sister's husband. Once they got the money, they could move out of here, she said, which would ease the problems both her family and their hosts were facing. She had been polite, she had been annoyed, but whatever her tone, Shankar Ghosh kept fobbing her off with talk about Bhopal or Bombay.

It didn't take long for Sudhamay to conclude that Shankar Ghosh had no intention of fulfilling his promise. But what could he do here in this foreign land? Nanigopal, his own distant relative from Manikganj, lived in Dum Dum. Sudhamay had made a futile request to him for a loan. Suranjan had looked for a job frantically, at a ceramic factory, at a wagon-manufacturing factory, at Texmaco, at schools in Belgharia, but without success. He had never felt so helpless. One night, he had drunk himself into a frenzy and punched

Shankar Ghosh in the jaw. 'Give back the money, you bastard, or I'll murder you right now.'

Suranjan didn't get around to murdering Shankar Ghosh. Or to murdering anyone at all. It wasn't as though he wasn't itching to kill, though. At a time when their life was almost unbearable, *Lajja* was proving to be a bestseller. Although Suranjan had stopped telling people about it, Sudhamay would tell anyone he ran into: 'It's our family that's been written about in *Lajja*.' Some would look at him disbelievingly, some would probe him for his motive, some would laugh, and some would actually believe him and make sympathetic noises, although this last lot was in a minority, and had not proved particularly helpful or beneficial to them in any way.

The inhabitants of Belgharia would turn up to stare at Sudhamay, follow him with their eyes wherever he went, gaping at him like a new arrival in the zoo. But far from going up because of this, the number of patients who came to consult him declined. All this was in the early days, when everyone had a copy of *Lajja* and was devouring it avidly. After this, Sudhamay no longer advertised the fact that he was the Sudhamay of *Lajja*. In fact, he would evade the question if anyone asked on their own. 'No, not me, must be some other Sudhamay' is how he would respond, with an indifferent air. Not that there had been no exceptions. Some of those who had believed him had brought sweets for the family, some had invited them home, many of them from neighbourhoods beyond Belgharia, chock-full of people tormented by memories, where you could still hear the flavour of Bangla spoken across the border.

Sudhamay had just the one copy of *Lajja*. Suranjan had bought several copies, one of which he had kept. He stashed it beneath his pillow, reading it whenever he had some time to spare. Calcutta had been flooded with pirated versions of the edition that had come out in Bangladesh, a slim volume, badly printed on inferior paper.

People were buying their copies wherever they could, and even those who never read books were lapping it up. The frenzy had to be seen to be believed. Sudhamay had witnessed it for himself – in the neighbourhood, in newspaper reports, in overheard conversations. Once, he read that the police had arrested a group of book pirates, and began to wonder whether Suranjan had got himself involved with all this. Several times he said, 'You must be careful, Suranjan. I don't know who you spend time with. It's a new country, we don't know too many people here, we have no friends. You'd better not get into anything dangerous. Let people do what they like with the book, you stay away from trouble.'

Suranjan didn't respond to any of this. He didn't even want to see Sudhamay's pinched, anxious expression. He wasn't going to get any peace of mind till they had a place of their own to stay. He hated going back home, where he had to sleep on a mat laid out on the floor, being bitten by mosquitoes all night. It was better to sleep on the pavement. Suranjan had chosen a city where he had no friends, no family, no one to call his own. They were surrounded by hordes of Hindu men, women and children, whom Suranjan had considered closest to himself when he left his homeland. But in truth there was not a soul to help him. Shankar Ghosh's ugly greed and atrocious behaviour, his making Kiranmayee work like a slave, the way he had grabbed their money, Sudhamay's failure to sell the assets they had left back home, Maya being raped – all of these had pushed Suranjan to the brink of suicide many times. But he had not killed himself eventually, and several years had passed since *Lajja* had been published. He still browsed through its pages sometimes; he had developed a strange relationship with it. He read about the Suranjan of *Lajja* now and then as though it were a different person whom he had nothing to do with. This Suranjan looked at his namesake from a certain distance, a certain detachment too. The truth was that despite Sudhamay's suspicion, he was not involved with those who had been pirating *Lajja*. But after his constant suffering, unending humiliation, helplessness, starvation and sleeplessness, Suranjan had in fact approached the Bharatiya Janata Party (BJP) to join them. Their people had put him on a stage, presenting him as the Suranjan of *Lajja*, felicitated him, given him flowers and sweets. Why should they be opposed to him? After all, he had declared that he was the Suranjan Dutta about whom the book had been written. None of them had doubted him. He had placed his faith in their actions and their ideology. They were the ones who had arranged for ration cards for the family, and had assured him that they would find him a job.

Suranjan had spent days on end at the party office, hearing of *Lajja* being pirated everywhere. Some people had arranged for copies to be printed in large numbers and sold as cheaply as for ten or even five rupees all over the city. He had tried his best but had not been able to identify them. He would have made fat sums of money had he been involved with the piracy, but despite the temptation, he had not been inclined to do anything dishonest. For now, he had realized that the BJP was the only one among all the political parties to speak up for the persecution of Hindus in Bangladesh, to protest against it. And so this party was his greatest sanctuary now; its members were the only ones who had come forward to try and relieve his terrible mental suffering. Shankar Ghosh's house was no refuge for him. He had found his real shelter here, in the arms of the Rashtriya Swayamsevak Sangh (RSS) and BJP workers. But Suranjan abruptly withdrew his membership on the day he had asked for a loan of five thousand rupees. He had to find a place to rent, and the landlord would ask for an advance. He would also have to buy some furniture, no matter how cheap, for the new home. Suranjan had pleaded for a loan, tears running down his face, but since no one knew how someone without a job could repay such a loan, the party workers had fobbed him off with excuses such as 'I have no money', 'I'm hard up myself', and so on.

Suranjan was thinking of those days, and was wondering whether he could possibly say all this to the author of *Lajja*. Perhaps these were the very details she wanted to hear, all the things that had taken place since they had arrived in Calcutta, what sort of life it had been. Although he knew she wouldn't write another book like *Lajja* about him, Suranjan still experienced a strange compulsion to meet her. Even if no one else in the world had the right to know the minutiae of his life, he felt that she certainly did. Suranjan decided to visit the author again. It was as though she were an old friend of his, someone he had been very close to, someone whom he was much more intimate with than with any of his other friends. What led him to these thoughts, though? Why was Suranjan impatient to disclose everything to her? Was it possible to feel such closeness to someone whom he had met for the first time, who was neither a relative nor a friend, simply on account of this one book? What she had written could be the story of any Hindu family. Suranjan's story was nothing special. Did he exist only in those printed words, was he not a flesh-and-blood person in his own right? He wanted to escape the confines of the letters in black ink; he wanted to open up his entire life to the author; he wanted to tell her: 'All you did was pack me into the pages of this book. Did you never want to see the real person? The Suranjan in your book seems like a robot to me, madam writer. You haven't said anything about his suffering, his agony, his love for Parveen, his grief at losing her, none of it, nothing at all. You've stuffed your book with facts, you've pulled a gigantic hoax under the guise of writing Suranjan's story. You have written without a heart ... A dry essay. Everything in there is copied: accounts of what was done to Hindus, a list of whose houses were burnt, who was abducted, who was threatened. Kajal Debnath supplied all the books to you, I know everything.'

Suranjan leapt out of bed in agitation. 'You didn't go around the houses to see things for yourself, or, I don't know, maybe you did. The lack of security amongst non-Muslims is something you claim you understand, but do you really? And even if you do, how much of it do you understand?'

Then he told himself, what did it matter if the Suranjan of the book was lifeless? Maybe the writer had failed to depict her hero's inner emotions, but why should that matter to him? How many people in the world knew that the practically jobless young man who lived on the dark and dingy ground floor of the crumbling house in Park Circus with the plaster peeling off was in fact Suranjan Dutta? He hesitated to think of himself as young now. Did the author know that the Suranjan from *Lajja* was not stuck at the age he was in the book? But what if she did? Why should Suranjan's age matter to her? How would it help for *anyone* to know his age, his name, his address, the story of his life? Who was he, after all? No one, really. Just a big zero. Even a blade of grass was more valuable. He had no friends in this city, and this was the greatest truth of all. Suranjan paced around his room as though in a state of delirium, saying, 'How are you, Suranjan? How have you been?' 'I've been in all kinds of situations, but the strange thing is that somehow or the other I'm still alive. And ...' 'And? And I'm very lonely.' 'Why?' 'I have no friends.' 'Did you have a lot of friends back home?' 'I did.' 'Aren't you in touch with them?' 'No, not at all.' 'Why don't you go and meet them, pay them a visit?' 'I don't want to.' 'Why not?' 'I don't know.' 'How can you not know, surely you do.' 'I feel shame.' 'You feel *what*?' 'Lajja.'

Suranjan had tutored his students, but he had been pensive throughout. Afterwards, too. He couldn't sleep till late into the night. He had given up smoking, but he had bought a packet of cigarettes today, and proceeded to smoke his way through it. Staring at the damp wall, he felt that the marks on it resembled human faces, or a house, or trees. The images changed over the days, taking on new shapes. Propping his head on two pillows, he lay back and folded one leg across the other, gazing at the wall, nothing but the wall, and smoking all the cigarettes. He finally went to bed at 4 a.m. Some nights were for doing nothing at all, for not *wanting* to do anything at all. They were nights for sighs. There were some nights that could not be explained to anyone.

Three

'Who did you say has come?'
'Suranjan Dutta,' Sujata answered.
'Suranjan Dutta?'
'Yes, that's what he said. He came earlier too.'

I told her to open the door and give him a seat in the drawing room. No one comes to my house this way, without advance notice. Things like this used to take place in my childhood, when people could visit one another's homes at any time. They would knock on the door, the unannounced guest would be given a warm welcome and served tea and biscuits and payesh. The practice had disappeared by the time I grew up, especially after I had spent twelve years in Europe and America. I live in Calcutta now, but I haven't observed it here either. No one visits anyone without prior warning. Was Suranjan continuing with old habits from back home? I wondered. He had come a week or so ago, what did he want from me again? Would I have to do all the talking today as well? Or would we just sit there in awkward silence?

I was writing on my computer. This is what I've been using for the past sixteen years to write. Abandoning my work, I went to the drawing room to find Suranjan sitting there. He was looking more energetic than the other day. He was dressed in a blue shirt with a floral pattern – I had no idea someone could look good in a shirt like that. Black corduroy trousers, and shoes in far better shape than during the previous visit. No stubble either, and a bluish tinge to his cheek. His eyes weren't trained on the floor; they were wide open. A gentle smile played upon his face. Suranjan had no gem-studded rings on his fingers or a red thread fastened around his wrist. I must say I was surprised. Here in Calcutta, everyone had a red thread around their wrist, whether they were educated or uneducated, rich or poor, an artist or a genius, a politician or a writer, a doctor or an engineer, a scientist or a pilot. The sight of a bare wrist was surprising. Did this man not believe in religion? My enquiry revealed that he did, but he hadn't been for a pujo or a religious ceremony lately. But that was the reason I had expected to see the thread, for Suranjan had gradually become communal. He had sunk from being an atheist to becoming a religious believer. This was the biggest shame in *Lajja*. The indifference of the state had ruined an entire secular, idealistic generation. Imagine a socialist like Suranjan, a follower of the Communist Party, turning into a hardcore Hindu who lumped all Muslims into a single group, othering them. Suranjan didn't forgive anyone. What about Taslima, did he forgive her? Or did she win his forgiveness because she had forsaken Islam?

Gazing at his wrists, bereft of red threads, I said, 'What's new with you? Were you passing this way?'

Suranjan looked directly at me. 'No, I came to see you.'

'I see. You don't have my phone number, do you?'

Suranjan showed no interest in taking my phone number. Still, I wrote it out on a piece of paper and gave it to him, so he was forced to accept it. But though he did it, he didn't bother to even glance at it, putting it into his pocket instead. He must have come here to tell me something.

'Tell me. How are you?'

He nodded, he was well. He didn't ask after me. In this city, I'd noticed that many people tell me how they are when I ask, but never ask about me. Nor is anyone in the habit of saying thank you. I had just given Suranjan my phone number, surely he ought to have thanked me in return. But then Bengalis believe that thanking someone amounts to demeaning them, which was perhaps why Suranjan had not thanked me. He hadn't said a word after nodding in response to my question. We would have to sit facing each other on the sofas now, which was impossible for me. Say something, or go. My expression reflected my impatience.

'Are you always so reticent, or is it just with me? You weren't the quiet sort before. Have you changed a great deal?'

Suranjan smiled. It wasn't an innocent smile. I felt explaining it would be difficult. I didn't know what to do with him. I asked, 'Did you want to tell me something?'

Suranjan bowed his head. I'm not very comfortable with people who do this. It seemed he did want to say something. I expressed my wish to meet his mother and Maya.

He lifted his eyes now and nodded. Yes, he was ready for this.

'Come, eat with me today. Do you have some time? You aren't busy, are you?'

Suranjan grabbed at my proposal. I took him to Marco Polo for lunch, where they had laid out a buffet. As he ate, Suranjan told me he had got married in '96 to a girl named Sudeshna. Both of them used to teach at a private college in Dum Dum; Suranjan's subject was history.

'And then?'

'And then nothing. We got divorced.'

'Why?'

A cold question in response to a cold reply.

There was no direct answer to this. Suranjan rose to get himself another helping. It seemed to me he had been served delicious food

after a long time, for he was eating ravenously. He took several
helpings of crab, and the waiter gave him the instrument for cracking
the shell. Using it, he said, '498A, you know. She framed me in a
case of domestic violence two years after we got married.'

I looked at Suranjan critically. This man used to torture his
wife, and here I was, treating him to lunch. I sighed. Would I
never learn; would I keep doing good things for bad people all
my life? Yes, many people had been persecuted in Bangladesh, but
was becoming communal the only way to confront communalism?
What quality of Suranjan's could make me favourably disposed
towards him? I thought about it. Nothing. In the past, he did not
differentiate between Hindus and Muslims, he judged people as
human beings, he did not believe in religion, he used to criticize
religious rituals. But that aspect of the man was history now. The
truth is that a real humanist-atheist cannot turn into a Hindu
overnight. I doubted whether he had ever been a firm and resilient
non-believer. He couldn't have been, or this change would not have
taken place. What reason could there be for my sympathy? I began
to eat quickly, planning to leave as soon as I'd finished; I even took
a quick look at my watch. Not only did my ideology not match his,
but I also shouldn't have been spending time with someone who
had tortured women.

It wasn't as though I had to accept every misconduct of his just
because I had written a novel based on the story of his life.

Suranjan said faintly, 'I did beat Sudeshna.'

I almost shouted in response, 'Admirable! A remarkable
achievement. You beat her. That night that when you abducted
a woman from the street in Dhaka and raped her, you beat that
woman too, didn't you? You're so strong that you cannot help
demonstrating your strength on women. You probably beat your
own mother too. Or do you spare her because she's your mother?'

'I was drunk that night.' Suranjan answered me calmly.

'You mean the night you beat Shamima?'

'No, when I beat Sudeshna.'

'Are you blaming alcohol?'

He was silent.

Through clenched teeth, I said, 'Don't blame everything on your drinking. It's *your* fault. Plenty of people drink; they don't beat anyone up. Didn't you have to go to jail?'

'I was in jail for a long time. The divorce came through afterwards. I lost my job too.'

'Excellent.' I breathed a sigh of relief. 'Appropriate punishment. Sudeshna is still working at that college, I hope.'

Suranjan nodded. 'She is. Her job's permanent now. We were both assistant teachers; she's become permanent now. I'd have become permanent too, if I hadn't lost my job.'

'Did you try to get a job in another college?'

'I did. In schools too. No luck. It's hard to get a job if you have a jail record. And there's no political party now to get me a job.'

To tell the truth, I savoured this information. No matter that he was the protagonist of my novel, no matter that I had known him a long time, I was happy because he had been punished for his violence towards a woman.

'Why did you hit her?' I asked in some agitation.

'Because she couldn't tolerate Maya,' replied Suranjan.

'Why couldn't she?'

Sighing, he said, 'Why isn't Maya getting married? Why can't she go away? This was her problem. She wanted Maya to get married. It didn't matter if the man was a doddering old fool or a scoundrel. I was not in favour of this.'

'And then?'

'Sudeshna and I separated. Maya did eventually get married, though.' Suranjan looked at me with melancholy eyes.

I said, 'The dessert's on that table. Help yourself. Don't you like ice cream?'

'No dessert,' announced Suranjan.

Settling the bill, I decided to get rid of him right there, at the restaurant. But when we walked up to my car, I said, 'I'm going home. What about you?'

'Would you mind if I came with you?'

'Not at all, why should I mind?'

Suranjan came home with me. I had never been in the habit of a post-lunch siesta, so I was fine. Did he want one, though? He denied it vehemently when I asked. But was there something he wanted to say, surely there was, for why would he have accompanied me home otherwise? Long ago, I wrote a story about him, about his family and social crisis. Would I have to pay the price for it now? All right, he had dropped in, I had treated him to lunch at a swank restaurant – why couldn't he go home now? I didn't want to waste my time probing him for his story. I had enough stories to write. He and his family were either comfortable here, or unhappy, like any other human being. I had no reason to write another story about them. It wasn't as though Suranjan was too obtuse to realize these things. He should understand that being the protagonist of my novel didn't give him the right to turn up at my house whenever he liked. Still I was attentive to him. To tell the truth, perhaps I was attentive to him only because he was Suranjan. But how long could I go on this way if he proved to be devoid of any sort of personality or even humanity? These were my thoughts as I sat on the rocking chair in the veranda, gazing wistfully at the sky.

The door leading to the balcony is usually open all day and night. Getting up from his sofa, Suranjan came up to my chair and said, 'I know I'm disturbing you. If you'd rather rest or have some work to catch up on, please do.'

'What about you?'

'I'll just sit here. Don't worry about me, you don't have to keep me company or play the host.'

'Is there anything you want to tell me? Why should you just sit here? Say what you have to.'

'No, I have nothing to say.'

'Well, then?'

'You want to know why I am still sticking around in your flat?'

I gave no answer. I didn't nod either.

'It's because I feel close to you.'

Who knew what Suranjan meant by 'close'? Was he under the impression he was visiting an elder sister or a childhood friend? I thought of asking, but didn't. I considered him close too. The word had a magic to it. Perhaps different people interpreted it to mean different things. I love you, I feel close to you, I cannot live without you – statements like these put pressure not just on the mind but also on the body. Mine went limp when I heard him use the word, as though all the strength had been drained out of me.

It actually took me some time to get out of my chair. I was feeling unsettled. For some reason, what he had said had given me a warm sensation. Possibly no one had ever said such a thing to me. How many people can I call 'close' to me anyway? Those whom I think of as close do not consider me close to them. I have a cousin in a distant country; she asks after me when I fall ill or when she misses me. Back home in Bangladesh, I have family everywhere, so many friends too, but none of them, even though they live so close by, only a half-hour flight away, has ever come to see me. They haven't even bothered to find out whether I'm alive or dead. So, despite my problems with Suranjan, what he had said gave me a strange sort of pleasure – there was *someone* who considered me close.

Our society does not believe in closeness. Whenever anyone fulfils their duties or responsibilities towards someone, we assume it's out of love, but actually no one does anything out of love, they do it because they don't have a choice.

I led Suranjan to a room – to my bedroom, in fact – to rest, and asked Sujata to give him tea or anything else he needed, before going into my study and lying down on the bed there with a book. My intention was to read, but after a few pages, I realized that while I may have been reading, reading every single word in fact, I wasn't really comprehending. I had merely been taking it all in with my eyes; none of it had entered my head, because of which I had no idea what I had read all this while. But why not? Because my mind was elsewhere, thinking about Suranjan. I was furious with him, but it was also true that I felt close to him. And yet I couldn't unravel the mystery of why someone whom I hardly knew, someone whom I had met and spoken to only a few times, should seem so intimate. How easily I had let a virtual stranger into my bedroom! I was certain he was no threat to me; if at all he did anything, it would be beneficial, not harmful.

Around five, I decided to kill two birds with one stone by dropping Suranjan home in Park Circus and meeting his mother Kiranmayee. Whenever I go out in Calcutta, a five-member police squad escorts me everywhere; if I go out of town, a pilot car full of policemen in uniform leads the way, its siren blaring. In the city, a police car always follows mine, with four people in it, while my personal security officer or PSO sits in my car. They put their foot down when they heard I wanted to go to Park Circus. Apparently, it wasn't safe to enter a Muslim locality, where fundamentalists could kill me at any moment. I brushed aside their objections.

'Of course not, nothing like that will happen.'

'What do you mean? Anything can happen.'

'It can happen anywhere; it doesn't need Park Circus in particular. Are you really suggesting someone's waiting there to kill me? Even if they are, that's what you're there for. I have nothing to fear, I'm not going alone.'

The police officer stood quiet.

'Besides, I simply must go there.'

Yes, I absolutely had to visit Kiranmayee at home. I had never entered a lane like that one since moving to Calcutta. It was so narrow that if a car were to stop in this lane – with shops named Great Medical Stores, Hotel Shaan-e-Firdous, Indian Cycle State and Jagannath Jewellers – leave alone a second car, not even a rickshaw would be able to go past it. The houses were decrepit, brimming over with poverty.

Garbage was piled everywhere. The uncovered drains gaped at us with their dirty mouths. I felt my skin prickling as I entered the dank lane. It was almost eerie. Kiranmayee ran up and flung her arms around me, not letting go for a long time and talking constantly: 'Maago, how are you, ma? Are you well, ma? I'm heartbroken every time I think of you, maago. It's been so long since you came to see me.' When I finally managed to ease myself out of her arms, I saw she had tears in her eyes. Was someone really crying for my sake? I had never seen anyone but my mother weep for me. My body began to give way again, while a whirlwind raged within in my heart. It wasn't as though I wasn't used to receiving love; many people showered me with their love every day in response to the courage and honesty in my writing, and I accepted it.

I wasn't sure how to address Kiranmayee. Mashi or mashima, those traditional terms of respect for elders? One of the bad habits I'd picked up from years of living abroad was addressing people by their names, which I do these days even with those twice my age. I continue with the suffix of -da and -di with older acquaintances, but I no longer use them with those I've met recently. Still, it can be uncomfortable if they glare disapprovingly because of this. So I opted to use the traditional 'mashi' for Kiranmayee.

'How are you, mashi?'

I had probably addressed her the same way when we met in Dhaka.

'Shuro must have told you how I am. Why couldn't you have come a few years ago, ma? Shuro's father used to talk about you so much, whenever there was news about you in the papers, he would keep a clipping. All he would say was, how she must be suffering because of us, having to live in a foreign land without her family, who knows how she is. He wept for you often. And look, you're here now, but he's gone.'

Kiranmayee burst into tears. I reached out and took her hand, held it in mine. Once the crying had subsided, she said, wiping her eyes, 'He would sit in front of the TV all the time, in case they had some news about you. He would be there an hour in advance when an interview with you was scheduled. There wasn't a single thing you wrote that he didn't save. He had several scrapbooks with your pieces glued to the pages. They were stored carefully in the cupboard. Sometimes he would fetch them and read them. We didn't buy every newspaper, but he made friends with the newspaper sellers and checked all of them for news about you, in every language – Bangla, Hindi, English – and always bought the paper when there was an article about you. We lived hand to mouth, but he took great care of the clippings. Never allowed dust or grime to settle. He kept saying, I'm sure she'll be able to go home soon. I placed many of his favourite things on his pyre, maago. I put the clippings too. I didn't know if he was going anywhere, but if he was, I wanted those to go with him. Not that he had too many things of his own, just things from his own country, ma. Things from his home. You wouldn't believe it, a flag of Bangladesh, his freedom fighter's certificate, he'd got someone to get him some bakarkhani from back home, he'd break off a little every day and eat it, how excited he was about it, just that old piece of bakarkhani and those scrapbooks of your pieces and news about you. What was the point of holding on to them? I put them on his breast, let him take them wherever he was going – we wouldn't be able to honour them the way he did. How happy he would have been to see you.'

Kiranmayee began to sob loudly once more. She cried for a long time, while I sat by her side, immobile. My body began to give way again; my hand withdrew slowly from hers. I couldn't say a word now, I just sat silently for a long time, tears gathering in my eyes too. Crying can be quite infectious sometimes.

I didn't want to hear elaborate stories about how Sudhamay Dutta had died. Maybe it was heartless of me not to show any interest in the person being spoken of, but the fact is that I really have no desire to learn anything about death. I want to neither talk about it nor hear about it. Let the conversation be about life, instead. About being alive.

Looking around the room, I asked, 'Where's Maya?'

'At her husband's.'

'I see. What does she do?'

This is a question I always ask whenever a woman comes up in a conversation. I really want to be told that she works, that her identity is not limited to being someone's wife or mother, that she's economically self-reliant, either employed or a businesswoman, that she works for a living. I hate hearing things like she doesn't do anything or that she's a housewife. I insist that all adult women be self-reliant, and I feel pity for those who depend on others. I even feel angry sometimes at those who take no initiative to be financially independent. There's just this one life, you live only once. There are bound to be difficulties, but that's no reason not to take risks. There will be defeats, not one but several; no one smoothens the way for women, they have to clear the path themselves.

Kiranmayee did not appear any older than the last time I'd seen her, save for a few grey strands near her temples. Physical labour usually prevents old age from claiming one's body. Because my work is sedentary, I feel I've added thirty-four years in fourteen. The fat has accumulated unchecked, and I have more grey hair than both my grandmothers. I look like a wreck. I have a double chin now, and yet, when I wrote *Lajja*, I was considered one of the most beautiful and accomplished young women in the city. My perpetually lean and slim body weighs 80 kilos now. Kiranmayee, though, looked unchanged. Suranjan had become much heavier, and yet his face belonged to a much younger man. He had grown older but his face had not. His eyes – I might have been mistaken, or not – seemed deeper. What did Maya look like? Had she changed? I didn't ask either of them this question, mulling over it myself when Kiranmayee went off to make tea.

Two rooms and a tiny kitchen – that was all there was by way of a home. There was a large bed, which was where everyone sat. Two steel cupboards, a clothes rack with the clothes arranged neatly on it, small curtains on the windows. There was an alcove in one wall with a temple-like dome, which held small idols of gods and goddesses, along with red hibiscus flowers. On the other side of the room was a table with a television set on it, draped in a red-and-yellow batik cover. The other room held a small bed, a table and a few chairs, besides a wooden cupboard and some books on a rack hanging on the wall. A helmet, too. There was no dining room or dining table; I assumed they ate on the bed. Kiranmayee spread a newspaper on it and laid out the teacups. The house Suranjan had lived in with his family in Dhaka was a much better one, their standard of living distinctly higher. Here, they could feel the sting of poverty every moment. But despite their hardships, at least they had security of a kind – they were no longer victims of the ignorance and lack of education of fundamentalists. But why did Suranjan choose to stay in Muslim-majority Park Circus instead of Hindu neighbourhoods

like Belgharia or Dum Dum? The question persisted in my head; it
made me wonder.

'A job. Not too far from here, near Bondel Gate. A drug company.'

'Good salary?'

'Nothing special. Six or seven thousand.'

'What good is six or seven thousand today?'

'She has to manage on it. She doesn't even get to *see* her husband's
earnings.'

'What does he spend it on?'

'What do you suppose?'

Kiranmayee's eyes were brimming with tears now. Suranjan
slipped into the other room with his cup of tea.

'What about Suranjan? I don't suppose he has...'

'He tried several jobs after losing his post as a teacher. But he
gave them all up because he didn't enjoy them. I sell saris to run the
household now. He pays for his own expenses with whatever he earns
from coaching students. He does contribute a bit to the household,
but then what kind of household is it anyway? Can you even call
this a household? I can't think of us that way any more, ever since
Suranjan's father passed away. We're just surviving. The sooner God
takes me, the better.'

I waited for her to stop sobbing. When she quietened down,
I said, 'What about your relatives? Do they check on you? Do they
help you?'

'No. Not at all,' said Kiranmayee, shaking her head vigorously.

'We have no relatives to speak of in Calcutta. Almost all of them
live back home. Those who came over to India live in Bhopal,
I believe. We have no contact with any of them.' Kiranmayee
continued, sighing deeply: 'This place is nothing like our own
country. Everyone's so selfish. Any number of people could have got
Suranjan a good job, but none of them did. When we came here,

we stayed with a distant cousin of mine – it was harrowing. They're a disgrace to the idea of family, ma, they have ruined us.'

'Who?'

'The people whose house we put up in when we first came to this country.'

I didn't take the initiative to ask how they had been ruined, although I did want to know. But I was keener to hear about the possibilities ahead rather than the calamities she believed had befallen them. Kiranmayee looked at me with pleading eyes – why, I couldn't tell. Was she under the impression that I was well connected in this city and could get Suranjan a job? What she didn't know was that I did not have so much power. Why, I was not on strong ground here myself. The authorities could throw me out any time, at which point I would have to pack up and leave.

After the tea and biscuits, I asked Kiranmayee to show me some of her saris. She had nothing by way of a shop; anyone who wanted to buy had to come home to choose. She designed the patterns for the saris herself and had them embroidered by a group of women in Tiljala, which enabled a slightly higher price. She sold salwar-kameezes too. Opening the cupboard doors wide with great enthusiasm, she brought out a bunch of saris and laid them out on the bed.

Most of them were ordinary cotton saris; some were silk. A few of the saris had animals hand-painted on them, and others, embroidered patterns. To be honest, none of them appealed to me greatly, but I still picked seven, and said, 'I'm buying these.'

Kiranmayee gulped. No one had ever bought seven saris in one go.

'Can you tell me what the price is?'

'Why should you buy all of them? Tell me which one you like; I'll gift it to you.'

'I'm going to buy them all. I like all seven.'

Kiranmayee looked embarrassed. 'But will you wear saris like these? They're…'

'I don't really wear expensive saris; I prefer cheaper ones. The ones I get at Dakshinapan are quite inexpensive, and in any case I like thin cotton saris the most; they're ideal for this hot land.'

Kiranmayee was hesitating. She obviously wanted to give me all the saris as gifts, but pragmatism was coming in the way. She might have been able to do it if we'd been in Dhaka. In Bangladesh, people were extremely generous. No one here was similarly inclined. Kiranmayee kept wiping the perspiration off her face with the end of her sari. I noticed the dark circles under her eyes.

'You're not ill, are you?'

'No, not physically ill. The heart, though – that's a different matter.'

Kiranmayee smiled wanly.

'Are you sleeping well?'

'Not always.'

'Take sleeping pills if you can't sleep.'

'Suranjan hasn't changed. He's as lazy as always. I have no idea where he wanders about. When he got the college job, I thought he was going to settle down. Who'd have imagined he'd remain as much of a good-for-nothing as ever? He wasn't working at all. I had to beg and plead with him to start coaching students.'

'Doesn't he have any friends?' I looked in the direction of the other room.

'None that I can see.'

Someone entered the house, going directly to the next room. From the snatches of conversation I overheard, it seemed that someone named Amjad had come to return Suranjan's motorcycle. Fragments from their exchange floating into the room made it clear that Suranjan and Amjad were quite friendly with each other.

Suranjan came in with a smile on his face, saying, 'Can you give us two cups of tea?'

'What do you mean *give*? Make it yourself.'

Both Suranjan and Kiranmayee were taken aback by my response. Here was a son asking his mother for some tea, and here was I, butting in and asking him to make it himself. I smiled at their expressions. No, nothing I said would change anything, but at least I elicited a comeback from Suranjan.

'Feminism burns bright in the cottage.'

'My feminism is not just for palaces, it's for cottages too. For you too.'

Suranjan was smiling engagingly. It was a lovely smile, probably the first time he was bestowing it on me. I had no idea what he was so pleased about.

I could hear him discuss the Communist Party of India (Marxist) [CPI(M)], Nandigram and Singur with Amjad; then he sounded worried about Amjad's business venture in Khidirpur. He had been talking to someone who felt the project should be relocated to Beckbagan. There were too many terrorists in Khidirpur; Amjad was risking his life; why do it? Though I kept talking to Kiranmayee, my ears were keenly focused on the conversation between the duo in the adjoining room. Their voices were faint but clear.

'What made you choose this neighbourhood of all places?' I asked Kiranmayee.

'We were living in Belgharia, but he didn't want to stay on after his father died. Still, we didn't manage to move. But this year, he simply refused to stay there any longer; I have no idea why. So we decided to move. And he was adamant that if we moved, it had to be to Park Circus. I don't know why or for what purpose. It would have made sense if his workplace was nearby.'

'Why, then?' My voice shook with anxiety. Suranjan was still chatting pleasantly with Amjad in the next room. I didn't care for his intimacy with a Muslim. Was he getting involved in something? Why did he want to live here? What could the reason possibly be? I was worried. Was he working as a BJP or RSS spy, with the intention of getting inside information and then finishing them off one by one?

Whose side should I be on, the innocent Amjad's, or Suranjan's? Who knew whether Amjad was really innocent? I tried to stay out of his sight. You never knew – if he was a fundamentalist, he might slaughter me on the spot. Suranjan had plunged me into a mystery. He had already thrown a couple of sharp glances at me, and must have seen the curiosity and suspicion on my face. I couldn't read his eyes now. What did he want? I hadn't committed a crime that had to be avenged. All he had to do was tell me: 'I have turned into a hardline Hindu. Now I'm here to help establish a Hindu nation, which is why I'm living in disguise in a Muslim neighbourhood.' That was all it would take. What pleasure would he get out of making me worry?

'Do Suranjan and you spend time with the Muslims here?'

'Yes, yes we do. Very nice people.'

'Nice?'

'Of course.'

'Are they locals?'

'Yes, they are. They're Bengalis.'

Kiranmayee may not have made the mistake specifically because she was from Bangladesh. People in India have this terrible habit of referring to Bengali Muslims as Muslims, and to Bengali Hindus as Bengalis – the outcome of poor education and ignorance. In Bangladesh, Hindus and Muslims mingle with one another because they live in the same localities; but the neighbourhoods are segregated here. It's practically impossible for a Muslim to live in a Hindu area, while here in Park Circus, it's all Muslims, with just a Hindu family or two. And apparently Suranjan was here by choice. He had forsaken a country, his own country, because it was filled with Muslims. So what was the motive behind moving to a Muslim locality? I wouldn't be at ease till I found out. I wanted to tear apart this veil of mystery around Suranjan.

The price for the seven saris came to five thousand five hundred rupees. Kiranmayee finally accepted the payment with great hesitation and embarrassment, but she insisted on giving me a fine silk sari as a gift.

Amjad should not become aware of my presence, but whom could I possibly say that too? My security guards were waiting outside, having escorted me into the house. They had no idea that this man was in the house now. Amjad alone knew what was on his mind. Did Suranjan know?

'Do you know the person visiting Suranjan?' I asked Kiranmayee in a whisper. I must have looked anxious.

Kiranmayee laughed. 'Are you frightened? He's a very nice boy. His name is Amjad; he's practically family. He had been to Medinipur on business and had borrowed Suranjan's motorcycle. He was away for a month. Must be here to return the motorcycle.'

You had to be on good terms with someone to lend them a motorcycle for a month.

Kiranmayee was perturbed at the way I was pacing up and down restlessly. I could not leave either, for I would have to pass through the other room, and then this Amjad was bound to recognize me. And once he did, would he block my way, or do something much more chilling? Would Suranjan save me in such an eventuality?

I was now full of suspicion for someone I had been thinking of as close to me in the morning. Kiranmayee noticed my discomfort and diagnosed it correctly. Calling Suranjan into the room, she told him softly to get rid of Amjad. Naturally, he didn't understand why – after all, it wasn't as though Maya was at home or something. Kiranmayee pointed at me out of the corner of her eye to hint that there could be danger.

Suranjan gave me a probing look, which I returned. Maybe we were trying to size up each other. But he ought to have had no trouble gauging my situation. Muslim fundamentalists wanted to kill me, not just in Bangladesh but in India too. According to a fatwa issued by the Imam of Tipu Sultan Mosque, anyone who smeared my face with ink or placed a garland of shoes around my neck would get twenty thousand rupees. More recently, a new fatwa had promised fifty thousand rupees to anyone who could kill me. Didn't Suranjan know how many of my effigies they had burnt? There was no knowing what was being planned.

There was suppressed anger in Suranjan's voice. 'There are some good people in the world, don't you think?'

'Of course. But you know her situation.'

'Hmm.'

Suranjan went back and saw Amjad out.

'I want to meet Maya.' I said this with my hands on the frame of the bed, in contact with the blue mosquito-net, touching the days of my childhood.

'Maya?' Kiranmayee was startled. 'But she's at her husband's house.'

'So what?'

'You'll visit her there?'

'I don't care whose house it is. I want to meet her.'

'Why don't I ask her to come meet you at your house? Or if that's a problem, she can come here and so can you.'

I realized that Maya lived in a forbidden place, which could not be visited. Taking my hand, Kiranmayee forced me to sit on the bed.

'Must you leave so soon, ma? I cannot believe you are actually here. It feels like a dream. What will you have? You can't leave without having a meal with us.'

A meal was the last thing on my mind. All I could think of were the implications of the connection between Suranjan and Amjad, although those thoughts had been intruded upon by reflections on the state of affairs at Maya's husband's house. Had she been living there happily, Kiranmayee would surely have been pleased at the possibility of my visiting her there.

I asked for another cup of tea. As Kiranmayee was making it, I said, 'Don't you or Suranjan visit Maya?'

'She visits us. She has two children; she brings them too.'

'She never comes by herself?'

'Sometimes she does.'

'Doesn't her husband come with her?'

Kiranmayee remained silent. The sigh that followed was mine, not hers. I had thought she might say, 'Maya's husband is too busy at work to visit us, so she drops by on her way home from work.' But no, she said no such thing.

As I was preparing to leave, I saw a young woman enter Suranjan's room. Short, dark, dressed in a green cotton sari. Her smile held a certain grace. Her age was impossible to gauge; it could be anywhere between twenty-three and thirty-three. Her eyes were wide, her expression suggested uncertainty, but she held her head high. Standing near the door, Suranjan performed the introductions only because he had no choice.

'This is Zulekha.'

A faint smile played upon my lips, though I had no idea why it planted itself there. As I was leaving, Suranjan settled Zulekha in the room and walked me to the car. Kiranmayee followed him, wiping her eyes. Giving her a goodbye hug, I said, 'Why are you crying? You mustn't.'

Kiranmayee spoke in a muffled voice: 'I don't like it here, ma, I wish I could go back.'

I got into my car without answering. Behind me stood Kiranmayee's white sari, and, holding a sigh, a cityful of darkness.

Four

Suranjan didn't go out later that day, although he was supposed to leave for Khidirpur with Amjad. The reason for his reluctance was Zulekha, whom he was meeting after nearly a week. They would spend several hours together now. She was like a gentle breeze in the stifling room. Even the searing heat didn't seem unbearable when she was present. Suranjan had never told Zulekha that he loved her.

All he had said, before lifting her face to kiss her, was: 'You look lovely because you don't use make-up.'

Zulekha wanted to hear more. Suranjan did tell her, but only when she was naked.

'You're like a mermaid. You dive into the water, then float up; you float and then you dive again. I don't know which depths you swim up from when I call out to you. I know you and yet I don't. You're not a creature of the land, you're not anyone I know. I don't know, are you for real or a figment of my imagination?'

His fingertips explored the recesses of her body, as though he were painting on the canvas of her skin. From the brow, down the nose, climbing the peaks of her breasts and then straight down to her stomach and groin, and lower towards the junction of her thighs. From there, along one leg to the knee and then all the way down to the toes before climbing back up the other leg and retracing their steps back up to her brow. Only when the fingertips touched her closed eyes did Zulekha open them.

Earlier, this play, this game on the bed, used to take place in Zulekha's house, when her husband was at work and her child in school. But a cussed street dog would invariably stand outside the window and howl whenever Suranjan arrived. No one could tell why. Eventually, Suranjan had had to stop the game and leave. While no one had actually gathered near the window at the barking of the stray dog, there was always a risk. Those in the neighbourhood who were excessively inquisitive about Suranjan were under the impression that he was a relative of Zulekha's. Her family lived in Birbhum district, and there wasn't so much as a peep out of them, year after year. For several months, Zulekha had exercised great caution while sleeping with this suddenly arrived relative. During fiery afternoons in the deserted neighbourhood, she got her fill of physical love – which had eluded her during the tedious sex over several years of married life with Mohabbat – from Suranjan.

Suranjan had no quick answer if asked how he had come to know Zulekha. Was it a very old relationship, or was it recent? It wouldn't be easy for him to answer this either. Suranjan knew a man named Amjad who lived in Park Circus. He used to visit this neighbourhood to meet Amjad, who had introduced him to someone at the tea shop where they chatted over cups of tea. This person was a distant relative of Zulekha's – she was his brother-in-law's niece. It was from him that he had heard about a woman named Zulekha, educated and married to a bad-tempered businessman. She had been pointed out to him once, walking past absently with a little boy in tow. Since that very first glimpse, Suranjan had found himself in a haze, spinning a story in his head. He had sown the seeds of this story in every cell of his brain and watched it grow swiftly, sprouting leaves and branches and flowers that had wrapped themselves around him.

And, most of the time, when he visited Zulekha for their moments of intimacy, the story no longer seemed imaginary. He felt that the events in it had indeed taken place. Eventually, the story became completely real, his unconscious mind accepting it as the truth.

No doctor or relative or friend or even Zulekha herself had found out yet about Suranjan's delusion. Even he didn't know that a false story was rearing its head like a demon within him. He hated the truth of his relationship with Zulekha; so it was his fantasy that he believed in. In this story, he was the hero, although no one in the city knew him or even of him. Still, he had no regrets about it, for he was proud of this imaginary story. It was his wealth, though it was also a source of embarrassment. This was the only secret fantasy in his life, which made him feel both honoured and humiliated.

This fantasy – or it could be called the reality within Suranjan's unconscious mind – held the blueprint of a murder. A group of people from Belgharia, among them Suranjan and Achinta, had hatched the plan. Suranjan and Achinta had been friends for a long time. They had only recently started consorting with the other members of that group. The person who had to be murdered was Mohabbat, for the crime of having mercilessly beaten up two young men. If killing him was not possible, his limbs had to be mutilated so badly that he lived out the rest of his life as a cripple, in constant agony. Mohabbat Hossain had a crockery shop in New Market, where he sold Indian and imported dinner sets, tea sets, glasses, cutlery, electric kettles, non-stick pans and similar things. And what was poor Mohabbat's crime? That a couple of young louts, drunk to the gills, had demanded money from him. Money? For what? Oh, nothing in particular, just money. So Mohabbat and his friends had thrashed these two within an inch of their lives and handed them over to the police. Incidents like this took place in the city all the time, too trivial to even make it to the newspapers. But a little investigation would reveal that it was far more sinister, or, even if it

wasn't, that was how those looking to stir up trouble would view it.
For, those who had been beaten up were Hindus, and those who had
beaten them up were Muslims. News of the incident had spread like
wildfire within the circle of Suranjan's friends. The Hindu men who
had been thrashed were from Belgharia – familiar faces for Suranjan,
Achinta and the rest of them. Despite being beaten up, they were
in hiding, lest the police went on the rampage in Belgharia. No one
could say for sure that this was an unfounded fear; you just couldn't
be too careful.

One afternoon, Achinta arrived at Suranjan's house with several
friends in a Sumo SUV, picked him up, and set off for Park Circus.
They had hidden rods, sticks, knives and daggers under a black cloth
in the SUV. They began to drink as they drove, with Suranjan joining
in joyfully. Since it was Sunday, they had assumed Mohabbat would
be at home, but when they arrived there in full strength, he was
missing. His wife was home alone. So she was dragged into the SUV.
On Achinta's advice, they sped off towards Gariahat, to their old
friend P.K. Majumdar's restaurant. Achinta and Suranjan climbed
upstairs to the small room on the first floor which was primarily
meant for siestas and the occasional important meeting. The rest
left, saying they'd be back in ten minutes. The room was furnished
with a cot, a thin mattress and an oil-stained pillow, along with
two plastic chairs and a bare wooden table on which were scattered
some old documents. Strangely, Zulekha did not have to be forced;
she walked up on her own. Achinta kept drinking from his bottle,
which held pre-mixed whisky and water.

'Where's Mohabbat? Where's the bastard?'

Zulekha answered calmly, 'He's closed his shop and is visiting
a friend.'

'What's this friend's name?'

Zulekha remained calm. 'Taukir.'

'Where does this Taukir live?'

'Rai Bahadur Road.'

'Where's that?'

The question came from Suranjan.

'I know, it's near the Chanditala bus stop, right?' Achinta asked Zulekha.

She nodded.

Suranjan couldn't make out whether the situation was turning into an abduction, or whether the woman had been brought there only to extract information about Mohabbat's whereabouts. He said to Achinta, 'Why did we have to bring her here? We could have found out on our own and gone to Rai Bahadur Road.'

Taking a swig of his whisky, Achinta said, 'Call him and ask for cash.'

Suranjan said, 'Which bastard will pay a ransom for his wife? And a mullah on top of that. If it had been a rich man's fat son...'

Achinta said, 'Why didn't you bring the fat son too?'

'No sons at home.'

Suranjan didn't know just how Mohabbat's wife was going to be used in this drinking session. Achinta was leaning back comfortably against the wall. He had taken off his belt, which he was waving gently, his eyes fixed on the wife. It was difficult to interpret the smile on his lips. Suranjan was concerned that things could take a different turn. Mohabbat was not the target at this moment, his wife Zulekha was. Was Achinta going to take off his trousers, or would he use the belt as a whip? Suranjan was not prepared to witness either eventuality.

Picking up Achinta's bottle, Suranjan took a swig from it. He knocked it back like water, the way people drink when they're dying of thirst. The other three – Subrata, Vishwa, Gopal – came in through the door. Subrata was carrying two bottles of Teacher's whisky, Gopal had some plastic glasses, and Vishwa, three bottles of water. They made appreciative noises, all of them staring at Zulekha, who was sitting on a chair with her back to everyone. Suddenly, Vishwa grabbed her breast from the back. Suranjan observed that she was making no attempt to shake off the hand. He assumed she was gritting her teeth.

Achinta laughed loudly. 'How dare you touch those boobs before me?'

All of them were Suranjan's friends. He had spent hours with them, drunk with them, got drunk with them, talked politics, throttled any Muslims they could get their hands on, or at least wanted to. If there was one person among them with real courage, it was Suranjan, but still, his instinct told him that it would be best to take Zulekha home. It would be disastrous if the news got out. They could go to jail or even be hanged. There was a communist government in the state; they didn't care what happened to Hindus, but the slightest scratch on a Muslim would mean no one would be spared.

He was feeling dizzy now, his head flying off his body and rolling along the gutter to Gariahat. Suranjan had taken off his belt too. Would it be his turn first or Achinta's? Or the others'? They were gulping down the Teacher's they had bought. Suranjan drank by turns from their bottle and Achinta's. He had never drunk as much as today, nor were his friends the type to drink Teacher's whisky. But it was a special day, a day for special food and drink; it was a celebration. Suranjan looked on as Subrata jerked Zulekha up from the chair and flung her on the bed, on to the filthy mattress and pillow. Subrata's head was drooping now, his body swaying. He tore Zulekha's sari off her body, her blouse and petticoat as well. A naked woman in front of five pairs of male eyes.

Suranjan gazed, mesmerized, at Zulekha's body. He had not set eyes on a naked woman since his separation from Sudeshna. A young body, firm breasts, not the kind that babies had suckled at. A little fat on the lower abdomen, the kind Suranjan liked on a woman, the kind that seemed natural. Shedding this fat through dieting and running and swimming seemed artificial to him. Was he aroused? He was. His penis wanted to burst out of his pants now. Suranjan looked away. Achinta was splashing alcohol on Zulekha's body, laughing uproariously. The woman – how strange! – was not crying at all. She had hidden her face and eyes behind her sari; she couldn't see anything. Anticipating that she might scream, Achinta stuffed a rag into her mouth. As soon as she tried to take it out, he slapped her hard. Still, she managed to spit it out, but without screaming. She didn't resist either, only kept her eyes tightly shut. With loathing.

Suddenly Vishwa began to hop up and down, and threw himself on Zulekha. Dragging him away, Achinta said 'me first' and jumped on her. Then Subrata shoved him away.

None of them was shouting – even in their drunkenness, they were wary. Still, anyone passing by would hear the commotion, and would assume that a group of young men were having a good time. No one would know that a woman had been dragged in to be punished.

Suranjan remembered Shamima. They say history repeats itself. Was that what was happening today? He had done something similar in another land, but the woman in that case was a prostitute, it was legal for her to offer her body in exchange for money. But today he had brought the wife of a Muslim man here by force. He had not actually been able to avenge anything by raping Shamima. Raping Zulekha would mean punishing Mohabbat. That was what the rest of them kept saying, their words lodging themselves in Suranjan's mind like arrows. If they found Mohabbat, they would knife him in the stomach; but even without killing him, they could punish him severely by raping his wife. She would be raped not by Muslims but by Hindus. 'The next time you try to attack a Hindu, we'll slit your throat, Mohabbat, you son of a bitch.' Suranjan had no difficulty reading the message. And so, the more he drank, the more he readied himself. The faster his head was carried away in the wind, or rolled in the gutters of Gariahat, the faster did his doubts disappear. But his eyes kept returning to the woman's sari-covered face and mouth, from where a constant groan seemed to be emerging. Suranjan's eyes were riveted to the sight. Vishwa jumped in as soon as Achinta rose. Turning Zulekha over on her stomach, he began to cackle, biting and clawing his way to his climax.

It all seemed so very simple to all of them, as though they were having legitimate sex with their legally wedded wives in their own bedrooms – as though none of them could remember, even if they wanted to, that this was nobody's bedroom, that there was an audience, that the woman wasn't married to any of them, that she was someone else's wife, that she belonged to a different caste and creed. None of them could remember, even if they wanted to, that this wasn't a country like Bangladesh; even if you could do anything you wanted with the minorities there, you couldn't do the same thing in India. None of them seemed to realize that if the word got out, they would all have to be on the run for life, or rot in jail. Or die at the hands of Muslim thugs. All of them had forgotten that they were miles away from reality. They were behaving as though they were no longer on the planet on which they lived. It looked so straightforward that they seemed to be a bunch of friends visiting a brothel for sex and revelling in it. There had not been even a murmur from any of them about whether it was right or not, nor was anyone thinking about the repercussions. It was all just for pleasure.

Suranjan's eyes were stilled now. His penis began to soften; his body was going limp. Once, just once, he said, 'enough'. Softly. No one heard.

The second 'enough' came a little louder. Suddenly, his body was coiled in tension, and the third 'enough' emerged as a shout. Subrata burst into laughter in response. Suranjan balled his hand into a fist and kept drinking, silently. Suddenly, he no longer felt that the whole thing was taking place right in front of his eyes. It was as though he was reading about it in a newspaper, or watching a documentary, in the process of which it appeared that he had also been present. When he woke up, or when the haze had lifted, he would realize he had been a spectator or something like that.

Subrata pulled the woman out of the bed and made her lie spreadeagled on the table. She was finally resisting, trying to get up, but Subrata dissuaded her with a series of stinging slaps.

His method of raping involved pinching Zulekha's skin and biting her nipples. Suranjan got up and tried to shove him aside, but Subrata retaliated so forcefully that he was dashed against the wall and bounced off it on to the floor, taking a knock on his head. But he charged at Subrata again, grabbing the hand with which Subrata was pinching Zulekha's skin. Rape her if you must, why hurt her even more ... maybe that was what Suranjan was trying to say. He didn't let go of the hand, punching Subrata on the nose when he tried to free his hand. He said, 'No one else must touch her.'

'What do you mean?' Gopal stepped up. 'I haven't done her yet.'

'No one's doing anyone any more. Not another step, Gopal, I'm warning you.'

'I see, you want to go first. Go ahead, I'll wait.' Gopal sat down on the floor again, sipping his drink.

'I'm not doing anything.'

Achinta looked at Suranjan sharply: 'You're not?'

'Ohmygod. What's going on here?' Gopal laughed.

'She's a human being. Is she a human being or not?' Suranjan was shouting.

Sounds of laughter.

'The bastard's gone mad. What's the matter, Suranjan, we're not fucking your sister, are we?'

More laughter. Suranjan kicked out at them indiscriminately, and then fell on his face while trying to pick his glass up. At once, Subrata delivered a mighty kick on his buttocks.

'Motherfucker!'

Three of his accomplices piled on to him, Suranjan lying flat on his back on the floor. Vishwa was pissing on him. As Gopal threw the woman back on the bed and concentrated on raping her, Suranjan reached out with his feet, entangled them with Gopal's and dragged him down on the floor.

Suranjan jumped to his feet and threw himself at Vishwa. But even though he was more than a match for Vishwa, when Subrata and Achinta joined forces with Vishwa, Suranjan found himself back on the floor, on his stomach, absorbing the kicks aimed at his back, shoulders and legs. He didn't feel he was conscious any more.

Then they left, all of them. Before going out, Subrata grabbed the collar of Suranjan's shirt and pulled his head off the floor, saying, 'Do her and dump her. Don't be late. Mention our names to anyone and your body will be found in the river.'

He remained on the floor for a long time. The door was wide open. Anyone who entered would know what had happened. Bottles and plastic glasses were strewn on the floor, along with a belt someone had left behind by mistake.

Suranjan sat up and told Zulekha, 'Get up, I'll take you home.'

'Don't you want your turn?' Zulekha's voice was icy, metallic.

'No.'

She tried to get up, but could not. Suranjan had to get up and help her out of the bed. He was aching all over, his body covered in cuts and bruises, some of them bleeding. Still, he managed to put the petticoat, blouse and sari on Zulekha. Her head was probably spinning, for she tottered forward upon getting to her feet. Supporting her with an arm around her shoulder, Suranjan led her downstairs slowly and helped her into a taxi. Passers-by must have assumed the gentleman was taking his ailing wife to the doctor. Suranjan had indeed become a gentleman today. Depositing Zulekha on the staircase outside her front door, he melted into the darkness. Someone would open the door for her, her husband or someone else.

Zulekha could have returned home by herself in the taxi, and Suranjan wouldn't have had to take any risk. But he had not considered there was a risk in escorting her home. He could have been arrested by the police or cornered by local residents; Muslim thugs could have broken his bones. He had either not entertained the possibility, or had not been inclined to. That evening, Suranjan had gone directly from Park Circus to Sealdah station, buying a ticket to Siliguri and boarding the night train. He hadn't decided where he was going, but it wasn't as though he was escaping the police – he was escaping himself.

He had frightened himself greatly that day for having helped take Zulekha away from her house to be gang raped. Only once had he thought of Shamima during the whole thing. He had raped Shamima purely for psychological pleasure, not physical. He had actually sought her permission for the act. So, the incident with Shamima had occurred to him briefly, but the rest of the time, he had wondered whether this was how they had raped Maya. No, he had not been able to channel his anger against Maya's rapists into raping Zulekha. She had appeared to him to be a human, an innocent young woman, a Maya. Not for a moment had he thought of her as a Muslim. He had not felt even an iota of hatred for her. Instead, he had experienced hatred for himself, for the four other rapists. He had cut off all ties with Achinta and the rest, for ever.

Suranjan reached Siliguri without getting a wink of sleep, staring fixedly out of the window all the while. He neither spoke to anyone on the way, nor ate anything. And the next day, he returned to Calcutta, exactly the same way. Was Achinta's friend

Vishwarup Mitra connected to the BJP and RSS in any way? The question occurred to him suddenly. To find out, he went directly to the party office on returning to Calcutta. There, he hunted through the documents for Vishwa's name, but couldn't find it. The people he met told him that Vishwa was not associated with any of the Hindutva parties. An elderly man in the office who was observing Suranjan told him without hurry, 'Don't leave the party because of anger with someone. That will be a mistake. The party stood by you when you were in trouble; it will do the same in future too.'

Suranjan was aware of this. He had got his college job because of his connection with the party. Sure, it was a part-time job, not permanent, but still a job. He left without replying.

He visited Zulekha's house on two successive days, in the afternoon. There was a maid there, and Zulekha herself, struck down by a high fever, almost unconscious. That night, Mohabbat had beaten her up with anything he could lay his hands on. There were bruises beneath her eyes, her lips were cut, blood clots on her back and breasts, arms and thighs. No medicines were given to her at home, no doctor had examined her either. She had informed neither the neighbours, nor the police. Perhaps she had thought of Suranjan as an ally in trying times. She had told Suranjan what had happened that night after she went back home.

'He saw the state I was in when he returned home. I was groaning in pain. A neighbour came by to say I was picked up by Hindus. That was all it took.'

'How did they know?'

'They didn't. But they knew that this would lead to an explosion; people just want to watch the fun. I kept telling him it was Muslims, they were thugs, I had no way to save myself, but he refused to listen.'

Zulekha didn't know the truth of the matter like Suranjan did. She was under the impression she had been abducted by someone named Amjad, from whom Mohabbat had borrowed two lakh rupees and, far from repaying the loan, had denied taking it altogether. Amjad would often come home to ask for his money back, during which time he would stare at Zulekha. She had told her husband many times to return the money if he had borrowed it; that she didn't care for Amjad's frequent visits. Mohabbat would flare up in rage at the suggestion. Amjad even dropped by when Mohabbat wasn't home, asking for a drink of water, or to come in for a few minutes. He had told her several times, 'What are you doing with this bastard, bhabi, come away, I'll marry you.' Zulekha couldn't tolerate such propositions, and had even berated and insulted Amjad and thrown him out. He had picked her up, taken her to a house in the neighbourhood and raped her with some of his friends. Suranjan listened to this version of the events that Zulekha told him. She added that Mohabbat had behaved like a beast that night, tearing her sari off her body, stripping her, spitting his hatred all over her body, and asking what they had done with her.

She had not answered. Mohabbat's eyes were flaming, his veins had turned bluer, threatening to burst out of his skin. Pacing up and down, he had said, 'I'm asking you again, whore, did they fuck you?'

Zulekha was silent. Then Mohabbat had pounced on her, grabbing whatever he could find and beating her with it. The leg of a broken chair. A glass flower vase. Boots.

Zulekha had said, 'Yes, they did what they had to.'

'What did you just say?'

'You heard me.'

'Say it again.'

'The swine did all the things they're capable of. Was it my fault?' Zulekha was screaming. 'Was it my fault? What are you beating me up for?'

Mohabbat did not answer her question. Suranjan had asked himself the same questions as he listened to Zulekha recount what had happened. Mohabbat had had no answers. Nor did Suranjan. What was Zulekha's fault?

He had picked up Zulekha, who was burning up with fever, in his arms, deposited her in a taxi, had her examined by a doctor at MD Hospital near Bridge No. 4, bought the prescribed medicines, and had taken her back home. When the maid asked who he was, Zulekha had replied, 'My cousin from back home in Birbhum. Shafiqul.'

Shafiqul went out, wandering around the city like a man possessed.

He lay in parks or on benches, staring at the sky, calling at hourly intervals to find out if he was needed, whether the fever was better, whether the pain had subsided, whether a doctor should be sent for. He couldn't get Zulekha's stricken, pitiable expression out of his mind.

Much later, Suranjan had asked why Zulekha had not screamed the day she was raped, why she hadn't tried to attract the attention of people, why she hadn't tried to bite and scratch her rapists in a bid to escape. Zulekha had explained, speaking slowly, with her head on Suranjan's chest, her teardrops falling on his bare body. His left arm was draped around her back, while his right arm covered his own eyes.

Suranjan was in a daze while the story unfolded, disturbing the soporific state he was in. He could see it all playing out in front of his eyes, how a gang of criminals had abducted Zulekha, how he had saved her from those rapists.

He began telling her this story, slowly. She didn't want to believe it, but she liked the idea of believing it.

'I was blindfolded, I couldn't see anything,' Zulekha was saying.

'Who blindfolded you?'

Zulekha answered harshly: 'A man named Amjad.'

'How did you know it was Amjad?'

'I know.'

'But Amjad is a friend of mine.'

'No, not this one. He's Mohabbat's friend.'

'My friend could be Mohabbat's friend too.'

'I doubt it.'

'How do you know?'

'You think there's only one Amjad in the world? This is a different one.'

'How can you be so sure?'

'What does your friend Amjad look like?'

'Ordinary. Like all of us. Like me.'

'No, he's not remotely anything like you.'

'Where does this Amjad live?'

'Here in Park Circus.'

'Amjad of Park Circus is my friend.'

'Then was it your friends who did it?'

'Yes, my friends. But they give friendship a bad name. I have abandoned them. But you know what?'

'What?'

'There was nobody named Amjad there.'

'There was. It happened right here, in this neighbourhood.'

'No, not here, it happened somewhere else.'

'They were Muslims.'

'No, they weren't. They were all Hindus.'

'No, Hindus don't have so much courage. They've never had it. I know Amjad was the leader.'

'You're wrong.'

'I was blindfolded. I don't know when they removed the blindfold.'

'Your eyes weren't covered, Zulekha, you saw everything. You saw me too.'

'I didn't see you.'

'I was there.'

'How could you be there? You're not a thug like them.'

'I'm not a thug, so I didn't behave like one. I saved you from them. I wanted to be a thug too, but I couldn't be one, eventually.'

'Why are you saying these things, Suranjan? You have nothing to do with Amjad, you weren't there when it happened.'

'How do you know? You said you were blindfolded.'

'But you're saying I wasn't. And I didn't see you.'

'You're denying it now.'

'What for?'

'To protect me.'

'Why would I want to protect you?'

'Because I rescued you from that hell.'

'You're making it up.'

'Don't turn it into a mystery.'

'I'm not.'

Suranjan took a long drag on a joint and passed it to Zulekha. Both of them fell under its influence, their vision grew blurred, the sounds rolled around one another, and Suranjan's stories began to spin, with the incident concerning Zulekha spiralling into oblivion within them, at least for the time being.

'My uncle is just like you. He too doesn't want to admit it was Muslims who took me away, he says it was Hindus, Hindus. But I know it wasn't. Amjad was there. Amjad is Muslim. No Hindu would dare touch a Muslim woman.'

'There was no one named Amjad there. Amjad is my friend.'

'I told you already, this Amjad isn't the one who's your friend. A different Amjad. People call him Badshah.'

'No.'

'What do you mean *no*?'

'You know my friend Amjad, don't you?'

'This Amjad has a beard. Your friend Amjad doesn't.'

'How do you know?'

'I know.'

'You said you were blindfolded.'

'I was, but still I know.'

'Why would they have abducted you?'

'There were reasons.'

'What reasons?'

'Why should I tell you?'

'Was Mohabbat a reason?'

'No.'

'Revenge on Mohabbat?'

'No.'

'What was it, then?'

'Amjad wanted to marry me. I didn't agree.'

'Liar.'

'Why should I lie? He used to threaten me.'

'Liar.'

'I'll murder you, he would say.'

'Why didn't you file a case?'

'Who's going to go to the trouble of filing one? You think these things can be done alone? And will I be spared if I file a case? I'm not suitable for this society. That's why I can do as I please. With you.'

'As you please?'

'Yes, as I please.'

'I was rotten, Zulekha. I was one of those rapists. You know everything. Achinta, Vishwa, Gopal, Subrata, you heard their names.'

'I didn't.'

'You've heard me talk about them too.'

'You've gone mad. How can you blame Hindus when you're a Hindu yourself?'

'You're blaming Muslims when you're one of them.'

'I'm blaming them because they're the ones who did it.'

'No. I know who did it. I took you home. Do you remember that at least?'

'No, I was blindfolded. I don't know who brought me home.'

'I did.'

'You didn't. Amjad dumped me on the staircase.'

'So what was my contribution?'

'You took me to the doctor, bought me medicine.'

'And where did I turn up from?'

'You were passing by; you saw me lying on the stairs.'

Suranjan began to laugh. Still laughing, he said, 'You're fine now, Zulekha. You don't have to file a case against anyone. Forget the past, look at me, think of pleasant things, talk of love. Forget about rape and abduction.'

'Don't utter those words. They feel like hot lead being poured into my ears.'

After a pause filled with heavy sighs, Zulekha said, 'Actually, I was raped every single time, Suranjan. Do you think my husband ever touched me with love? What he did to me was no different from what they did. This child is the outcome of his assault. I'm telling you the truth: sex with him was never anything but rape and assault for me. I got no pleasure from him. It was only with you that I got pleasure. You're the first person to have made me aware of it.'

Another pause. Wiping her tears with the back of her palm, Zulekha continued, 'When they took me away, I knew at once they would gang rape me. They were all drunk. I didn't dare scream – What if someone throttled me? What if someone pulled out a knife and slit my throat? What if they killed me? I wasn't unused to rape, but I had no wish to die. So I tried to bear it in silence, so that no one would get angry and kill me.'

'Don't blame Amjad when he isn't guilty.'

'What would I gain from it?'

'You're taking revenge.'

'For what?'

'He wanted to marry you. But that was as far as he went. You want to take revenge on him for not forcing you to marry him.'

Astonishment was writ large upon Zulekha's face.

Suranjan continued, 'I don't believe a woman as courageous as you would not have filed a case if it was indeed Amjad and his friends.'

Zulekha saw no need to respond to Suranjan's meaningless charges. She remembered how Mohabbat would spit out his hatred at her every night after how one. She had become an extra person in the house by then, a fallen woman whom Mohabbat did not want. Let her leave. But informing her parents and her uncle served no purpose; no one came to take her away.

Mohabbat had tried to throw her out physically several times, but Zulekha had resisted, threatening to call the police. If she left, she said, it would be for good, and she would take Sohag with her. Mohabbat was extremely attached to his son, and couldn't possibly live without him. Six months had passed this way, after which Mohabbat had got a new bride for himself.

A village girl, the second wife hadn't studied beyond class VI. Mohabbat slept in the bedroom with her at night, while Zulekha spent her nights in a smaller room, holding Sohag in her arms, racked by fears and anxieties. In this house, she was spending her days like a tattered doormat. The day he returned unexpectedly in the afternoon to find Zulekha's cousin Shafiqul at home, Mohabbat uttered three talaqs on the spot. Suranjan was sitting on Zulekha's bed, not exactly in the manner of a cousin. The curtains were drawn; the room was dark; Suranjan's shirt was unbuttoned. When Mohabbat entered, Zulekha was caught standing dumbfounded with a tray holding two kababs on a plate and two cups of tea. She had barely straightened up after placing the tray on the table when she heard the words. Talaq talaq talaq. The divorce was done. This meant she would have to leave this home now. But when she tried to take her son with her, Mohabbat refused. And where could Zulekha go without her son? She had to move into her uncle's house in Beniapukur.

Mohabbat lived nearby, Sohag with him. The boy had begun calling his father's new wife 'ma'. Zulekha was a woman who accepted reality. She wasn't one to beat her breast and weep and commit suicide. By now, she had realized that women, especially Muslim women, had to all but give up their lives just to keep living. Zulekha hadn't shed a single tear when Mohabbat divorced her. She had only glanced at Suranjan with stony eyes, asking without words, 'And what are you going to do now? Run away, of course.' Zulekha had known that Mohabbat would divorce her sooner or later. He would have thrown her out the night she was raped, but had held back only because of Sohag.

Mohabbat had not turned to the police. If he had tried to find out who had raped his wife, he would have got to the truth, he had no lack of resources. But he hadn't done any of this, for a couple of his friends had said it would serve no purpose, and might just end up endangering his life. Mohabbat had a long-running business feud with Amjad, and had heard that it was Amjad and his cronies who had abducted Zulekha. Still, he hadn't wanted to probe further, for it was convenient if Amjad's anger had abated after raping his wife. In this case, Mohabbat's rage was directed at Zulekha. Although he knew it was not her fault, he convinced himself that she was responsible. She must have enjoyed the whole thing and not bothered to resist the rapists. Now that she had tasted blood, she would go back to them for more whenever she had the opportunity. Whatever the provocation might have been, after her pleasure cruise on the ocean with other men, she wasn't going to limit herself to the backwaters with Mohabbat. In fact, he suspected Zulekha of being involved in the abduction. She was trying to say a group of Muslim men were responsible, though Mohabbat had heard rumours that it was actually Hindus. Although there was no proof, some derived great happiness out of making such allegations, driving a wedge between people, and sparking off conflicts. Mohabbat wasn't interested in Hindu-versus-Muslim; a minor abduction and rape couldn't even touch him. But he wouldn't be at peace till he had cast that bitch out of his sight. He hadn't been able to stand her ways from the very first day – used to divorce her in his head all the time. Now this mishap had given him an opportunity to actually divorce her; it wasn't going to come again. He would breathe again only after it was done.

Zulekha was afraid that Suranjan would make himself scarce if she got into trouble. This was what men were adept at: sparking a crisis and disappearing when it erupted. Suranjan's ardour, his propensity for turning his back on everything to run to her, had given Zulekha much pleasure. He was her greatest joy in an existence full of strife. But her fears had not come true; he had not run away. The day Mohabbat had pronounced the talaq, that was all he had done, he had not tried to hit either Zulekha or Suranjan. She had not cried, and had only sat there, turned to stone. She had asked Suranjan to leave, but he had not. She had considered leaving instantly with Sohag, but her thoughts were jumbled, plunging her into a void.

None of the neighbours found out what had happened. She had maintained a distance from them ever since she had moved in here after marriage, not even bothering with friendly visits. She was more or less alone at home. Mohabbat's relatives lived in Jangipur in Murshidabad, from where they visited sometimes. Mohabbat went too, once a month, occasionally with his wife and son, but mostly by himself. Now he had ordered her to get out at once, and forbidden her from taking Sohag with her – she shouldn't try to get in touch with the child at all. Zulekha had left in the clothes she was wearing, Suranjan by her side. She had left her home of six years with him.

Zulekha was a college graduate, from Suri College, not that anyone had acknowledged her education. She had studied on her own initiative and passed her examinations. A professor named Rabiul Islam used to encourage and inspire her, telling her, 'Education is the most valuable thing a woman can have. If you're educated, you can always put it to use. Knowledge never goes waste.' He would say, 'You're intelligent, you will do very well for yourself if you study.'

Zulekha hadn't got around to doing very well for herself. Mohabbat had enough money to ensure she didn't have to work like a slave to run the household, but it had never felt like her home. He had never asked her about her BA degree. Zulekha had many qualities, but as a woman, her college degree was her greatest disqualification. Her in-laws had never taken kindly to the idea. Mohabbat himself had only studied up to the Intermediate level, and considered his wife's BA degree a source of humiliation.

The attraction of earning money for himself had led him to break away from his family's timber business in Jangipur to take a friend's advice and plunge into his own venture, the crockery shop. His elder brother had taken the responsibility of running the family business, and Mohabbat himself had no other desire in life besides making money. Getting married and having a wife meant procuring a maid for household work. Having a child would ensure there would be someone to look after him when he grew old. Mohabbat had never bothered with the namaz or the roza or with any religious rituals. He fasted during Ramzan only because of social pressure, and he read the namaz on the two days of Eid, not so much for himself as for others. He neither smoked nor drank; his only addiction was to paan.

The match for Zulekha came after she graduated. A business in Calcutta, the family was from Jangipur, a well-behaved and decent young man. Her father and relatives wasted no time getting her married. Her father paid her extra attention because her mother had died when Zulekha was a child, but being physically handicapped, he was obsessed with settling his daughter into married life as soon as possible. Surely, Zulekha could get herself a job in the city!

She was still trying to get one, as was Suranjan. Still, irrespective of his success at job hunting, he had succeeded in moving to Park Circus from Nandan Nagar in Belgharia. This was no less an accomplishment than getting a job. Suranjan wanted both of them to make a living by coaching students for now; something was sure to turn up later. But Zulekha was not keen on waiting passively. She wanted a job, no matter how insignificant. She wasn't willing to coach students. With some effort, she got the job of a salesgirl at Shoppers Stop in Inox mall. Her employers did not know she had a child; they assumed she was not even married. Suranjan was not keen on this job. They make you work to the bone, he would say, but pay you so little. How can anyone manage on such a small salary?

Zulekha poured most of what she earned into her uncle's household expenses. She had no choice. Whatever little was left over went towards buying things for her child. When she visited Suranjan, she would be penniless. He would say, 'I like this. Neither of us has any money, neither of us is better than the other. We are equals.'

Suranjan was adamant about not visiting Zulekha at her uncle's house. He lived nearby now and had moved to be near her. Zulekha could visit him at his Park Circus house whenever she liked. Even if Suranjan wasn't home, Kiranmayee would be there.

Zulekha didn't talk much about her uncle's family. Suranjan didn't think she was very happy there, her only source of joy being Sohag giving his father the slip and coming to meet her sometimes.

She would buy chocolates and confectionery, clothes and toys for him, smothering him in kisses and showering him with gifts whenever he came. She asked about school, whether his father was good to him, what his new mother was like, was she looking after him, and so on. Sohag nodded in response to every question. The boy had been forced to accept the cruel truth early in life: that he wasn't allowed to live with his own mother. If Zulekha suffered, it wasn't for herself but for Sohag. Her bond with him was umbilical. And the person whose love she desired with all her heart and body was Suranjan.

Until now, the more inquisitive among the neighbours had known Suranjan as Shafiqul. She had even passed off the same story at her uncle's house. But since Zulekha hadn't been given a room to herself, she couldn't spend any time with her cousin in privacy there. She slept on the floor in the same room as her aunt and her cousins. Having Suranjan over would allow for little more than offering him tea and biscuits in her uncle's room. Her uncle had a meat shop in Bhawbanipur. They were not hard up, but when there is no culture of spending money, the standard of living often deteriorates. It wasn't as though Zulekha's own parents had been affluent, and she could adapt to any economic standard. She had been to the homes of rich classmates in college, even stayed in one after her hesitation had melted. The faith of her teacher Rabiul Islam and his insistence on a life free of regressive practices, his civilized behaviour, his taste and sensibilities, had influenced Zulekha greatly during her years in college.

To her, Suranjan was a human being, not just a Hindu man. And especially on the day of the rape – apparently he was Amjad's friend – he had done so much, taken her to the doctor, bought her medicine, it was all Suranjan. Leave alone seeing it for herself, Zulekha had never even heard that a rapist could have tears of compassion for his quarry. Suranjan may not have been a rapist himself, but he was the rapist Amjad's friend. Zulekha was convinced that this compassion, these tears, would not come her way from either community, Muslims or Hindus. This was a different community, rising above religion. Zulekha was accustomed to cruelty. She had wilted under Mohabbat's stern, unrelenting expression every single day for six years. They had never gone anywhere together, and even if they had, it was to the house of a relative on some urgent matter. Or to Jangipur. Friends or relatives had never gathered at their home. Mohabbat wanted to make a lot of money through his business in Calcutta and move back to Jangipur with his wife and son, where he would either get into the second-hand-wood business or start a furniture shop. Mohabbat was a prudent businessman. Zulekha didn't care for prudence; she was thirsty for love.

That evening, after he had doused the fire in twenty-seven-year-old Zulekha's body with the one in his thirty-seven-year-old one, Suranjan said, 'Do you know who was here?'

'Who?'

'Don't you know who that lady was?'

'I don't.'

'I'm sure you do.'

'No.' Zulekha shook her head. She could not identify the visitor.

'Taslima Nasreen.'

Suranjan lit a cigarette, leaning back against the headboard. Zulekha threw a displeased glance at the cigarette, she detested its noxious smell.

'Haven't you read her books?'

'A long time ago, in school. *Selected Columns.*'

'You haven't read *Lajja*?'

'No.'

'Really?'

'What's so strange about that?'

'Everyone but you has read *Lajja*.'

Zulekha laughed. 'So why is the writer visiting your house?'

'We knew her back in Bangladesh.'

'Countrywoman?'

Kissing Zulekha on the cheek, Suranjan replied, 'Like you're a neighbourwoman.'

'Hmm.'

Suranjan had never suggested that Zulekha move into his house. It wasn't as though he didn't know how unbearable the atmosphere at her uncle's home was. Ever since she had walked out of Mohabbat's house, Zulekha had hoped that Suranjan would come to her support, that he would say, 'Why do you have to live in such misery, move in with me, we'll live together here.' When there was a perfect union of hearts and bodies, Zulekha saw no sense in living apart. What was Suranjan's problem here? But she didn't ask. The one thing she no longer did was to expect anything. That way, whatever she got gave her great happiness. If Suranjan asked her to move in, she would come at once, without a moment's delay, but she wouldn't bring it up unless he did. She was afraid: what if he said *no*? Their relationship might end in that case. It was still possible to shut herself off from everything and stay on in her uncle's house, but this relationship was more valuable than diamonds to her right now.

But why wasn't Suranjan asking Zulekha to move in? If only he knew the answer himself. He hadn't shifted from Belgharia to Park Circus just for the sake of his love life. He too could have some dreams of his own, couldn't he? He felt both pity and compassion for Zulekha; he loved her too. How innocent, harmless and yet resolute she was! If only Sudeshna had been the same way. He had fallen in love with Sudeshna and married her. It had been a short affair, but it was definitely love. Was he in love with Zulekha in the same way? Suranjan was plunged into doubt. He was driven primarily by a sense of guilt where Zulekha was concerned, which in turn had led to pity, and pity, to affection. Just the way he felt a constant affection for Maya. He had sex with Zulekha, but it wasn't just a physical exchange, his heart was in it too. But Suranjan couldn't quite accept the idea of marrying her and having her live with him. He had a group of Muslim friends in the neighbourhood, whose numbers were swelling. They might not burst into anger if he were to marry Zulekha, but would the conservative Muslims in the neighbourhoods sit by and watch as the wedding took place? Suranjan was apprehensive, not so much for himself as for Zulekha. They might slaughter her like a sacrificial goat one day. Suranjan realized that he was no longer as fearless as he used to be. He had demonstrated whatever was left of his courage on the day of the rape and had saved a helpless woman from Achinta and his gang. But could he really be said to have saved her? Four men had raped Zulekha, and he hadn't stopped them, he hadn't even tried to in the beginning. On the contrary, he had even considered the possibility of raping her himself before the others. He was 100 per cent responsible for what had happened to Zulekha. The abduction. The divorce. Her existence on the floor of her uncle's house. A life of being constantly ignored, of being at the receiving end of utter contempt. At least she had had some rights in Mohabbat's home, the rights of a wife, even if they were far fewer than the rights of a husband. And her greatest source of comfort, Sohag. She would have had Sohag in her life. The greatest loss for Zulekha – more traumatic than the rape and the divorce – was that of Sohag, and it was all Suranjan's doing.

Suddenly he jumped out of bed, putting on his clothes and telling Zulekha, 'Come on, get dressed quickly.'

'Where are we going?'

'I'll take you home and then go to a friend's house. It's urgent.'

'Who's this friend?'

'No one you know.'

'Tell me the name, maybe I do know them. Didn't you say you weren't going out today?'

'I did, but I have to go.'

'Where? To Amjad's house?'

Suranjan did not reply. Zulekha looked downcast. She was certain Suranjan was not going to a friend's house but somewhere else.

Five

Suranjan's life was a mystery, but not Kiranmayee's. Usually it's men who have more secrets, while one woman can easily read the life of another. It has been this way all my life. I have never quite figured out a man. And the more I tried to understand Suranjan, the more I found myself hitting a wall.

Kiranmayee had fed me lovingly, wept with me, treated me like a daughter. Not that someone can suddenly become my mother, but how many would even address me as 'Ma'? Because of this, and because Sudhamay's death had led the family to hardships, I sent an envelope for Kiranmayee through my driver, Tarun, with ten thousand rupees in it. Suranjan brought the envelope back to me at eleven at night. As soon as I opened the door, he held it out to me, saying, 'You sent this by mistake.'

I invited him in. He entered, reeking of alcohol. Handing the envelope over, he said, 'Don't demean yourself.'

I was annoyed. 'Demean myself? When did I do that? Am I not allowed to give your mother a gift?'

'No, you cannot give her so much money as a gift. We get by. Even if not as well as you do, we manage. We're not penniless. We have a house to live in.'

This was true. Millions of families in India lived the way Suranjan's did. In fact, many lived in far worse conditions. Returning the money was a message – they were not desperate. I felt a surge of respect for Kiranmayee and Suranjan. Not that I would have lost my respect for them if they had accepted the money … In fact I would have concluded that they considered me close enough to take money from and that if their circumstances improved, they would try to return it. I didn't want that, though. Maybe I want people to be in my debt. I've noticed that if I owe anything to anyone, it makes me very uncomfortable, I cannot be at peace until I have turned the tables on them and made them owe me something instead. Perhaps indebting others to me while I don't owe them anything is a technique that allows me to hold my head high. Have I been using this technique unconsciously? Maybe, or maybe not. I sliced myself with a sharp knife, then took pity on myself and put the knife away.

'Come on in, sit down.'

'No.'

'Why not? Come in.'

So he did.

'Have you only been drinking, or have you eaten?'

'I haven't eaten.'

'Eat here.'

'No.'

'Why not?'

'I'll eat at home.'

'Your mother will have to get out of bed at this hour to serve you.'

'Like she does every night.'

'Most considerate of you, troubling an old woman.'

'She enjoys it.'

'People do enjoy such things when there isn't much else to enjoy. Eat here.'

'It's not just my mother; you're no better. It seems to me you'll be overjoyed if I eat here.'

I laughed, and Suranjan joined in.

'I don't want a meal; I could have a whisky if you have some.'

I don't drink whisky myself, but I have it at home since friends do. Handing Suranjan a bottle of Black Label, I said, 'Pour yourself a drink.'

Sujata brought a glass and water. Suranjan said, 'Don't you have something less expensive? I'm not used to all this.'

'Don't you like good whisky? No need to be a revolutionary, all right? Eat bad food, wear cheap clothes, live in a slum, won't work anywhere, anti-establishment, anarchist, that's how to be an ideal revolutionary. You think it's so simple?'

'It's not as simple as you think either. Can you live without a fan or AC when it's so hot, the way millions do? Can you survive on rice and vegetable scraps day in and day out?'

'I love green vegetables. Who says it's bad food?'

'You love them because you get meat and fish to eat whenever you want. These things are on rich people's plates now for nutritional reasons. Now that you people have started eating the fish we do, our food has become expensive. Can you tell me what kind of food you dislike?'

'What do you mean?'

'Simple, what don't you like eating?'

'Karela.'

'Can you eat nothing but karela and rice every day?'

'Listen, just because I eat good food or live in a nice house, it doesn't mean I'm insulting those who are forced to starve, who are deprived. I want everyone's standard of living to improve, I want everyone to be affluent.'

'It's easy to say that when you lead a luxurious life yourself. Nothing easier than saying it. But you won't be happy if everyone attains your standard of living. Because you won't have your luxuries then. You won't find a maid to work for you, a gardener to water your plants, a driver to drive your car.'

'It's true that these conveniences have spoilt us. Why don't you ensure they are not available any more? But all this is communist talk; you used to believe in communism once. You haven't joined the CPI(M) here?'

'No.'

'Why not?'

'There's no communism anywhere in the world. They're more capitalist than capitalists themselves.'

'Everything evolves.'

Suranjan smiled. 'That's just an excuse, claiming to be marching with the times when all you're doing is protecting the interests of the rich.'

A long silence followed. Suddenly, I asked, 'Is this an act of repentance, Suranjan?'

'No.'

'What is it, then?'

'Not repentance.'

'What are you doing with Zulekha, then?'

Silence.

'You don't love her. You're not in love with her. Why are you ruining her life?'

'Who says I don't love her?'

'You don't.'

Suranjan glared at me, speaking through clenched teeth: 'How do you know I don't love her?'

'You mean to say you love Zulekha, Suranjan?' I laughed.

Suranjan's brow was lined with creases.

'You love a Muslim woman?'

'I do.'

'I don't believe it.'

'Because...?'

'Because you hate Muslims. Simple.'

'Life isn't black and white, Taslima.'

Suranjan had never addressed me as 'Taslima' before. He used to call me Taslima di.

'Why have you suddenly become sympathetic towards Muslims, Taslima? You had no sympathy for them earlier. You filled pages and pages of *Lajja* with descriptions of the way Muslims brutalized Hindus.'

'I was telling the truth.'

'Yes, you were. So why can't you see the truth here? Or have you chosen to be blind?'

'What are you implying?'

'You know perfectly well what I'm implying.'

'No, I don't. Explain clearly. Are you trying to say that the truth here is just the opposite of what it is in Bangladesh: that Hindus are brutalizing Muslims? No, I haven't seen anything like that for myself. Hindus here don't know much about Muslims and Islam because they don't live with them. Yes, Muslims were attacked in Gujarat, but it was Hindus who protested the most strongly. So did I.'

'You protested because you cannot be an intellectual otherwise.'

'Don't talk rubbish, Suranjan. Hindu, Muslim, Christian, it doesn't matter to me. A human being is a human being. That's the only identity I acknowledge, nothing else. Everyone's a mixture of good and bad, some are conservative, some are progressive. Some have a fundamentalist mindset, some are secular. Some...'

Suranjan did not allow me to finish. He said, 'Have you ever left your home to visit the slums? To see what sort of lives they lead?'

'Who?'

'Muslims.'

'Are you telling me there are no Hindus in slums? That Hindus don't suffer from poverty? Some are rich, many are poor. There's a huge gulf between the rich and the poor. These are political conspiracies. It's not about Hindus and Muslims. Are you telling me there are no Muslims among the wealthy? Have you any idea how many rich Muslims there are in India? You could say Muslims are lagging behind. Now if they choose to turn their religion into the law, if they build madrasas and send their children to study there, if they reject scientific education, if they pack women into burqas, if they prevent them from becoming self-reliant, how will society improve? There will be neither economic nor psychological improvement. I have started a group – the Religion-free Humanist Platform. Atheists born in Muslim families have been brought together on this platform to fight for the replacement of religious laws with a uniform civil code based on equality: a secular society, secular education, human rights, women's rights. One must do this if one is genuinely sympathetic towards those who have been left behind. Nothing can be achieved by shedding copious tears over poverty. Useless…'

Suranjan was listening carefully. He had lit a cigarette. Smoking is not allowed in my flat. Anyone who wants to smoke must go out to the balcony and use the ashtray there. This is what I tell visitors. The balcony was suspended in the fragrance of night-blooming jasmine. Suranjan was drinking whisky; I was neither drinking nor smoking. I had tasted freedom after escaping the clutches of tobacco.

My curiosity about Suranjan was not to be satiated. I asked the old question again: 'Weren't you a Hindu fundamentalist once, Suranjan?'

'I was. Very much so. I wanted to stay that way.'

'What happened after that?'

'I don't know.'

'I'm sure you do. How can someone not know what's going on within them?'

'It can happen. Things can change without you being aware of them.'

'Are you not a fundamentalist any longer?'

'I don't know.'

'Yes or no? Don't beat about the bush.'

'I told you already, I don't know.'

'That's impossible. You may not know about others, but you surely do about yourself.'

'*I* certainly don't.'

'Are you confused?'

'Perhaps.'

'Why did you pick Park Circus of all places to live in?'

Levelling his eyes at me in the light and shade of the balcony, Suranjan replied: 'Zulekha.'

'Zulekha?'

'Yes, Zulekha.'

Suranjan left after smoking his cigarette, leaving me astonished as he walked out the door. I remained sitting for a long time. In front of me lay the envelope with the ten thousand rupees he had returned. I felt lonely.

Six

Zulekha might have tried to hide in her uncle's house, but all her relatives everywhere, those who had neither been to her wedding nor checked on her after she was married, materialized suddenly to condemn her. Not one of her uncles or aunts, not even the children, spared her in their denouncements. How could Zulekha do this, how could she bring calumny upon the family? Zulekha had never been told of the glory of her family. She hadn't ever been told of anything to be proud of. Strangely, no one blamed Mohabbat. Zulekha alone was the target of their criticism. They had abducted Zulekha and raped her. Still, Mohabbat loved her so much that he didn't divorce her. On top of all this, she was up to no good with a Hindu. While her uncle did allow her to stay, he kept saying, 'Impossible, I can't live in the neighbourhood with honour; this girl may have no shame, but I do.' Zulekha had no idea that her uncle, a professional butcher, was so highly thought of by his neighbours. Her trouble was her BA degree, which told her that even if the world rejected her, she would survive on her own. Her trouble was also her intellect, which asked, why can't I rent a house for myself somewhere in the city if I want to? Without her education and her questioning mind, she could have stayed comfortably in any relative's or any husband's house, or even in a brothel. She could have got herself work as a manual labourer or a maid. But her BA degree told her, don't do that, you deserve far better. But it didn't actually help find her a job. She was desperate to run away from the viciousness in her uncle's house, but where to? If she had a place to go, she wouldn't have allowed herself to be slaughtered day in and day out, her honour to be sliced every day by people's tongues, in a butcher's house.

She didn't want to let herself die so easily. That was why she had not resisted while being gang raped. With no one to support her, she had tolerated her husband raping her cold-bloodedly year after year. She hadn't protested – where would she go if she did? This question had threatened her constantly. No one looks for a place to go to till they're evicted. Only when they've lost their way do people feel the urge to find it again. And so she had managed to find a shelter and a job of some sort after her husband had thrown her out. Although things had looked dark for Zulekha, there was a silver lining too. Her father was crippled, and none of these relatives was particularly close to her family, which was why they had neither held out a helping hand nor abandoned her. They had made their feelings known from a safe distance. Even her elder sister's in-laws had been vilifying her. She had called Sulekha, who had told her that everything was out in the open and that everyone was blaming Zulekha. You wouldn't find another instance in all of India of a Muslim woman having an affair with a Hindu man in her Muslim husband's home. That Mohabbat had only divorced her bore testimony to his kindness; anyone else would have chopped her body into pieces and thrown them into the river. Sulekha's husband had been abusing her: 'If your sister's such a bitch, you can't be much better.' Apparently, he had lost face in front of everyone because of his sister-in-law's shameful behaviour.

Zulekha had told her: 'I won't go back home to Suri again. Make sure to check on Baba regularly. Tell yourself I have disappeared, women disappear all the time from villages and towns, they're sold off in distant places.' Zulekha had called from a phone booth, wiping her eyes continuously with the back of her hand. She didn't tell Suranjan about the slurs she was being subjected to, which would amount to putting pressure on him. There was only one way to rescue her standing in society, and with her family and relatives, which was for Suranjan to convert and for the two of them to get married. But that word, 'marriage', it had never escaped Suranjan's lips. Zulekha would derive no pleasure from forcing him into something he was reluctant about. She knew Suranjan as someone who had terrorists for friends, men who had abducted an innocent woman and raped her to take revenge on her husband. How could Zulekha consider marrying such a man? At the moment, it appeared Suranjan was attracted to her, but was it because he really had fallen in love with her, or did it stem from a sense of guilt? Maybe he wanted to atone for it this way. 'Some of my friends have made you suffer greatly; because of them, you have had to tolerate sex without love. I will compensate for it with countless occasions of loving sex.' Certainly, this would amount to a most pleasant kind of expiation, but it wouldn't lead to a genuine relationship between them, of love or friendship. It wouldn't even lead to real enmity. From time to time, Zulekha asked herself whether she was indeed in love with Suranjan. It seemed to her that she was, but she had her doubts about him, for she didn't trust him. Was it possible to love someone when you didn't trust them? Most definitely it was, for she did love Suranjan after a fashion, even without trusting him.

But was this only physical love? Zulekha didn't think so. If it was just a matter of a physical relationship, why had she never climaxed during sex with Mohabbat? Because she had never loved him, that's why. From the very first day, they had failed to build an emotional connection. Mohabbat had always felt like a machine to her, with no inflexions in his voice, never a smile on his face. When he called her name, it was like a sound emerging from the mouth of a machine. 'Come here, can't you hear I'm calling you, lie down.' When she did, he would stare for some time at her stiff form wrapped in a sari. Then he would lift the lower half of her sari, lift his own lungi as well, spit into the palm of his right hand with his sinuous, snake-like tongue, rub the saliva on the tip of his cock, and push his way into her. Zulekha would groan in pain every time. For a minute or so, Mohabbat would run his penis in and out of her as though he was playing with a toy car, and then move away. This was how Zulekha paid for being a woman; this was what she had to bear. If you were born a woman, you would be forced to marry some man you didn't know, who would do whatever he liked with your body, and you couldn't protest. Zulekha didn't break the mould. If she'd wanted to be a rebel, she would certainly not have married a crockery-shop owner. The proposal had been presented to her father, who had insisted on the match. None of their relatives had suggested that Mohabbat might not be suitable. If they considered a teacher or a doctor or an engineer a better choice, why hadn't they found such a match for Zulekha? She hadn't met anyone in college she could have fallen in love with. Even her college education may have been cut short had Sultana Kabir, a schoolteacher from Nalhati, not persisted in drilling into her the importance of education for girls, especially Muslim girls. Without an education, she would have to accept the life of a maid. Zulekha's father believed that girls should not study and should marry a decent boy instead. Luckily, he didn't fancy maids' lives for his daughters either.

It was Rabiul Islam who had introduced Zulekha to Sultana Kabir. Zulekha had been inspired to live with pride, but eventually things hadn't worked out, and she was forced to get married. Her father Maniruddin didn't have an option, for neighbours were already beginning to talk: 'The girl's growing up, aren't you going to get her married?' They had waited long enough, time to do something.

With no matchmaker or even a well-wisher in sight, when a proposal came from Mohabbat's family, Sulekha's husband approved, so did a couple of Zulekha's uncles, and that was all it took to send for the priest and complete the rituals. Life appeared rather strange to Zulekha. Sohag resembled Mohabbat, and his nature, too, she feared, was turning out to be like his. He hadn't cried even once after his mother had been forced to leave home, nor had he demanded to go with her. He was the apple of his father's eye, and was closer to Mohabbat than to Zulekha. His father had power and influence – qualities everyone realizes are advantageous from an early age. Children learn quickly whom to mirror in order to enjoy the perks, and usually feel attached to the person early on.

Zulekha had asked Sohag, 'What do you call your abba's wife, babu?'

'Amma.'

'Why do you call her Amma? She isn't your amma, I am.'

'Abbu said I should call her Amma. So I do.'

'But I'm asking you not to. Won't you listen to me?'

Sohag remained quiet. Zulekha realized he wouldn't listen to her, that he would follow his father's instructions.

'Do you remember when I was there?'

Sohag nodded a yes. He did.

'Do you want to live with me? Let's you and I live together.'

'What about Abbu?'

'Not him, just you and I.'

Sohag was silent.

'You won't live without Abbu?'

Sohag shook his head. No.

Suddenly, breaking free from his mother's arms, he raced out of the front door of Zulekha's uncle's house. The maid at Mohabbat's house never let go of his hand. Zulekha stood watching till he disappeared from sight. She feared that Sohag would gradually stop coming to meet her. Perhaps he had been told by the maid Maryam that his mother was a loose woman, that she had run away with a Hindu man, and so on. Mohabbat and his new wife must have maligned Zulekha, making the boy believe bad things about his mother. The older he grew, the more he would hate her. Zulekha felt utterly lonely, a pain eating away at her heart. She stood holding the door frame, gazing at the world outside. It was such an enormous sky out there, a yawning emptiness. Perhaps this was the moment when women killed themselves. Zulekha didn't want to kill herself, she wanted to live, she had always wanted to live, on her own terms, but hadn't succeeded. Still she had wanted to live on, in whatever manner the society and her family permitted. But now her life didn't suit her tastes at all, not even slightly. Her demands were not big, nor were her dreams sky-high. If what Suranjan claimed was right, that he was indeed connected to the group that had abducted and raped her, then he had gone from being avenging enemy to abductor to a man harbouring a guilty conscience to lover – or, at least, to someone whom Zulekha considered her lover, even if he himself did not. Still, she had not built any dreams around her relationship with him. Whenever she felt unhappy, whenever her body was on fire, whenever her heart yearned to be swept away, there was Suranjan, but only as long as he was physically there. It had happened many times that he had promised to meet her but not shown up. He had forgotten his promise; he had not been at home though he had said he would be. When Zulekha went over, Suranjan would be missing, so she would be forced to chat with Kiranmayee, who liked her and commiserated with her when they met. But Zulekha could tell that the older woman didn't want the relationship to deepen.

One day, Kiranmayee asked her, 'Look, it's a difficult time for you. You must consult a doctor. This is no time to be unwell.'

'But I'm not sick.'

'Be careful you don't get pregnant and get into more trouble.'

Zulekha bowed her head in embarrassment, unable to respond. She knew there would be no culmination of her relationship with Suranjan, that it would stay this way till their mental and physical attraction for each other waned. Living together was not possible. Had they been able to do that, even without getting married, she would at least have been released from the misery of living in her uncle's house. Her earnings from her job at the mall were not enough to even rent a place where she could stay safely. She had no choice but to live in Calcutta. There was no reason to go back to Suri, where she could well imagine the unbearable life she would have to lead. Everyone would tear into her there and she would have no choice but to kill herself. She knew people – even her father – would be happy if she did that. But she wasn't interested in pleasing them. Her life didn't belong to anyone else. It was hers and hers alone. Why should she allow others to trample over it whenever they wanted? She had done no wrong. Some people had taken revenge for her husband's wrongdoing by assaulting her. And far from apologizing to her for this, far from giving her all the love and compassion possible, he had beaten her up. No relative or father had come to her aid then. She had called her father; he was the only one she had told, sobbing, of all that had happened, to which her father had said, 'Beg for forgiveness from your husband, Zulekha.'

'Why should I? What have I done that's wrong?'

'Beg him for forgiveness. He's your husband. He can always beat you.'

'Why should I beg his forgiveness? Explain to me how I have wronged him. Some people abducted me – is that my fault? Don't you feel bad for me? You don't have a single kind word for me. All you're doing is shout at me.'

Her father was furious. He refused to forgive her until she apologized to her husband. Zulekha did not seek her husband's forgiveness, for she didn't know what crime she had committed. She hadn't done anything wrong; it was Amjad and his friends who were guilty, Mohabbat who was guilty.

Zulekha should ... Zulekha didn't know what she should do. Her confusion had taken her to Suri, where she had first tried to meet her sister. But she was told on the phone that she wasn't welcome at Sulekha's in-laws' house. If anyone got to know that Sulekha had met her sister, her in-laws would create trouble for her. It would be better if Zulekha came back a month later, when things had calmed down. Sulekha would have no problem meeting her.

After this, Zulekha had visited Rabiul Islam and Sultana Kabir at their homes in Suri. She had been given tea and biscuits, but neither had wanted Zulekha to linger. She had visited them for their support, to reassure herself that they were with her. But she hadn't received sanctuary from anyone. Both had advised her to return to her father. What would she do there? Everyone would spit on her with hatred and her only option would be to kill herself. Or to marry some other thug. No decent, well-educated man would want to marry Zulekha. Her crime of being divorced by her husband was overshadowed by her crime of being abducted and raped. And her greatest crime was to have had an affair with a Hindu.

Zulekha was desperate to meet her crippled father. His household comprised a servant and a distant nephew. Rahman, his son from his first wife, Zulekha's stepbrother, had left for Kashmir at seventeen, when Zulekha was very young. He used to write at first, but the letters stopped after a while, and they never heard from him again. There was a framed photograph of Rahman on the wall. Zulekha had never found out why he went to Kashmir, why he had not returned. Not a day passed when her father didn't gaze at the photograph and sigh.

Both his wives had died young. His second wife had had to suffer much humiliation for being unable to give birth to a son. On her way to the railway station, Zulekha recollected the scorn heaped upon her mother, who would be at the receiving end of abuse, swearing, and even spit all day, and would weep in a low voice deep into the silent night. Sulekha and Zulekha had not been able to reduce her suffering. No one knew what illness she had died of. She didn't receive any treatment, so how was anyone to know? She used to have intense stomach aches, which her father responded to with 'she's probably overeaten'. For eleven years, that was all he had said: 'She's overeaten.' Apparently, she would eat anything she could lay her hands on, indiscriminately. Zulekha walked faster towards the station. Behind her lay her home, where she had been born and brought up, which had been her house till she got married.

Her retired schoolteacher father was lying on a cot in the yard. Rahman's photograph hung on a wall inside. The servant boy handed him whatever he needed. When he spoke to friends and relatives who dropped by, he declared he would disown Zulekha. In reality, he wanted her to die. Zulekha kept walking, perspiring profusely. She couldn't help feeling she was walking towards a new life, one in which no one else but she existed. The society she lived in had buried her; she was headed for a new society now, one that would accept her. She was incapable of living outside society, and was not willing to dedicate her life in a red-light area to calming the bodily passions of those who lived amidst nothing but green lights. If it was ever time to go there, she promised herself, she would kill herself.

Zulekha did not tell Suranjan what had happened in Suri. He had asked, 'So what did you do there?'

'So many things.'

'So many things, what? Did you meet your old lovers?'

'Of course. I'm going to run away with one of them. They're more handsome than you are.' Zulekha was laughing.

'Why did you come back, then?'

'I came back. To check.'

'On whom?'

'You, obviously.'

'To see what? Whether I'm pining away for you?'

'I have no such hope.'

'You didn't do anything untoward in Suri, did you?'

'You think I have the ability? It's the others who do untoward things, I'm either a witness or a victim.'

Zulekha had no idea whether her barb had hit home with Suranjan, but she thought not. He didn't ask any more questions about Suri. Zulekha didn't have any information to volunteer. She could tell anyone about the way her sister and other family elders had treated her, but she couldn't tell Suranjan. If she were to confess that they had in fact thrown her out, Suranjan might conclude she was seeking shelter with him now. So she pretended that nothing unpleasant had taken place, that everyone had supported her decisions, that her friends and family had unanimously promised cooperation, that she had been told to live her life the way she wanted to, that she had been reminded that everyone's good wishes were with her and would always be with her. To her family, her community, her society, she was an object of admiration.

Why should she tell Suranjan what had happened? Her self-respect was still intact; she wanted to keep living with it. She wanted work – if only she could get a schoolteacher's job. Suranjan knew so many people, he had worked as a teacher himself for a long time, surely he could have helped her out. Zulekha didn't expect anything from anyone, she didn't want to, and yet somewhere in the back of her mind expectations lurked. Like those from Suranjan; or from her elder sister Sulekha, that she wouldn't turn Zulekha down; from Rabiul and Sultana too. Zulekha had only a handful of people to rely on, not an entire army. She continued battling single-handedly against her expectations. If only she could get rid of them from her life altogether! It wasn't as though those who had nothing, no one, no dreams, didn't survive in this city. There were many who breathed only because they were alive, who gazed upon an infinite emptiness with empty eyes and an empty heart. If only Zulekha could have been like them! She had to sleep on an oil-stained pillow in her uncle's house, wrapped in a sheet that reeked of urine, facing the open door of the lavatory. What if Suranjan could see where she slept, how she lived in this house every single day! She doubted whether her anguish would elicit any sympathy at all. At most, he might cluck his tongue in commiseration, nothing more.

Zulekha consoled herself with the thought that his powers were limited too. Suranjan himself lived in a state of hardship. His economic backbone had collapsed long ago. Being privy to Zulekha's plight would only increase the pressure on him. It was better that he didn't see her living conditions. If he did, Zulekha might expect him to take her away, and then what if he didn't? That was her fear. She wanted the attraction and intimacy between them to last at any cost. It was her only way to dispel wretchedness now. Without Suranjan, her world would fall to pieces. In him, she had found a man who had entered into a physical relationship with her without raping her. He never touched her without her consent. Unknown to himself, he had grown to become the only source of joy in Zulekha's life, and so she didn't want him to feel the slightest sense of responsibility or dutifulness. Freedom and not bondage was what was needed to keep the relationship going.

So there was no need for Suranjan to know the truth. Let him assume that she wasn't being inconvenienced in any way at her uncle's house, that her job was fine too. Her salary at Shoppers Stop was five thousand a month; let him take it for granted that there would be increments every year, that Sohag cried for his mother all the time. Let him imagine some good things in Zulekha's life. Without these, Zulekha would be nothing but a gang rape victim, a helpless woman who had been beaten up by her husband. And she did not want a fresh wave of pity from Suranjan. Love had replaced sympathy – if at all anything had, that is – and she did not want sympathy to replace love now and ruin her life.

Sometimes, Zulekha was racked with doubt: was there really any love for her in Suranjan's heart, or was it just that he had found a way to have sex without having to pay, without having to assume any responsibilities? He couldn't have had a relationship like this with any other woman in this city – they would have demanded a lot more, even marriage.

The other option was Shonagachhi, but visiting a brothel involved both risks and expenses. Zulekha was not threatening Suranjan's finances, family or social relationships in any way. On the contrary, she was giving both her heart and her body to him, unhesitatingly, unconditionally. Was it possible to keep giving all your life? Zulekha felt herself alone, absolutely alone.

This feeling was essential. Zulekha held back her tears when they threatened to burst forth – she couldn't afford to cry. She bought several newspapers every day to pore over the jobs columns. She realized that she was qualified for a far better job than one that involved standing constantly behind a sales counter in a uniform. If she found such a job, she would move out of this neighbourhood. Sohag was fine. If he loved his mother, he would seek her out. So would Suranjan, if he loved her. No matter how much he claimed that was the case, she didn't believe he had moved to Park Circus after all those years of living in Belgharia for her sake. He must have had some other reason.

Seven

Maya had become incensed after learning of Suranjan's relationship with Zulekha. She had given her brother an ultimatum: 'If you maintain this relationship, you and I are done. You have to choose, Dada.'

Suranjan could not imagine not hearing Maya call him 'Dada'. The world could be swept away for all he cared. He was willing to sacrifice everything for her.

Kiranmayee didn't want him to marry Zulekha either. The girl visited him at home, she was well behaved, decent, Kiranmayee enjoyed chatting with her, and, most importantly, Suranjan was happy. When she visited, the two of them went into his room and locked the door in front of her eyes, obviously because they loved each other. In fact, Kiranmayee thought it was preferable to meet a lover at home, rather than go out and get into bad company. Her son's wife had divorced him and left. He was a lonely male; he couldn't be happy without a companion. This was how she rationalized the whole thing to herself, and tried to explain it to Maya too.

But Maya was adamant. Not only was there no question of marrying her, Suranjan must not even maintain a relationship with Zulekha. It was not for nothing – she had obviously not forgotten the nightmare of the riots in Dhaka, when those Muslims had torn her apart. Maya could forgive anyone in the world except Muslims. Just imagine, the same Maya for whose sake Suranjan's marriage to Sudeshna had ended was now insisting that if her brother couldn't find anyone else, she would be happy for him to patch up with Sudeshna. Sudeshna had not remarried, which meant the option was always open. He must break off his relationship with the Muslim woman at once, this very moment.

This was what Maya was saying through her tears, seated on Kiranmayee's bed. Her mother was sitting on a chair, while Suranjan was standing in the doorway. There was a commotion just outside the window, where residents were collecting water. The window curtain was flying in the breeze. Some of their neighbours here were Hindu. Anyone could hear Maya crying if they wanted to. Sighing, Kiranmayee said, 'I will never have happiness in my life.'

Maya looked daggers at her. 'Maybe I have given you no happiness, but why is your favourite child depriving you? Why have you moved *here*, of all places? Nothing but a den of terrorists. Down the road it's nothing but Muslims all the way. Who's going to ensure your security here?'

Maya sobbed, and Suranjan's heart went out to her. He didn't know what to do. Maya was his only sister, his beloved little sister; they had grown up together in their house in Tantibajar in Dhaka, where she used to be devoted to her elder brother. He understood the agony in her heart; he knew each of her utterances, her non-utterances, her sighs, her smiles, and the reasons for them. He would have snapped off his relationship with Zulekha if it were possible – right now, this instant. Not because she was Muslim, but for Maya, because Maya wanted him to. He needed no other reason. He wasn't going to get back together with Sudeshna – a relationship that could break so easily, at the slightest of knocks, was not worth putting back together – it would break as easily again, with another knock. It was better to be single.

And just as he was reflecting upon this, Maya said, 'It would be preferable if Dada were alone. So many people are, I am too, I'm alone for all intents and purposes.' Now Maya burst into tears, crying for a long time. She cried with her head on Kiranmayee's shoulder – there was no other sound in the room besides her sobs. No one asked her to stop; no one's request would stop her. The purpose behind Maya's visits was to cry without restraint for all the dissatisfaction and unhappiness in her life. Without these tears, she wouldn't be able to spend the rest of the week the way she did, dry-eyed. She gathered all her suffering in her heart like ice, which melted into a river only in the company of her mother and brother.

Suranjan sighed. If he had unlimited money, he would have taken a nice house on rent in a fine neighbourhood, and brought Maya and her two children home to stay with him and Kiranmayee. Not for himself, not for Kiranmayee, not even for Zulekha, Suranjan's regret about being poor was only for Maya's sake. He had told her one day: 'If I could get a good job, or some work with lots of money, you wouldn't have to suffer, you wouldn't have to live with that bastard.' Maya had hugged him then. Controlling his tears, Suranjan had said, 'Don't forgive your incompetent brother before I can do this.' If only Maya didn't have to bring her complaints and weep over them. If only she could be happy.

'My fate doesn't hold happiness for me, Dada…'

Suranjan didn't believe in destiny. He knew there was no such thing, nothing was predetermined. Maya could have had the life she wanted if they had a lot of money. Not that he believed money could buy happiness – he knew plenty of unhappily rich people. There was no doubt that he had a better life now than when he had a great deal more money. Whenever he and Sudeshna fought after he got home, he would hit the bottle in their Nandan Nagar house. Sudeshna would be in one room and he, in another. Finally, Kiranmayee would try to take the bottle away late at night, saying, 'Who do you think you're troubling besides yourself? Do you think you're taking revenge on anyone? No, nobody will be affected by your drinking. If anyone has to die because of it, it will be you, no one else.' But none of this helped, Suranjan would keep drinking till he passed out in the wicker chair. None of this made any difference to Sudeshna, who had figured out soon after the wedding that Suranjan was nothing but a bundle of rage, both within and without. People might mistake it for a strong personality, but the fact was, he was extremely selfish, and indifferent at the same time. He could cold-bloodedly kill someone, but also dive into a river to rescue someone who was drowning. Both these personas existed side by side. Sudeshna had realized that no normal person could live with him.

Suranjan hadn't been able to save Maya; it had only been a fantasy. Maya's abduction by Muslims had turned him into a madman. He was willing to save her even at the cost of his own life. But he had failed. Frustrated, he had decided to leave the country – a country where no Hindu was safe, where his beloved younger sister was not safe. While he was packing to leave, he'd opened the door one morning to find Maya's body lying near the stairs. He had screamed at the sight. Maya was dead. He had thought Maya was dead. He had carried her inside in his arms, Sudhamay had checked her pulse, his hands shaking uncontrollably as he tried to listen for a heartbeat with his stethoscope. Kiranmayee had kept stroking Maya's cold body. All that Sudhamay could mutter was, 'Take her to the hospital at once, she's alive.' Kiranmayee had begun to wail at the top of her voice, and Suranjan had left with Maya in his arms, followed by Kiranmayee. Sudhamay would have gone too, if he had the strength. They had got into a rickshaw and gone directly to PG Hospital. Saline, blood transfusion, strong injections.

Maya had opened her eyes and spoken two days later. But they didn't change their decision, leaving for India as soon as Maya was released from the hospital, handing over their house for safekeeping to a relative. They had never asked Maya what happened, what those men had done. Maya would start crying sometimes, without saying why. Kiranmayee or Suranjan would draw her head down to their shoulder, letting her cry on it, or stroke her back, or put their arms around her to let her know they were with her.

The news of Maya's disappearance and return was kept a complete secret from the distant relative whose house they had put up in. After all, they had decided, this was not the kind of news that should be broadcast to everyone. Although they had given detailed descriptions of the Muslims' attacks on their home, they hadn't said a word about the assault on Maya. India being a Hindu-majority country, their address being Calcutta in West Bengal, Prafulla Nagar being a neighbourhood primarily for Hindus, and their relative's home being a safe place, none of them had had to fear Muslims any more. All that Suranjan knew, all that his parents knew, was that although there was no warmth, there was security here. But Sudhamay's world had come crashing down when his life's savings of four lakh taka were stolen. In desperate need of a place to stay, they couldn't afford to reject the shelter they had. They had originally been given the extra room in the yard, but suddenly Shankar Ghosh had shifted them into his three-room house. Anyone would imagine he was being generous, but no one knew then that he would touch Maya at night, clamping his hand over her mouth. After the first time, even that had become unnecessary, for Maya wouldn't make a sound at all, lest they be thrown out the next day, or even the same night. If they were evicted, they might have nowhere to go but the train tracks. And this possibility made Maya picture an eyeless locomotive running over her like a fierce monster. Her body was being crushed to a pulp, her blood and flesh shooting out to fall on her parents and brother.

Maya would live in a state of perpetual fear. Those Muslim men had already mauled her body; she had died; her life had been saved by accident. If a Hindu also wanted her body now in exchange for offering the family a place to stay and two meals a day, well then, her body was no virginal vault that she had to protect fiercely. She had not objected.

Suranjan was apprehensive that something was going on, that something was being done to Maya, and she wasn't resisting. Kiranmayee probably realized it too. Maya wouldn't look her brother or mother in the eye when talking to them. She behaved oddly. Sometimes she had dark circles under her eyes, sometimes her lips would be swollen, or there would be bruises and scratches on her neck and arms. If asked, she would say 'Why do you need to know' in a voice full of hurt or fury or something like that, though no one understood whom it was directed at. Or perhaps they didn't wish to understand. No one knew at that time how Sudhamay would set up his practice in this new place, or how Suranjan would get a job. There was no one to help them. And Suranjan didn't have the strength to ask Maya any questions or to hear her answer. Knowing would mean having to take on the responsibility of rescuing all of them from this hellhole.

Maya would say, 'Can't you get a job, Dada, is it not possible? If you can't, tell me, I'll go looking for one. You have more qualifications than me for a job, but can you at least arrange for me to coach students? Can't you find us a place to rent?'

'I'm trying, I go looking every day,' Suranjan would reply.

'Liar. You're not searching hard enough.' Maya's eyes held no plea, only contempt. When she looked at her parents too, her eyes radiated loathing. None of them had known that helplessness could devour a family in such an ugly way. They had all turned mute. Suranjan, unworthy brother, had failed completely. Sudhamay was the one who had had to see patients almost round the clock for the meagre fee of five rupees, while Maya tried to coach children. But here in India, the textbooks, the methods of teaching, were all different. Getting work in Calcutta after moving from Bangladesh was proving to be difficult. She was looking to tutor children, but the work she had found involved massaging children with oil and bathing them, as well as washing their clothes. At home, though, she said she gave them lessons. This back-breaking work brought her only three hundred rupees a month. On her way back home in the evening, she would see young women in their finery lining the pavements. Soon, she realized that men paid for their bodies. Once, Maya had gone up to one of them to ask, 'How much do you make?' The woman had smiled and held up her palm with the five fingers spread apart. Maya hadn't understood: had she meant five, fifty or five hundred? Just to get out of the house they were in, Maya had considered joining the women on the pavement too. It seemed far better than the 300 she got at the end of the month. If she could make fifty each time her body was used, six times was all it would take to make three hundred and she wouldn't have to slave the entire month. The possibility began to swirl in her mind – since she no longer had the responsibility of preserving the sanctity of her body, using it to get out of this hellhole should be her only objective. There really was no point expecting her useless brother and father to do anything.

Suranjan had resigned from the political party because he hadn't been given a loan. He was far too emotional, lacking in practical sense. Maya knew this too; she knew it was futile to depend on him, and yet she did. Suranjan appeared helpless. It didn't seem like he was the elder of the two and she often felt he was her adorable younger brother. While Maya no longer met his eyes, she knew that

uncertainty and anxiety flickered in them. She didn't want to look
at such eyes.

I would murder Shankar Ghosh one day, she told herself
repeatedly, every day; all she needed was some firm ground beneath
her feet. She had considered telling him this the day they left his
house for good, but she didn't, for the place they had taken on rent
was not far. From Prafulla Nagar, they had moved to Nandan Nagar.
She hadn't spoken out of fear, lest he mount another attack on them.
Maya was no fool. She knew only too well that evil men had all
kinds of evil designs. There was no telling when he might set their
house on fire, or poison all of them, or frame them in a crime he had
himself committed. Suranjan had wanted to extract four lakh taka
from Shankar Ghosh by hook or by crook, he had said, 'I will murder
him and bathe in his blood and only then will I leave this house.'
Maya had said, 'Forget about it, if you want to survive forget all this,
Dada.' But to forget was not to forgive, and Maya had not forgiven
Shankar. She had forgiven those monsters of Dhaka even less. The
other person she had not forgiven was Taslima Nasreen, who had
ruined her life by writing *Lajja*. Anyone who came with a proposal
for her found out that *Lajja* had been written about their family.
Maya had been abducted; she had been raped. So, marriage was
impossible. Maya had met more than one young man who was keen
on romance and marriage, but had backed off on hearing rumours
that her virginity had been taken. Muslim men had raped her – a
prospect even more horrifying than Hindus raping her. No marriage
proposals came, and it became obvious to Maya that she wasn't going
to get married. She would have, had *Lajja* not been published. Not
everyone was willing to believe it was the story of Suranjan's family,
but there was no dearth of people ready to believe that it was about
Maya being raped. She cried loudly, burning every copy of the book
that could be found in the house. She was on the brink of insanity.
There was no greater curse than starting life afresh in a new country;

it wasn't possible without money or the help of others. It was easier
to end one's life than to restart it. Maya had been on the verge of
suicide several times, though she had desisted eventually.

The hardships of the family worsened rapidly, and Maya chafed
constantly. Finally, she married a man named Tapan Mandal, an
unemployed drunkard, whom some referred to as a lower-caste
person. Caste was of no concern to Maya. The main thing was that
she was marrying a Hindu and not a Muslim. She had accepted
Tapan's proposal with alacrity and had willingly moved into her in-
laws' house, dressed as a demure Bengali Hindu bride. There, she
had to cook for twenty-five people, serve them their food, and make
sure they were looked after. Rice for lunch, ruti for dinner. She had
to personally make fifty rutis for dinner every day. Technically, the
responsibilities were divided between the four sisters-in-law, but
effectively she had a mountain of work. Maya had never worked
in the kitchen. She didn't know how to. But here at her in-laws',
she was not going to get any respite by claiming she didn't know
how to cook, that she had never done household work before. Her
husband came home some nights, but not all. He was apparently
taken care of lovingly by a middle-aged woman in Jadavpur. Tapan
lived on her ample wealth. Her husband was dead, and both her
children lived abroad. Alone in Calcutta, she had Tapan as her
only companion. A drunkard with no income was precisely what
she was looking for. All he needed was a supply of alcohol to be at
her side constantly, wagging his tail. Maya had come to know all
this from her sisters-in-law soon after her wedding. She had tried
her utmost to bring him back to her, to free him of drinking and
from that woman, but in vain. In the course of these efforts, she
had offered her body to him repeatedly, and his casual sex with her
had planted the seeds of two children, without her achieving her
purpose. Tapan had not reformed. He had married her because
marriage was a social necessity. He had slept with her because he

enjoyed sex, but he had developed no attraction for either his wife or his children. Since it was a large family, the children grew up in the company of their cousins, with their uncles and grandfather playing the role of their absent father. The real responsibility was Maya's. She had got a job at a pharmaceuticals company at a salary of one thousand five hundred rupees a month, a number that had climbed to six thousand five hundred. She had to contribute eight hundred rupees to the family kitty for food, the rest being spent on clothes for her children and herself, school fees, bus and metro fares, and snacks. She couldn't save any of it. Nor was there any means of borrowing from her brother or mother when the need arose. Still, Maya stayed on at her in-laws', sporting all the symbols of a married Bengali Hindu woman. Her room was lined with deities, and she personally was a staunch devotee of Goddess Kali, visiting the temples at Kalighat and Dakshineshwar whenever she could. She had no other interests, such as watching films or plays or going to concerts or even spending time with friends. After moving to India, she had had to put away all the passions she had developed back home. As a matter of fact, Maya had no friends. The creature she called her husband was more of an absence than a presence in her life, and still she had a line of vermilion powder in her hair. Why? She had asked herself this question and then answered it too: so that no one considered her easily available. A husband, a family, in-laws, children, the line of vermilion ... all of these yielded respect, but without them, women were at the mercy of predatory men. To Maya, her in-laws' house was not hell, it was a place that allowed her to survive. Her husband came home once a fortnight, sometimes once a month. On some occasions, she had had to haul him in from the pavement in a drunken stupor. He had often vomited on her. Still, Maya hadn't considered leaving her in-laws' house. Where would she go, it wasn't as though she had a safe haven elsewhere. She didn't want to earn a bad name for herself again by leaving.

She didn't want another storm of uncertainty. The children were growing up in a ten-foot-by-ten-foot room, Maya slept in the same room, with them on either side. They ate on the bed, studied there too. With the large bed, there was very little room for anything else. Maya lived for the day when her children would grow up and support themselves and take care of Maya too, at which time they could all leave this house.

A few months later, Maya bought Suranjan a shirt, and Kiranmayee, a sari. Suranjan was delighted to get a shirt from his sister, but what could he give her in return? Nothing. Maya cried, complained, shouted, exploded in rage, but Suranjan knew she loved him fiercely. The one who is loved always knows this better than the one who loves. Maya couldn't stand it when Kiranmayee wept over their former life in Bangladesh. 'Don't even mention that country to me, it has ruined us, it has killed all my dreams, all the possibilities my life had,' Maya would say.

Kiranmayee found it more comforting to talk of Bangladesh to Suranjan, who listened quietly. At the market, she would buy things imported from Bangladesh and cook them for her son. Belgharia had been filled with people from her country, but here in Park Circus, she hadn't found a single such person. Everyone and everything was from this side of the border. The young men from north Calcutta who visited Suranjan occasionally were locals too. With Maya, Kiranmayee had no opportunity to indulge herself in nostalgic memories from back home – their family visit to Sudhamay's friend's house in the hills of Chattogram, the trip to Rangamati from where Maya didn't want to return, the boat journey to the Sundarbans, those happy-go-lucky days, celebrating the rains with khichuri and hilsa, Maya going out to play in the torrential downpour. Remembering those days was like paddling in a pool of little joys. These were the only occasions worth reminiscing about when looking to cheer oneself up. Kiranmayee wanted to keep the painful memories as far away as possible. But Maya didn't want to be reminded of anything at all about her life in Bangladesh. She didn't want to remember being abducted from Zindabahar Lane; she didn't want to remember being mauled and bitten and mangled by a group of Muslim men in ways that words cannot describe. Kiranmayee gazed at the rain wistfully in Calcutta, where there was no Maya to go out and play, no Sudhamay to buy fresh hilsa. They couldn't afford such expensive fish right now. When the prices dropped later, Kiranmayee would try to get a small one and invite Maya for a meal. But she knew that her daughter would eat it as though it were a bitter vegetable curry. The hilsa couldn't be separated from the river Padma, and the Padma, from Bangladesh. Maya didn't care for all this, and while she ate the fish at her mother's insistence, she derived no joy from it. Still, the sight of her children eating hilsa made tears of joy run down Kiranmayee's face. The family wouldn't have been in this situation today had Sudhamay been alive. Whenever she saw her children happy, Kiranmayee thought of Sudhamay and shed a few quiet tears. It had been many years since he'd died, but she still had some tears stored away for him. She combated the hardships, fought the battle alone when she had to, and suffered from loneliness too. Uncertainty clamped its teeth on to her like a leech, though none of this could make Kiranmayee cry. But when Suranjan put his arms around her and said, 'Ma, I'll make you a house by the river, we'll go out on a boat on a moonlit night,' or when Maya made her put on a new sari she had bought for her and said, 'How beautiful Ma looks, how beautiful my mother is', those were the times Kiranmayee remembered Sudhamay and her eyes grew moist. He had not stayed long enough to witness even these fleeing moments of happiness.

When she felt utterly desolate, Kiranmayee called Suranjan to her room, running her fingers through his hair and saying, 'Let's go back home.' Suranjan didn't reply, going away without a word, leaving Kiranmayee crying in a thin whine. After moving to Park Circus, Kiranmayee said sometimes, 'Let's go back to the old neighbourhood, rents are higher here. Suranjan refused, saying, 'Those who were friends there are enemies now; we would have been in trouble if we hadn't left.' Suranjan wasn't one to lie, Kiranmayee believed her son.

But why should they have become enemies? Why had Suranjan made enemies? Was he going to make enemies here too? Would the family have to run from one neighbourhood to another constantly because of him?

She couldn't speak her mind as easily with Maya as she could with Suranjan. It was with much trepidation that she had told Maya, 'Taslima wants very much to meet you.'

'Taslima who?' Maya frowned at her.

'Taslima Nasreen.'

'What does she want? What does that witch want? Does she want to do even more harm to me? Hasn't she done enough? How do you know what that she-devil wants, how do you know she wants to meet me?'

Kiranmayee didn't respond. Maya went up to Suranjan, ready for battle. 'Has either of you met that bitch Taslima? Have you spoken to her?'

Suranjan was leafing through a book. Continuing to turn the pages, he said, 'Yes, I have.'

'Where?'

'I went to her house.'

'And Ma? How did she meet Ma?'

'Why do you need to know so much?' Suranjan was barking at her. 'You don't want to meet her, fine, end of story.'

'No, it's not. I don't want either of you to be in touch with her ever again. If you are…'

Maya began sobbing.

'If you are, that'll mean you've accepted everything that happened to me in Bangladesh, the fact that my life has been ruined. Accepting Taslima means accepting my plight, my humiliation, my being raped day after day, my getting married to a drunken beast, to an imbecile, my death. Nothing less.'

Suppressing her tears, Maya stormed out of the house. Kiranmayee and Suranjan remained behind, stunned into silence.

Eight

Suranjan was a man, so he was answerable to no one; he was allowed to do as he pleased. He could start a job today and give it up tomorrow. You don't feel like doing anything today? No problem. His mother lived under his protection. She earned enough selling saris and other garments to keep the household afloat. Suranjan had his mother to look after him, his clothes were washed and ironed, his bed was made, he got food whenever he wanted, he had nothing to complain about. Kiranmayee was all right too. Her husband was dead, their economic status had deteriorated, but at least she had her son, the apple of her eye, right by her side. He wasn't married; she didn't have to share his affection with his wife. When Suranjan was married to Sudeshna, he had no time to sit with his mother or take her anywhere. All his attention was reserved for his wife. They would leave for the college together, come back together too, and then go out in the evening. Kiranmayee used to feel lonely. It was true her son didn't have a family; the presence of children would have brought such joy, but then it wasn't so bad without them either. Suranjan belonged entirely to her now; when he came back home, it was to her; it was her he called out to. Kiranmayee's heart was full. Her son had never spoken to her hurtfully, he ran to fetch the doctor when she fell ill, or took her to the hospital, and sat by her bed all night when she had a fever.

So Kiranmayee was happy even in sickness, for then her son was even closer to her. How many women of her age were lucky enough to have their son by their side? These days, sons moved out after getting married, or went abroad, or, even if they remained at home, were so zealously guarded by their wives that they didn't dare go anywhere near their mother. Suranjan brought her fruit sometimes. 'Eat these, Ma, they're good for your health.' Kiranmayee's joy came from the fact that her son had got them for her, that he had thought of her, though she ended up feeding the fruit to him. Suranjan handed over the money he earned from tutoring students to her, keeping only a little for his personal expenses. It was not a large sum of money, but it was a source of enormous comfort to Kiranmayee. She wanted to die while her son still loved her.

It wasn't Suranjan or Kiranmayee I was worried about, it was Maya. Women can never have happy lives; society doesn't allow it. Maya couldn't be happy either. My heart bled for her. One day I spoke on the phone to Suranjan and Kiranmayee. As before, I told them I wanted to meet Maya. She could come to Kiranmayee's house and I could go over to meet her, or she could come to mine. And if neither was possible, I would visit her where she lived.

Although Kiranmayee did not respond to my request, Suranjan said he would call me later to talk about the meeting. I waited all day, but there was no sign of him. It was the same story the next day. I simply couldn't imagine what he was so busy with. Finally, I messaged him: 'you were supposed to let me know'. No response to this either. Men really are not to be trusted. Kiranmayee had no phone, or I would have spoken to her directly. She had bought Suranjan his phone, but hadn't felt the necessity to get one for herself. Out of compassion for Maya, or perhaps for the entire family, I bought two saris for Kiranmayee, four for Maya, and a panjabi for Suranjan from Treasure Island in Gariahat – seven thousand rupees' worth of gifts in all – and, once I felt calmer, told Tarun to drive me to their house in Park Circus. Suranjan was not at home, but Kiranmayee was. I wanted to just hand over the gifts and leave, but Kiranmayee took my hand to stop me: I mustn't leave without eating something, when would I have a meal with them? She wanted to buy some good fish and cook it for me, such was her desire, her ardent desire.

When I asked about Maya, she burst into tears: 'Don't talk about her, ma, she really is not all right in the head any more. I know you want to meet her, but you won't enjoy it.'

With a sigh, I said, 'Do you suppose I enjoy seeing you this way? Something tells me Maya isn't happy, that's why I want to meet her.'

Kiranmayee said, 'I'll explain to her, I'll tell her to meet you. She has no friends; she doesn't lead a normal life at all. Considering what those men did to her in Bangladesh, it's a miracle she's alive. How can she wipe out those memories, it's still a nightmare for her. She's trying to force herself to lead a normal life, but it isn't that simple. But at least she's got a job that she's held on to. I'm constantly worried that she might lose it. Apparently, she starts shouting even at her workplace whenever the subject of Bangladesh comes up. She abuses anyone who's from back home. She's angry with the entire country. I've tried very hard to make her understand that there were some good people in Bangladesh too, but she doesn't agree.'

I listened in silence, trying to understand the reason for Maya's fury. I began to feel more compassion towards her.

'Still, I want to meet her, mashima.' My voice was choked with emotion, but I realized that Maya's emotions were different from mine. Kiranmayee didn't say it, but it was obvious that Maya was particularly angry with me, probably because I wrote about her abduction in *Lajja*. As far as I knew, they had killed Maya, but it turned out she was alive. And precisely because she was alive, she was being forced to experience the agony of death. She would have been saved if she had died; women are never free till they die. My eyes filled with tears for Maya.

The tea went cold, Kiranmayee sat there, I left. I decided that I was not going to keep knocking on the doors of those who had misunderstood me and didn't want to see me ever again. I would live as I wanted. I had enough anxieties about my own existence. I had moved to Calcutta and set up a household here, but I still didn't know whether it would be possible for me to live in this country. I might have to leave any time. I had no idea where I would go in that case. I had developed a large circle of friends after moving to Calcutta, but most of them were not real friends. I knew that only too well. What is one's own country anyway? Is it the land or is it the people? I think it is the people.

I was busy with my work, though I was still hurt by Suranjan's behaviour. He hadn't called despite his promise. He hadn't even replied to my SMS, nor had he bothered to thank me for the beautiful panjabi I gave him. And now he was calling after a fortnight, saying he wanted to meet me. High hopes! I had thought of saying, 'I'm busy, I can't meet you, call me some other time.' But I couldn't. This is my problem: I cannot say what I don't mean. I do as I please, as long as the hurt remains, I keep my emotions in check. But then how long do I remain hurt anyway?

Why did Suranjan want to visit me? I felt he might return the saris and the panjabi. I even prepared myself for this. I decided to distribute them among my friends if that came to pass. What else could I do?

When Suranjan came, though, it was not with a packet but a tiffin-carrier. Kiranmayee had cooked an elaborate meal and sent it.

'What's all this for, why all this food? My fridge is already full of food, I can barely eat it all myself, so much of it goes waste, and now more food, uff.' Going into the kitchen, I told Sujata to empty out the tiffin-carrier and clean the bowls. But I was tempted to see what Kiranmayee had sent. I found five or six items, all cooked the way we used to eat in Bangladesh. I stood in silence for a long time, gazing at the bowls, taking in the food with my eyes, which began to brim over with tears. A small note was attached to the tiffin-carrier, which I unfolded.

'Ma Taslima, I send you my love. You must eat everything. I've cooked a simple meal for you. Who will make these for you? I'm sure your maid cannot cook food the Bangladeshi way. Your life is the warrior's life. We are all proud of you. You must stay well. Take care, ma, and never lose heart.'

I kept holding the note, while my teardrops slowly blurred the words. I couldn't return to the drawing room immediately and face Suranjan. I had to stay in the kitchen for some more time to dry my eyes, to let the moisture drain out of my voice.

Suranjan had brought a young woman with him – the same woman I had seen entering his room when I was there. Yes, the same one. Her hair was tied in a braid, and she was dressed in a yellow blouse and a light green sari. She had a charming smile and large eyes, very sweet to look at. Not very slim, she had the kind of figure that could run to fat, but hadn't yet. Suranjan was standing next to her. Curly hair, a wide brow, deep eyes. His nose wasn't particularly sharp, but it suited his face perfectly. His lips and chin were the most pleasing parts of him, replicas of Kiranmayee's. And that mole on his cheek, which transformed his face. He could have dressed in the panjabi today, but he had chosen a white shirt and black trousers instead. I've noticed that men look extraordinarily handsome in white shirts.

Dr Subrata Malakar, for instance, looks best when he puts away his yellow and green and red and purple shirts for a white one. He treats my vitiligo – I developed white spots on my hand some time ago. They're still limited to the back of the hand, without spreading further. Malakar is treating me, but there's no sign of a cure. Still, I have quickly become friends with him, which is usually the case with good people. But then quick friendships grow with bad people too. It takes years to tell them apart.

'You've met Zulekha already,' said Suranjan.

'Yes, I have,' I said.

'Please sit down,' I said to Zulekha, addressing her as 'aapni'.

'No need to say aapni to her, she's much younger than you, you can use tumi.'

'I cannot jump to tumi just because someone is younger, Suranjan. I cannot be informal with someone I hardly know.' I was so uncomfortable that I sounded brusque.

'Did you like the panjabi?' My question was for Suranjan. A short 'yes' was the answer.

'But you aren't wearing it.'

'I'm not used to such expensive clothes. I'm thinking of exchanging it for something cheaper.'

'But why? Keep what I gave you, wear it sometimes.'

'On my wedding day, in that case.'

Suranjan smiled at Zulekha, who smiled back at him.

I didn't know how to interpret this. Was Suranjan saying he loved Zulekha, that he would marry her? I couldn't believe my eyes. I had thought there was no truth more fixed than the fact that, whatever he might do with his life, he wouldn't fall in love with a Muslim, he wouldn't marry a Muslim. Why had everything changed suddenly? I didn't know what exactly I should say. Had Zulekha trapped Suranjan in some way, or was this real love? My head began to spin at the possibilities, and I went to make some tea. I could easily have asked Sujata, so why did I go myself? Was it because I didn't want to be there in their company? Why didn't I? I should have been the happiest person if they loved each other – it would mean Suranjan

was no longer a fundamentalist; he was liberal now; he didn't care
about the religion of the person he loved.

I took my time making the tea. Suddenly, Suranjan appeared in
the doorway.

'What's the matter with you?'

A direct question.

'Nothing. Why do you ask?'

'Why did you come away?'

'I'm making tea.'

'No need. Come back. Let's chat for a while and then we'll leave.'

'Have some tea first.'

Suranjan looked at me probingly, as though he was trying to
reach my soul; as though he wouldn't allow my thoughts to remain
private any longer. He simply had to know what they were.

'What's your relationship with her?'

'With whom?'

'That girl who's here with you.'

'Oh, you mean Zulekha. What can I say?'

'Say it.'

'We're friends.'

'Just friends?'

'More than friends, actually.'

'Is it love?'

'Yes, love … you could say that.'

'Yes, love … you could say that.'

'I see.'

'Why do you ask? Do you want to write a story?'

'Of course not.'

'You're in the habit of writing whatever you see and hear.'

'Are you saying it was wrong to write about your family?'

'How have we benefited from it?'

'I didn't write for anyone's benefit. I provided information, isn't that enough?'

'What use is information if we don't benefit from it? If nothing changes?'

'I don't understand what you're saying.'

'Let's say I've fractured my leg, and you inform everyone in detail about my condition. They listen and leave. I remain as I was with my broken leg. That's why I'm asking what use it is to inform people. It's pointless if my fractured leg isn't going to be treated.'

'It doesn't do any harm either, does it?'

I was angry now.

Suranjan sounded even more angry: 'Yes, it does.'

'What harm?'

'No one will take me in their team. I won't be considered. They'll assume I'm crippled. I'll become an outcast. Even after my leg mends, I won't be considered fit.'

'This is nonsense!' I interrupted him.

'It's not.' It was his turn to cut me off.

Looking him in the eye, I said, 'We'll talk about this afterwards.'

I took the tea into the drawing room. Zulekha stared at me inquisitively. 'Where do you live, did you go to college, what do you do, where's your home, how many brothers and sisters.' I asked her all sorts of questions, but not the one I really wanted to ask, the one nagging me: 'Are you in love with Suranjan?'

Zulekha answered my questions in a measured tone. She seemed to be just another small-town girl, a harmless sort. She wasn't a good match for Suranjan. I began to reflect on why she was not. I wasn't someone who cared about appearances, I examined people for who they really were. If there was no mental compatibility, there was no need to bear the burden of a relationship.

But then why was I bothered about their relationship? Suranjan was nothing more than the protagonist of my novel. I had run into him after several years. It was mere courtesy to ask how he was. But I must not forget that the Suranjan of India was a completely different person from the Suranjan of Bangladesh. The political landscapes were vastly altered. He was part of a minority community earlier, but he was a member of the majority now. All of society was aligned with the majority; so there was no need to feel sorry for his poverty. If he wanted to change his circumstances, he would have the opportunity for it. There was no permanent famine in this land. His relationship with Zulekha was purely his personal affair, why should I object if he wanted to be with a Muslim woman?

Suranjan was sitting next to Zulekha, quite intimately. I couldn't make out if their objective in coming here was to spend some intimate time together. Perhaps they were finding this difficult in their respective homes now, and so they needed some space elsewhere. Or were they here to actually meet me? But then they didn't seem to have anything important to say. I got up and went into the study. So much to write, so little written.

The shelves were lined with books. When would I read them? When would I capture the thoughts in my head on the page? Let Suranjan and Zulekha be alone in the other room. Sitting down at my computer, I answered my cousin Yasmeen's message: 'What are you doing, where are you', on Yahoo Messenger with 'Suranjan is here. I'm chatting with him.'

'Who's Suranjan?'

'Suranjan of *Lajja*.'

'Really?' Yasmeen proceeded to add two dozen exclamation marks. 'Wow, how are they?'

'Very well. Can you tell me if Suranjan ever visited my Shanti Bagh house?

'Yes, he did.'

'How many times?'

'Twice, according to you.'

'Didn't you meet him?'

'No, how could I?'

'But weren't you at Shanti Bagh in December?'

'No, bubu, how can you forget? Bhalobasha was born on 6 December. I was in Mymensingh.'

'Oh, yes, of course.'

At this point, Sujata came in to tell me, 'They're leaving.'

Abandoning the computer, I rushed out.

'Why are you leaving? What's the matter? What's the hurry?'

'We have to go.'

'You aren't staying?'

'No.' This was Suranjan's answer.

'What is it? Are you angry?'

'Of course not.'

'What's the problem, then?' I made Suranjan sit down on the sofa.

Zulekha said mildly, 'We have to go.'

Suranjan was on his feet again at this. I realized that even if he didn't want to leave, Zulekha had decided they were going.

'I didn't get a chance to hear any of your stories, Zulekha.'

She smiled. 'I'm nobody famous. Why do you want to write my story?'

'Who told you I want to write your story?'

'I did,' Zulekha answered with a smile.

Once again, there was talk about the benefit of writing stories.

'Whose benefit are you referring to?' I asked.

Zulekha didn't answer. I said, 'Are you under the impression I write about famous people?'

'Your writing makes you famous,' replied Zulekha, 'and those whom you write about also become famous overnight.' She had a quiet smile on her face.

'I don't agree. Suranjan hasn't become famous.' I sounded innocent.

Zulekha smiled mysteriously. I can interpret what is simple, but not complexity. Suranjan stood up and took Zulekha's hand. One warm hand in another. I couldn't take my eyes off their hands. They turned into crucial characters in my life, standing in front of me. All I wanted to do was kneel on the floor and watch them.

I buried my face in a pillow after they left. I realized I should have spent more time with them. I was an important person for Suranjan – that was why he had brought his girlfriend to meet me, but I had shown so little enthusiasm that they had left. Was Suranjan under the impression I was not interested in him at all? If he'd come alone, he'd have known how interested I am in him. For some reason – I didn't know what – I didn't like seeing Zulekha with him.

Nine

After dropping Zulekha off at home, Suranjan returned to his own in Park Circus and went to bed without having dinner.

'You must have eaten at Taslima's,' reasoned Kiranmayee.

Suranjan didn't reply.

'She's peculiar,' Zulekha had said today.

'What do you mean, peculiar?'

'She seemed rather odd. Not what you'd think if you know of her books.' Zulekha spoke slowly, pursing her lips.

'What were you expecting?'

'Not someone like this. She's very ordinary, isn't she? Peculiar behaviour too ... going off into her room, leaving her guests outside. Was that right, do you think?'

Suranjan nodded. 'Maybe she was busy. She writes all the time. That she even had time for us...'

'Listen, you're a little too devoted to Taslima. I don't like it.'

Suranjan began to wonder if he really was devoted to the writer. No, he was not. In fact, he did nothing for Taslima. Here was a woman who had chosen to live in Calcutta out of her love for the city. Had Calcutta acknowledged this love? It had not. And it hadn't expressed its own love for her either, not even once. Taslima wanted

117

so much to meet Maya, but Maya had put her foot down. He wasn't really able to do anything for Taslima, who only kept giving her love to others. People forget that those who give also like to get something in return. And so Suranjan wanted to give something to Taslima, but he didn't know what. What could he give her anyway, what did he have of his own? His life had changed greatly. This was a new life he was leading now, with no connection to his old one. In Bangladesh, he had had a life full of dreams; the people around him were cultured, aware, idealistic. Terms like class struggle, dialectics, dictatorship of the proletariat and socialism now seemed laughable, but these definitions, theories and debates had once leant meaning to Suranjan's life, making it seem important and essential. However, he had been living on a different plane since moving to India: one of harsh reality, of ugly poverty, of narrow-mindedness, or barbarity. No one knew Suranjan here. He could go wherever he liked, do anything he wanted. He could spend nights on end in Shonagachhi with prostitutes, he could drink himself into a stupor in Khalashitola, no one would try to rescue him or even shame him. Suranjan didn't have an iota of sentimentality about this form of existence. After he started teaching and married Sudeshna, she had begun to weave dreams in his head, but all of that had been destroyed and he was back to square one. He had absolutely no desire to get married again and settle down; he no longer dreamt of anything. Suranjan had no real interest in what he was doing or why. He had grown up in a political environment. Yet, today he had washed his hands of politics. He could see no difference between an Islamic fundamentalist party and a Hindu one. He had been quite passionate about Maoists at one point, but that too had died. No matter how sympathetic he was with the radical left, he didn't believe anything good could come of killing people. Steeped in politics once upon a time, he himself didn't realize when he had bid goodbye to it. It was impossible to develop an interest in anything when life was meaningless, when the world was meaningless. He was just sauntering through the days, without a past or a future, living only in the present, living in Zulekha. He went home nights only because Kiranmayee was there; else, he could have spent them anywhere at all, since it was just a matter of getting through them. This pessimism had begun to consume him from the time he was in Bangladesh, and it had not left him yet. He had assumed that he would be completely safe once he had left Bangladesh, that he would be cocooned by peace and happiness, that a dazzling life full of many dreams and numerous possibilities would be within his reach: 'All my joys await me across the border'. Leaving his own country with this belief and assurance, Suranjan received his first setback when the four lakh taka that was to be the family's assets in India were stolen. Suranjan had trusted Shankar Ghosh implicitly, and he had turned out to be the one who grabbed their money and calmly destroyed their well-being. Shankar Ghosh's behaviour at home was the second blow, on top of this were the rejection of his loan application by the party and their host's sexual assault of Maya. He could still have put all of this behind him, he could have settled down, returned to normal life, and been a source of security to his mother and sister, but Sudeshna's inability to get along with two perfectly harmless persons like Maya and Kiranmayee was also a big setback. As was her filing a case against him under Section 498A. He had tried to recover from each of these for Maya's sake, for Kiranmayee's sake. He was leading a completely unproductive existence at this point, but there was more to come. He had dealt the greatest of the blows upon himself, abducting Zulekha – a woman as blameless as Maya – like a goon, and then witnessing his companions' shameless savagery. He saw himself reflected in their actions: in Achinta he saw his own lust, and he began to loathe himself. Suranjan did not loathe anyone in the world as much as he loathed himself.

So, what could he possibly give to the writer of *Lajja*? He wasn't worthy. He would have taken Zulekha away from her detestable life had he loved her – after all, he was the cause of her misery. None of the things that had befallen her would have taken place had he not abducted her from her house. Suranjan realized that since he felt no love for Zulekha, all that he did for her was a form of atonement for his crime. And Zulekha would realize this sooner or later, at which point even she, Suranjan knew, would forsake him. But he had grown attached to her, in the same way that he was attached to Maya. He wanted to wrap his arms around both of them, hold them close to his heart. But Maya would not allow it.

Three living beings loved the worthless Suranjan – Kiranmayee, Maya and Zulekha. He added one more, Taslima. Maybe Zulekha would leave him some day, but he was Taslima's creation, a creator cannot withdraw too far even if she forsakes her creation. These were the thoughts that ran through Suranjan's sleepless nights. When he woke up at dawn and listened to the chirping of birds at the window, he did not feel he had been created by anyone; he was a flesh-and-blood, living being, with his own existence, although he doubted this at times. Even when he read *Lajja* and realized that the Suranjan of real life had done none of the things that the Suranjan of the novel had, sometimes he felt he had actually done those things. For instance, everyone in *Lajja* spoke a pristine Bangla, but nobody in Suranjan's family ever spoke it – theirs was a regional version, as was the language of their close friends. Only Jatin Chakraborty, Kabir Chowdhury and Saidur Rahman used a literary Bangla.

They no longer spoke the Bangla of Dhaka, and had become used to the Calcutta version. Kiranmayee did use it sometimes, but Maya never wanted to. As for Zulekha, she was from this part of Bengal; she didn't know how to speak Bangla like in Dhaka or Mymensingh. Suranjan's friends in Calcutta also spoke Bangla the

Calcutta way. How many friends did he have anyway! He was no longer in touch with most of his old friends.

Suranjan had deliberately cut off his friends from Belgharia. Just like his life in Calcutta was vastly different from the one in Dhaka, so too was his life in Park Circus different from the one in Belgharia. Suranjan had in fact lived many lives in the course of one. An ordinary young man had been turned into an extraordinary figure in *Lajja*. But he knew only too well there was nothing special about him. He had now made new friends in Beckbagan and Benepara and Tantibagan. He met Aftab, Hakim, Enamul, Sobhaan and Sadhan – whose mentality was completely different from those of his former friends from Belgharia – every day. He was trying to do something useful with them in their localities – blood-donation camps, health centres, adult education centres, children's parks.

Not everything turned out successful, and sometimes all of them felt a sense of despair. Suranjan was a past master at this, his credo being that life was a failure and would stay that way, that it was far wiser to give up all hope and smoke hash instead. When asked what he had failed at, he would say, 'I don't even know what I was supposed to have succeeded at.' Evenings with friends at the tea shop at the intersection of Park Street and Mullickbajar, at the liquor shop, or at Modern Pharmacy were now an addiction for him. He had spent no less time doing the same thing in Belgharia. They had a large circle of friends there who would gather at Feeder Road every evening. Drinking was a regular feature. If they ran out of alcohol, they only had to go to the station and ask for hashish. Gautam, Rupak, Manas, Tanmay, Jaidev, Achinta – these had been his companions earlier. Later, people began to whisper when he was seen in Sobhaan's company.

'Where does he live?'

'Feeder Road.'

'What's his name?'

'Sobhaan.'

'Not a Bengali?'

'Of course he is.'

'Have you checked his pockets? Are you sure he doesn't have bombs?'

'Rubbish!'

'All your friends are Bengalis; why did you have to start moving about with a Muslim?'

'Sobhaan is a Bengali.'

'How can he be a Bengali? He's a Muslim.'

'Muslims can't be Bengalis?'

'How can they be?'

'The same way that Hindus are Bengalis. Or Buddhists or Christians. Even atheists can be Bengalis, you know. One is race, the other is religion. You can belong to the same race but different religions.'

Some of his friends laughed mockingly. One of them poked him in the stomach, saying, 'Not been beaten up enough by Muslims, you bastard?'

Suranjan laughed. 'Enough and more. That's what made me leave Bangladesh. But whatever you may say, there are Bengali Muslims just like there are non-Bengali Muslims. You should know this. Don't forget there are Bengali Hindus just like there are non-Bengali Hindus.'

'No need to lecture us,' said someone.

'This is common knowledge. But you don't even know the basic facts.'

'Nonsense.'

'Read up history.'

'What do you know of history?'

'I used to teach history in college.'

'And which college is that?'

'Dum Dum College.'

'Oh, those private colleges just get teachers off the street. I can also teach physics there if I want to; no problem.'

Suranjan was from Bangladesh, where he had lived with a hundred and thirty million Bengalis, most of whom were Muslims. He knew the definition of a Bengali, but what he didn't know was that not even uneducated Bengali Muslims made the mistake of assuming all Bengalis were Muslims, while even educated Bengali Hindus assumed that being a Bengali could only mean being a Bengali Hindu.

When the argument began, it was Suranjan versus the rest. Trying to understand his friends' point of view, he reasoned that perhaps the preponderance of non-Bengali Muslims in this area was why they were referred to only as Muslims. But even when one of them spoke in Bangla, as Sobhaan had, in a form far finer than Suranjan's, Gautam, Manas, Achinta and Rupak said he was Mohammedan, not a Bengali.

Suranjan was furious now, not out of sympathy for Muslims, but because of the ignorance and lack of education of Hindus. He tried to explain to his friends the difference between Bengalis and non-Bengalis, but no, they didn't get it. It was impossible for them to understand that anyone but Hindus could be Bengalis. Even if the idea seemed to sink in briefly, it slipped out again.

Everyone on Feeder Road was a Bengali, with a handful of Muslims among them. But even though Suranjan's Hindu friends knew they were Bengalis, they never referred to them that way. Suranjan gave up. Perhaps it was inevitable that people who had seen segregated neighbourhoods right from childhood would speak this way.

But this was nothing, for when they saw Zulekha, some of them winked and sneered. 'Where did you get this bomb from? Which area?'

'She lives in Calcutta.'

'Not a bad-looking chick.'

'Mind your tongue.'

'Girlfriend?'

'Hmm.'

'What's her name?'

'Zulekha.'

'Mohammedan?'

'Can't you tell from the name?'

Suranjan's friends looked sullen and angry now. Their jaws had tightened. They looked like they would bash his nose in if they could.

After this, things grew heated over Suranjan's relationship with Zulekha. He had brought her over to Belgharia on a few occasions, mainly because it was easier to chat at home. In his small, two-room house, the two of them would sit and talk by the window, looking out to the lake. Suranjan never felt exhausted by their conversations. The company of friends was a huge attraction, which he felt in his bones every evening – he was drawn by habit, towards the alcohol, laughter and ribaldry. He shouldn't have suddenly felt the need to give up these pleasures and move to an outlandish neighbourhood like Park Circus. Kiranmayee had opposed the move vociferously, but Suranjan hadn't relented. On his request, Amjad had found the house in Park Circus. The rent was the same as in Nandan Nagar – 1,500. He had explained to his mother the benefits of living in the city rather than the outskirts. But Zulekha was always a factor. There was no obscenity that his friends had refrained from using when referring to her. They had declared that he wouldn't be allowed to live in the neighbourhood if he continued his relationship with the Muslim woman, and moved about with razors in their pockets. Walking Zulekha to Belgharia station one day, Suranjan had found Manas waiting there. Manas ran up to the train and jumped in.

Suranjan was not planning to go with Zulekha, but he got on too, to guard her. Manas got off at Bidhannagar; so did Suranjan, going up to him from the back.

'What did you get on the train for?'

'Watch out, Suranjan. End this relationship.'

'It's my relationship, none of your business.'

'Of course it's my business. You still don't know what Muslims are like? You used to live in their country.'

'Why shouldn't I know? I know them very well.'

'Don't you know treachery and villainy runs in their blood?'

'I know.'

'And you're still going ahead? Why?'

'Because I want to.'

'This can't be allowed.'

'Aren't you a CPI(M) supporter? Your entire family is CPI(M), your neighbours are all CPI(M), all of Belgharia is CPI(M). For decades. Why do you still have this kind of mentality? Think of a human being as a human being, nothing more.'

'You can have a relationship with anyone you want, but we won't accept your relationship with a Muslim.'

'You don't have to. I'm an independent individual, I can take my own decisions.'

'You're a part of society. If you live with other people, you have to follow their rules.'

'And what rules are these? That Hindus and Muslims cannot be friends?'

'No, they cannot. Muslims are terrorists. They've been oppressing Hindus for centuries. The country was partitioned. Muslims should go to Pakistan, which is where they belong. Why didn't they go? Let them go now. Our forefathers came away from Pakistan, why are *these* people staying here? This is a Hindu country. India was partitioned so that Hindus could stay here and Muslims could go to Pakistan. Why should we suffer because of them now?'

Suranjan listened in silent astonishment. 'What are you saying, Manas? Aren't Muslims supposed to be a CPI(M) vote bank? They're getting madrasas, mosques, they're getting all kinds of benefits.'

Manas sighed. 'That's politics for politicians, it's not for us.'

They walked up to the field outside Ramakrishna Mission and sat down. That night, Suranjan spent a long time talking to Manas, who worked in a government office. He had studied at a top college and even enrolled for an MA degree, although he hadn't taken the examination.

Suranjan drank cheap liquor to the gills with Manas that night, but did not promise to break up with Zulekha, as Manas had demanded.

Manas had kept saying, 'What you're doing won't go well for you, Suranjan.'

'I don't care. Whether it goes well or not for me is my problem.'

'Since you can't figure out what's good for you, someone has to take the responsibility of telling you.'

'Look, everyone has their own life to lead; everyone's life is full of problems, and it takes a lifetime to solve them. Who has the time to monitor other people's relationships or who belongs to which religion? Have I ever asked you what kind of relationships you have?'

Manas clenched his fists, his jaws tightened. He said, 'Mend your ways, Suranjan; there's still time, don't betray your own community. They're terrorizing the whole world, they hate non-Muslims. Marry anyone you want to. If you don't like any Hindu girl, marry a Christian, marry a Buddhist. But not a Muslim, not a Muslim. Never a Muslim.'

The next night, they beat Suranjan to a pulp and dumped him under the CCR Bridge. His friends. It took him five full days to recover. He hadn't gone back home during those days – Sobhaan had taken him to hospital, paid the bill and taken him home after he was discharged. He had been the only person tending to Suranjan during those five days, abandoning work and home just to make sure he gave him company.

Kiranmayee and Maya had been worried sick, although Suranjan had called home to tell them he was staying with a friend. When Sobhaan took him home, Maya had showered him with the choicest of abuses from the other room, without even having set eyes on her target. Muslims had abducted Suranjan, she was screaming, they wanted to kill him. Suranjan kept signalling to Sobhaan to leave – there was nothing else he could do; he hadn't even been able to thank Sobhaan properly.

Sobhaan was a software engineer who also ran a computer business. Suranjan had met him while teaching at Dum Dum College, where Sobhaan had installed new computers. He had observed Sobhaan introducing himself to everyone as Shobhon, even to Suranjan, who used to address him as Shobhon babu. Sobhaan had not objected. Then, when he decided to get a computer at home, Suranjan had asked Sobhaan to set it up, to install the software, to repair it when necessary. Even at this time, his name was Shobhon as far as Suranjan was concerned. Suranjan had made enquiries and discovered Sobhaan was giving him the software free, and had got him an excellent computer without making any profit from the sale. One day, he asked Sobhaan, 'You sell these things at double the price, why are you giving them to me so cheap?'

'It's fine,' Sobhaan had replied.

'Why don't you charge for the software? You didn't even take an installation fee.'

Lowering his eyes, Sobhaan said meekly, 'I had them with me already; why should I charge you?'

'What about the time you're spending on all this? Aren't you going to charge for that either?'

'No, it wasn't much of an effort. I like doing this.'

A very unusual person, this Shobhon, Suranjan had told himself. He had invited Sobhaan to tea at a roadside shop one day, and he had turned up without demur. Afterwards, he went to Sobhaan's shop on Feeder Road, where he had discovered what a busy man his new acquaintance was. And yet, even a good-for-nothing fellow like Suranjan only had to raise an eyebrow for Sobhaan to come running. Sobhaan had treated him to lunch and dinner on several occasions. They talked about nanotechnology, the Big Bang, stem-cell research, and so on. Sobhaan was soft-spoken, but discussing science seemed to charge him up, making him animated. Suranjan was an excellent listener; Sobhaan had probably not had such an attentive, intelligent audience before, and so had quietly befriended Suranjan.

From Shobhon babu to Shobhon to Sobhaan. This was how Suranjan had gradually come to know him better. He was startled when he got to know the real name. Sobhaan stood miserably in front of him, his head bowed.

'So you're not a Hindu?'

Sobhaan shook his head guiltily.

'Oh, shit.' There was anger, irritation and even humiliation in Suranjan's response.

Sobhaan had left swiftly.

The mild-mannered, gentle, well-behaved Sobhaan got busy with his own work. Suranjan could get by without him, and he, without Suranjan. And yet they could not. They were frighteningly lonely, both of them, and each had been a listener for the other one. Suranjan had talked of his parents and sister and former wife; he had told Sobhaan everything, even about his Muslim-hating friends, but he had never mentioned Zulekha. Asking himself why he was hesitant about this, the answer he had received was that Sobhaan was vulnerable, while he was assertive. Suranjan belonged to the majority, and Sobhaan, the minority. If Sobhaan came to know of his relationship with Zulekha, it would mean Suranjan was joining Sobhaan's ranks. A romance with someone from the minority community was different from a friendship, for a romance didn't just mean a romance, it meant a lot more – it meant marriage, and children. Children who would not be pure Hindus, for someone born to a Muslim womb would always be a Muslim.

But the bond broke after Suranjan discovered Sobhaan hidden behind Shobhon babu. Both of them knew their relationship would not proceed further and they stopped meeting or enquiring after each other. Things might have continued this way, but Suranjan, without any idea why, made an attempt six months later to get in touch. He could not go on without Sobhaan. Actually, he could have if he had tried hard enough, but he was too lazy for that. He took a risk instead, a leap, an experiment; he began to consort with the very people in whose blood, he knew, ran the seeds of treachery. He sought out Sobhaan, spending hours in idle conversation with him next to the Nandan Nagar lake, on the field in front of Ramakrishna Mission, at the computer shop. Possibly because they were in tune with each other, for what else could it be? Suranjan did not lack friends, after all. Sobhaan had never revealed whether he enjoyed Suranjan's company. A mysterious smile appeared on his face whenever the subject came up.

Suranjan's friends in Belgharia had not approved of his intimacy with Sobhaan, and he couldn't stop himself the day they had terrorized him. He was in Sobhaan's computer shop at the time. Achinta came in and said, 'So you're very thick with the mullah these days. Where's the asshole?'

'Cut the crap,' Suranjan had responded coldly.

'Tell him to pay up.'

'What do you mean?'

'The prick is making good money in the land of Hindus. Tell him to cough up 10,000, or else…'

'Or else?'

'Or else, we'll take him to Rajarhat and plant a loving kiss on his forehead.' Achinta had a mocking smile on his face.

Suranjan sat there, clenching his teeth. Even talking to them was abhorrent.

Ten days later, Achinta came back with some of his fellow hooligans. While he went in, his disciples took up their positions at the door.

'Make a contribution, Sobhaan saab.'

'Contribution? To what?'

'Pujo.'

'What sort of pujo?'

'Kartik pujo.'

'Kartik pujo?'

'Yes, 5,001. Hand it over.'

There was a long silence. Then Sobhaan said, 'I give money for Durga pujo, Kali pujo, Shoroshshoti pujo, I can't manage for Kartik pujo, dada.'

'But you have to,' said Achinta with a smile.

'I don't have so much money.'

'That won't work.'

'What am I supposed to do?'

'We need the money now, this instant, mister Sobhaan.'

Sobhaan gulped. His head was bowed.

Achinta pounded the desk. A glass full of water fell to the floor.

'Will a thousand do?'

'A thousand isn't enough.'

'Right now, I…'

Hauling Sobhaan to his feet by his collar, Achinta slammed him against the wall. Sobhaan asked his assistant to quickly borrow four thousand rupees from one of the nearby shops. The assistant raced out. Letting go of his collar, Achinta sat down on a chair, opposite Suranjan, who hadn't said a word, simply looking out the window at the pedestrians, cyclists, cars and buses passing by, some in one direction, some in another. The assistant didn't take too much time, returning soaked in perspiration and handing over the money to Sobhaan, who added a thousand and one rupees from his pocket and gave it all to Achinta. Counting the notes before putting them in his pocket, Achinta kicked Sobhaan in the stomach, spat on the floor, said 'fucking son of a Muslim' and walked out. Suranjan kept sitting for a while, turned to stone, and then ran out without a word to Sobhaan. Catching up with Achinta on the road, he tripped him from the back and tried to grab the money. 'Who do you think you're playing gangsters with?' he said.

Leaping to his feet, Achinta aimed a punch at Suranjan's jaw. 'With a Muslim,' he said.

Punching him back, Suranjan said, 'No, today you did it with me.'

Brushing the dust off his clothes, Achinta said, 'I'm warning you, Suranjan, don't touch me. I didn't do anything to you. I went to get his contribution, if he's your friend, that's your problem, not mine.'

Suranjan said, 'You want contributions for your pujo, take it from Hindus. Why are you extorting it from a Muslim? Do they take money from you during Eid? How much have you contributed till now?'

Achinta began to scream. 'There's still time, Suranjan, walk away from them. Haven't you found out yet what they're like? Haven't you suffered in Bangladesh? They're ferocious; you haven't seen their fangs yet. Don't you know who's responsible for all the crimes? Are you asleep? They live here, each and every couple produces a dozen children, don't you see the rate at which the Muslim population is climbing? They will kill all of us, they will bomb all of us, they

will take over our country. Wait and see. Why can't they all go to
Pakistan? When Pakistan wins against India at cricket, doesn't that
friend of yours join the victory parade with a Pakistani flag? He does.
He runs his business in our country without paying taxes. Go check,
he's probably building a house in Pakistan. A race of terrorists. I
wish I could kill the bastards.'

Achinta was panting as he spoke – panting and sweating. His
eyes were both blazing and tearful. Suranjan looked at him intently.
He remembered hearing the same thing in Bangladesh; this was how
hardline Muslims used to talk about Hindus: why don't they move
to India? They're happy when India wins a cricket match, they run
their businesses here without paying taxes, they're probably building
houses in India.

Achinta had been a Naxalite once, but he wasn't connected to
a political movement or party now. He had spent some time with
the people of Bajrang Dal, after which he had joined the CPI(M).
But – no one knew why – he had been expelled. Achinta followed
his own beliefs now, without caring for anyone. He swore at BJP
workers, saying 'you people are useless'. His band of followers wasn't
a small one – not only did it include ordinary people, but even
people connected with politics, who had voluntarily become his
disciples.

Achinta had declared that anyone who messed around with
him would not make it back home alive. Suranjan had gone home
without another word, and hadn't left home after that. He kept
thinking of what Achinta had said, of the horrifying amount of
hatred that had spilt out of him, the man's loathing for Muslims.
He had seen the same kind of loathing directed at Hindus. Hindus
and Muslims were unlike in many ways, but they were alike too.
The greatest resemblance was in matters of hatred. But did all of
them hate everyone from the other religion? Did Suranjan? Lying
on his stomach on his bed, he asked himself repeatedly: do I hate

Muslims, do I? Perspiring, he got up, had a drink of water, and lay down again, tossed and turned, then jumped to his feet and paced up and down, and lit a cigarette, then another, then another. He went out in his slippers, walked about aimlessly, returned, opened a book, shut it, got up to make tea, let it go cold, lit a cigarette, lay on his back, then on his stomach, then with a pillow beneath his chest. He buried his face in the pillow, then got up again to look for a sleeping pill, didn't find one, pulled the door shut and went to the pharmacy to ask if he could get a sleeping pill, was told he couldn't, went back home, lit a cigarette. His breathing grew faster, he felt a pain in his chest, he went for a bath, came out and lit a cigarette, paced up and down, made himself another cup of tea. The phone rang, he didn't answer it. Kiranmayee came to talk to him; he told her not to disturb him and went back to bed, lying on his stomach. Several hours passed. Suranjan remained in the same position.

That was when he had taken the decision to move out of Belgharia.

He had realized that something was crumbling inside him, that this worldview was changing, although it wasn't yet clear what form it would take. When he walked on the streets, he saw the majority of people sporting rings signifying astrological beliefs, red threads tied around wrists, crowds spilling out of temples, the ecstatic worship of deities at every street corner. This was not the Calcutta of his dreams. Everyone he came into contact with was religious-minded – the educated and the uneducated. Just as the RSS, Bajrang Dal or BJP members whom he had come across believed deeply in their religion, members of the Congress party or the Trinamool Congress or the CPI(M) were no less religious in their ways. All of them prayed, all of them believed in the gods. What had surprised Suranjan the most was that writers and artists, even scientists and doctors, engineers and those with advanced college degrees, were steeped in religion. Their counterparts in Dhaka – writers, artists, intellectuals, technocrats, scientists – had far less faith in religion; in fact, most of them did not. At least he had not seen any of them observing rituals.

In his own house, his father Sudhamay had never done it either. He was an atheist, and his son Suranjan had become one too, right from childhood. Kiranmayee alone was religious. Suranjan didn't know if she had turned more religious after moving to Calcutta, but he had noticed that she had become far more involved in rites and rituals. Was this an effort to forget something: Sudhamay's absence, perhaps, or her loneliness and poverty and fate? Or was it genuine faith that led her to get out of bed before dawn to visit the Kalighat temple, to make elaborate arrangements at home to mark religious occasions, and to do many other similar things that Suranjan didn't even know the significance of? Was it a desire to be like everyone else, or was it something else altogether? Suranjan was certain that Kiranmayee lavished a good deal of her earnings on her gods and goddesses.

'Times have changed; what use is all this any more, Ma?'

'Why does everyone else do it?

'Because they're fools.'

'So many people do it, are all of them fools?'

'Yes, all of them.'

Kiranmayee sighed. 'I'd hoped you might change your ways after moving to this country, you might start believing in god.'

'You pray so much to god, has this god of yours given you anything but misery?'

Kiranmayee sighed again. She didn't want to answer such difficult questions. Her religiosity had acquired a certain keenness after Sudhamay's death. Not that she lived like a widow who neither cooked nor ate meat or fish. Even Maya, who wouldn't so much as glance at the idol of a deity earlier, had become so extraordinarily devoted to the goddess Kali that Suranjan had no idea how to react. He had tried many times to get her to understand. 'Just because Muslims are bad, it doesn't mean you have to turn into a Hindu,' he told her. 'And even if you become one, it doesn't mean you have to be a blind follower. How will that help you?' But no, Suranjan's reasoning had made no impression on her. He felt she was growing increasingly ill, mentally. Kiranmayee at least was not unhappy when he mocked her, but Maya reacted by creating hell. The fact, Suranjan had realized, was that there was no use trying to persuade anyone. Why should Maya not be a blind devotee, considering it was on the ascendance everywhere? Only a handful of young people – members of science clubs, or genuine communists – Suranjan had seen, avoided religion, shunning all kinds of rituals. Suranjan had considered joining the CPI(M), a couple of party workers from Belgharia had even asked him. But the ideology of today's CPI(M) was so far removed from pure communism that he couldn't really consider it a communist party. How could religion be spreading its wings everywhere, how could temples be overflowing with devotees, how could shrines be springing up at street corners, how could astrology become so ubiquitous when the communists had been in power for thirty years? After so many years of their being in power, surely people's thinking should have reached a higher plane, even if the economy hadn't. Only if atheism and humanism had replaced belief in god and religion in everyone's hearts would communism have been successful; only then would there have been real socialism. Communism was not supposed to be in conflict with a humanism that had nothing to do with religion.

Suranjan did not understand why there was such a dearth of clear thinking in this state. College and university degrees obviously didn't make anyone genuinely educated. He realized only too well that he had directed his hatred at one country blinded by religious fanaticism, just to end up in another one. He had no belief in fate;

he knew this was not destiny – the decision to leave Bangladesh was entirely his, he did not regret it. Like the other members of his family, he did acknowledge the fact that, being Hindus, at least they had the security in this country of not being vulnerable to mob attacks. As he reflected on security, Suranjan trembled suddenly when he thought of the Mumbai train explosions and the fire in the train to Godhra. What if he had been on any of those trains? He would have had to die at the hands of Muslims. He corrected his choice of word to Muslim terrorists or Muslim fundamentalists. Terrorists, fundamentalists, militants – they were to be found everywhere, they flourished within all religions, all societies. And so, he concluded, nowhere would he or his family enjoy perfect security.

And, for the first time, Suranjan asked himself, were Muslims themselves very safe in this country? Who knew the answer better than him! To tell the truth, Suranjan was ashamed to go up to Sobhaan.

Leaving aside religious denominations, he also realized that the poorest of the poor around him were not safe either. Only the rich enjoyed real security, no matter what their religion or caste. It wasn't as though Suranjan didn't know this when he was in Bangladesh – he knew it very well. He might not have thought of leaving the country if they'd been rich, nor if he'd been a top political leader. Power had no caste or religion. Like a leech, uncertainty clamped its teeth on to the ankles of the insecure. Suranjan swayed between dreams and nightmares. Like a suppressed dream, his rational mind, his socialist instinct, his hope of a healthy, beautiful society, free of discrimination, tried to shake off the darkness of blind faith. His world grew illuminated, and surely he was beginning to recognize himself in this light. This was what he had prepared himself for. Then why was he destroying himself instead? Did he want to be a different person? Suranjan could not fathom many of the changes taking place in him, he felt an urge to kill himself in the waters of the Nandan Nagar lake.

Ten

I spoke to Suranjan on the phone sometimes, but hardly ever met him these days. It was Kiranmayee I met more often. Like Maya, she too was a devotee of Kali; so I took her to the Kali temple in Dakshineshwar one day. I'd been there earlier on Kushal Choudhury's request – I visit temples and mosques the way I visit old churches around the world; architecture interests me. Once she heard that I had been inside the room in Dakshineshwar where Kali's idol is kept, Kiranmayee began to plead with me like a child that I take her there. We fixed the date at once. As we drove to Dakshineshwar in my car, a police jeep with armed policemen piloted us with a blaring siren. This pleased Kiranmayee, for she now felt relieved that no one could kill me. The local police was waiting to escort us in when we arrived. The temple authorities took us into the inner sanctum, where devotees were throwing flowers at the idol through the door. I was carrying a basket of flowers too, which I handed to Kiranmayee. The priest took it from her, showered petals on the deity, and chanted prayers. Kiranmayee had tears in her eyes. The priest brought us the holy water – nectar flowing from the feet of the goddess, supposedly – which she sipped reverently, her eyes closed.

Kiranmayee was trembling with devotional passion. I gave the priest five hundred rupees before we left.

I put my arm lightly around Kiranmayee's trembling frame, and she put her head on my breast, sobbing, 'You have fulfilled my dream, ma!'

I replied, 'You could have come yourself if you were so keen; or Suranjan could have brought you.'

'Shuro doesn't take me to temples.'

I remembered the sari that Kushal Choudhury had given me as a gift – a red Benaras silk sari, once worn by a Kali idol. When we went back home, I gifted it to Kiranmayee, who began to sob for the second time that day. The sari gave off a fragrance: of flowers and perfume. Still weeping, Kiranmayee said, 'You were my daughter in my previous life.'

But Kiranmayee's devotion to the goddess was nothing compared to Maya's. When she found out about the sari, she demanded it for herself, even though she knew I had given it to her mother. I don't know if Maya forgave me thanks to this sari, but her mother did give it to her. I was sure she bowed her head to the sari every time she touched it, and thought about me in the process. After all, not only had I given her mother the sari, I was the one who had said it had been draped around the idol of the goddess. It was a claim I had made, there was no proof, which meant that Maya had believed my claim. But the question was, why. Was it because Kiranmayee had believed it in the first place? But then Maya didn't share Kiranmayee's beliefs about everything. She didn't believe that I had written about her with good intentions; that I had no ulterior motive. She didn't believe that I had wept for her suffering; she didn't remotely believe that her plight had torn me apart, that it had made me bleed. Now that Kiranmayee kept me informed about Maya, I didn't worry about her any more.

I got Kiranmayee to stay with me for a few days when Zulekha and Suranjan went to Rishop for a holiday to see the Kanchenjunga together. I gave her company throughout that period, taking her for plays and concerts, buying her saris, shawls and knick-knacks for the home at the Dakshinapan shopping complex, taking her to buffet lunches at Marco Polo and the ITC Sonar. I treated her like family, like my mother or aunt. I devoted myself to taking care of her, to ensuring she was happy. I gave my bedroom to her, sleeping in the study instead. She responded to all this love and attention by telling me repeatedly, 'There are relatives, of course, but no one invites me home or asks me to stay over. You're more than family to me, ma.'

Perhaps it was a sudden outpouring of emotion, but she told me many stories from her life, about her family, her husband, her children. Propping myself up on the bed, I listened attentively while she lay on it, talking. The stories made me grow more interested in Suranjan, but raised my suspicions about Sudhamay's death. Kiranmayee avoided answering whenever I enquired about his death. She refused to talk about it, despite my insistence. At first, I thought I had reopened an old wound, but soon realized she was hiding something from me. I kept asking about Sudhamay. How long could she go on evading the question? Finally, she blurted it out by mistake, forgetting that she had been trying to keep it from me. She told me as a confidante. What she revealed in bits and pieces was that Sudhamay had lost the will to live. He had left his country, but only physically – his heart had remained back home. Not all trees can survive when uprooted and transplanted elsewhere. Sudhamay was one of the trees that do not survive.

He had been unable to settle down here. Yes, there was poverty, but he could have borne that. What had hurt him more was people's duplicity and meanness and selfishness that he had witnessed every day. Still, if only he had waited longer, he might have built his medical practice and overcome poverty; Maya too would have escaped her misery.

But?

'He didn't think of us, not for a moment, how unbearable our lives would be without him. There was a period of hardship, yes, but it was passing. How many of those who came over from Bangladesh found everything to their liking right away? Everyone had to struggle initially. What made him think everything would be all right if he went away? We lost all we had.' Breaking into sobs again, she said, 'We had no idea that's what he was thinking.'

'How did he die?'

Kiranmayee did not answer.

'How did he die?' I asked again, placing my hand on her back.

'We don't know. He was found floating in the lake.'

'Did someone kill him?'

'We don't know. He was floating on the surface.'

'Did he have any enemies?'

'No.'

'Did he go for a dip?'

'No.'

'Why did he go to the lake?'

'He had been going for some time. He'd just sit at the edge of the lake and stare into the water. He had been depressed for some time – wouldn't eat, wouldn't talk.'

'Was it suicide?'

'That's what people say.'

'It could have been a heart attack.'

'I don't know.'

'Did he leave a suicide note?'

'No.'

As I was trying to sleep that night, I kept thinking Sudhamay's death had not been natural. Perhaps he had killed himself, after all.

He had drowned himself in the Nandan Nagar lake. What could drive an educated man to suicide? Betrayal? The guilt of leaving his homeland? The fact that Suranjan couldn't get a job? His medical practice not taking off? None of these seemed plausible. It was probably because of Maya. He may well have been a mute spectator to her downward journey. Perhaps he had been witness to Maya standing dolled up on the pavement and getting into the cars of strangers. I could not arrive at any other reason for him to have killed himself.

I remembered Suranjan telling me, 'Sometimes I have the urge to drown myself in that lake.' I think he said it on the phone. He was unhappy about everything. He was tutoring a few students, but only because he liked them; this was his only source of income. But he didn't want to go job-hunting any more either, and in any case he wasn't keen on being tied to a desk from nine to five; he'd rather enjoy whatever freedom he had ... how much money did a man need to survive? Who needed to be well off in this worthless world anyway? Millions of people were living in poverty. Kiranmayee's earnings supported the family. But what would happen when she wasn't there? What would he do then, would he live on the roads? Laughing, Suranjan had said, no, he couldn't do anything so romantic, he would rather drown himself in the lake. Which lake, had he identified one? Nandan Nagar lake, Suranjan had answered seriously.

None of this was proof, but still my suspicions weren't dispelled. Had Sudhamay been alive, he would have seen his practice flourishing within the year. Doctors from Bangladesh did not get many patients at first, but things tended to get better in a year or two. The family would not have been in such distress if Sudhamay had been alive. Kiranmayee knew she couldn't depend on Suranjan, which was why she had started her sari-selling business. She wanted to put in more capital to make it grow. The trouble was that the business would have run much better in Belgharia, for Kiranmayee did not frequent her Muslim neighbours' houses in Park Circus.

Who was going to buy her saris when people could easily get them in Gariahat or New Market. The only reason for buying them from Kiranmayee was that she provided better saris at lower prices. But she didn't get the kind of publicity she required. She knew Muslims would not be big customers since she had not yet built a relationship with them. She wanted to do that now for the sake of her business. She had begun to sell salwar-kameez sets and even embroidered burqas, and had even put up some posters in the locality. Just the other day, some people from the Bangladesh High Commission had purchased several saris, salwar-kameez sets and burqas from her, promising to come back. Kiranmayee had spoken in her native dialect with them to her heart's content. She had served them tea and talked about her homeland.

I wanted Kiranmayee to be happy. And if she became affluent, she would have some joy in her life, and derive satisfaction from doing something for Suranjan and Maya. Doing things for someone you love is the greatest pleasure in life. The weakest member of the family, who was completely dependent on others, had taken charge of the household after Sudhamay's death, while the one who was led purely by reason and rationality, Maya, had sunk into irrational prejudices and superstitions. As for the politics-obsessed young man, he couldn't care less about politics now. I reflected upon these transformations. And to think that the man who had been a warrior all his life, who was ready to battle every day no matter whether he won or lost, who took charge during crises, had chosen to give up and allowed himself to drift away from life, without a thought to how unmoored the family would become in his absence.

'If only Suranjan's father could have met you even once here. It would have brought him so much peace. He talked about you a lot.'

I interrupted Kiranmayee to tell her I had heard all this already, she had told me before. When I asked her about Zulekha, her already sorrowful face fell further. She admitted that Zulekha was a fine girl, that she could be trusted more than Suranjan, that she was more dependable. But Kiranmayee had had enough of all this already. Maya was deeply unhappy – the man she had married was not worth having as a husband. And if Suranjan suffered after marrying a Muslim woman, everyone from relatives to neighbours would speak ill of him. Maya was adamant that she wouldn't accept the relationship, and Zulekha too would be cast out of her community.

Marriage was nothing but a social more. As long as they didn't fall into a social arrangement, they were free.

'Can't they live together without getting married?' I asked.

'No.' Kiranmayee shook her head vehemently.

'Where is this relationship going, then?'

'I don't know,' answered Kiranmayee in annoyance. 'I've told Suranjan not to stay in this complicated relationship. He refuses to pay heed, he never listens to anyone anyway, except to you. Can't you explain to him?'

'Of course not,' I protested at once. 'Don't even imagine such a thing. I'm nothing in his life.'

Kiranmayee continued, 'No one will believe that you spend so much time with ordinary people like us, how close you are to us. If I told them I stayed with you and you looked after me, they'd think I am making it up. No one helps others nowadays, not even relatives. You know how they stole our hand-note money, they destroyed us. And now...'

'There's no point crying over what's gone,' I told her. 'Happiness does not come from money anyway. I've earned enough and more of it, and it has given me no happiness. I realize now how happy I was back in Bangladesh when I began working and lived on my meagre salary. I was hard up, but I had no sense of hardship. Actually, it's love that brings happiness, there's nothing more valuable than love.'

Kiranmayee listened. I couldn't tell what she was thinking.

After returning from Rishop, Suranjan came to fetch Kiranmayee. He spent a lot of time at my house that day. Kiranmayee cooked lunch – an elaborate spread made in the Bangladeshi style. We chatted over the meal. Suranjan was in a good mood after spending a week with his girlfriend. He had dropped Zulekha at her uncle's house on his way here.

'You could have brought her.'

Suranjan was quiet.

I said, 'They say you get to know your partner only when you travel together. Now that you've spent seven days with your girlfriend, how do you feel?'

Suranjan was forthright. 'I feel great,' he replied.

'Just great?'

'Best time of my life,' he said, looking directly at me.

It was clearly a poison-tipped barb. He kept staring at me. I lowered my eyes and concentrated on eating. Kiranmayee had emerged from the kitchen to serve us, but I forced her to sit down with us. 'I'm having none of this,' I said, 'No one is a servant here, nor crippled. Everyone can serve themselves.'

Unlike the local young men, Suranjan didn't spill food as he helped himself from the bowls. He did not need to be served, possibly because he was from Bangladesh. Men are spoilt there too, but at least they can serve themselves. This was possibly because men ate in a part of the house where women were not allowed to go. Even though the women do the cooking, the men eat at a separate table, or in a separate room. This was one of the positive outcomes of conservatism.

Suranjan was describing Rishop while I was musing over these things. I marvelled at the glow on his face when he talked about the beauty of the Kanchenjunga. They must have been so in love during those seven days. How did he show his love, I wondered. Did he kiss her all the time? Touch her hand all day? I held out my own vitiligo-afflicted hands and recalled how lovely they used to be once. Many men had wanted to touch them, but I didn't allow anyone, my conceit wouldn't let me. When had it fallen off? I could tell life was drawing to a close – something it does very quickly. Everyone's life was drawing to a close, but I had no one to touch my hand. And then I reflected: much of my life had been spent touching the wrong men; now I must let my hands be.

'Did you hold hands in the hills and walk?'

Kiranmayee and Suranjan were startled by my abrupt question.

'Of course,' smiled Suranjan.

'Deeply in love?' I asked.

'Deeply,' said Suranjan.

He scratched his mole. He was looking like Richard Thomas, the hero of *The Waltons*, a TV series I used to watch as a child. He had a mole in the same spot. I felt the urge to touch Suranjan's, but, restraining myself, I said, 'Don't scratch it, it's not good, scratching can lead to all kinds of diseases. If you scratch it, you…'

I realized Suranjan wasn't listening to any of this, he was lost in my earlier question and his answer. Deeply in love? Deeply. A smile flashed on his lips.

Suranjan's hand was in his food, his eyes on me, his heart elsewhere. Sounding overwhelmed, he said, 'There really is nothing bigger than love. Nothing is more valuable. I cherish it. It's the only source of happiness.'

How did he know what was on my mind? Was he reading it? How long had he been doing that? My eyes smarted.

'Are you saying money isn't valuable? You couldn't have gone to Rishop without money. Love was possible because you could go there together; without money, you wouldn't have found the atmosphere either. Which resort did you stay at?'

'Shonar Bangla,' came the swift reply.

I didn't tell him I had stayed at the same place. In a dry voice, I said, 'What are you going to do? What do you plan to do with Zulekha?'

'Going to do? Boys and girls travel together all the time these days.' Kiranmayee was trying to make me shut up.

'So, will you take her into exile?' My lips were smiling, my eyes too.

'I will.'

'Will you leave the country?'

Suranjan burst into laughter. 'I have no such desire.'

'Will you marry her?'

'If Zulekha wants to.'

'Do *you* want to?'

'I want many things, but marriage isn't one of them. I want Zulekha. If she wants to live with me without marrying me, I will. If she wants to marry me, then I'll probably have no choice but to agree. But I have no wish to get married. The whole thing is meaningless. I did get married once. After matching caste, creed, horoscopes, everything. Every last ritual was followed. It didn't last, did it?'

'Why'd you do all that? You could have settled for a registered marriage.'

'I wanted to be integrated into mainstream culture.'

'Why? Were you expecting to benefit from it?'

'Probably.'

'What happened, then? It didn't work out as you were hoping?'

'Probably not.'

'What will you do this time? An Islamic marriage?'

'Shut up.'

'Aren't you going to convert?'

Suranjan jumped to his feet suddenly, his food uneaten, and went off to rinse his hands.

Suranjan was no one, nothing. Hopeless. Worthless. A wastrel. No taste, no ideals. No healthy thoughts. No education. Darkness behind him, darkness ahead of him. He had hunted his quarry afresh and attached himself to her. She was a smart girl who'd get a good job. And Suranjan would live off her, justifying it as providing protection to a member of the minority. Zulekha couldn't rent a house in a decent neighbourhood since she was a Muslim, but this problem would be solved if she married Suranjan.

'Is Zulekha going to dress like a Bengali Hindu married woman?'

'It's up to her. Whatever she wants.' Suranjan's voice was harsh.

'You're pretending to believe in equality. But you will force it upon her.'

Suranjan burst into laughter again.

'What would you prefer?'

'Why do you want to know?'

'Just curiosity.'

'Are you going to write another novel?'

'I haven't decided yet. Maybe, maybe not.'

'Enough of novels.'

'What do you mean?'

'Enough of writing about me. Release me now.'

'Have I imprisoned you?'

'Yes, you have.'

'How do you mean?'

'You have, mentally.'

My heart trembled. I couldn't understand the reason for my irresistible attraction towards him. Was it because I was lonely? Or because, despite his rage and hatred and hope and despair and confusion and mistakes, he was still an honest man?

'What I do with my life is completely my business. Mine and Zulekha's. Please do not write about these things. Who knows what you'll end up writing, what trouble it will get us into.'

'You'll get into trouble because of what I might write?'

'Nothing but trouble.'

'You mean you're afraid of trouble?' I asked him in surprise.

'Do you take me for a superhuman? I'm nothing of the kind. Why would I have left my country if not out of fear? You think I have no fears in India? I'm definitely afraid of Muslim fundamentalists here too. As well as of Hindu fundamentalists. I want to live the rest of my days on my own terms, without trouble.'

Taking Kiranmayee's hand, Suranjan drew it closer to his heart. Not everyone knew how to express this love, this warmth. It was a beautiful sight.

'My driver will drop you,' I said.

I told Tarun to take them home, but Suranjan refused. He said they would get a taxi. I stood in the balcony as gusts of wind blew around me. Who was I for them? Nobody, merely a writer. Kiranmayee had spoken of ordinary people and special people. Apparently, they were ordinary and I was special. Once a person thinks of another one as special, they begin to push them away. Special people were good only to look at from a distance. Even when they came within reach, you still viewed them from a distance. When caste or creed do not matter, a Hindu and a Muslim can fall in love. But an ordinary person can never consider a special person close. No real relationship flowers between them. I saw gratitude, not love, in Kiranmayee's eyes and in Suranjan's, when they were leaving. I felt desolate, like an outcast.

Eleven

After she was widowed, Kiranmayee had removed her symbols of being married, but she neither dressed in white, nor gave up eating up meat or fish. Sudhamay used to say, 'I request you not to put on a widow's garb if I die. Be the way you are now; do all the things you like to do.' She hadn't honoured his wish initially, switching to white saris and a diet of boiled vegetarian food, but Suranjan came in the way. 'I'll leave home if you don't stop this nonsense,' he told her. There was no greater threat for Kiranmayee. With both her husband and Maya gone, if the last one, Suranjan, were to leave too, she would have no choice but to kill herself. And the boy was so headstrong that if he did decide to leave, Kiranmayee knew she wouldn't have the power to stop him. So she dressed and ate normally, but insisted that her wish to perform religious rituals be granted. With so many people doing the same thing, there had to be a god somewhere, she thought. But the problem these days was that she had too much time on her hands, and she didn't know what to do with it.

A terrifying loneliness gripped her when she was done with the chores. With advancing age, she felt increasingly alone – no one had any time for her. Suranjan spent all his time in his room, reading, tutoring his students, or with Zulekha or his other friends. Sometimes he would come into Kiranmayee's room and throw himself down on her bed; she would stroke his back – caresses that her son accepted. Kiranmayee had taken to paan. At times he demanded one from her. Like chewing cud, she would talk of the good days left behind. All her days were in the past. Kiranmayee saw life as meaningless and redundant – how could living in this dank, sunless lane be of any use to society, her family or to herself? Neither Suranjan nor she had the pleasure of leading the life they wanted to. Kiranmayee realized that had Zulekha been a Hindu, Suranjan might have married her and brought her home. But she also had the feeling that he would have left her if he could have, though she didn't know just why he could not do it. Possibly because nobody else would give him what he got from her. Or perhaps finding a girlfriend was not easy, especially for someone without much money. The unpleasant truth was that even love was transactional now. The poor romanced only with one another, as did the rich. But love was not bound by class distinctions, it was not uncommon for rich girls to love poor boys, or for a boy from an exceptionally wealthy family to be head over heels in love with a blind, orphaned girl. Even films and plays depicted such love stories. But those days were gone; those stories were from another era. Love was a calculated business now. Just as parents look for suitable matches for their children, boys and girls too look for suitable girlfriends and boyfriends. Romance came only after checking caste and creed and socio-economic status. Despite her best efforts, Kiranmayee could not imagine why Suranjan had chosen Zulekha, or Zulekha, Suranjan. She had still not fathomed the mystery of how a young Hindu man from Belgharia had met a Muslim woman from Park Circus.

Her son had not answered her question regarding this. She had asked Zulekha too, who had evaded the query. She didn't seem to intend Suranjan any harm, but she didn't appear inclined to run a household either. When she went into Suranjan's room, it was usually in a mess, with the mosquito net still hanging, teacups lying around, the ashtray overflowing, clothes and towels scattered on the bed and table and chair – but she had never tried to tidy it. Kiranmayee had said within Suranjan's earshot, 'What a strange girl, she's never even cleaned up the room, does she like it this way?'

One day, Suranjan had responded, 'Are you under the impression she's my maid?' Kiranmayee had been stung by this. She cleaned his room, did that make her a maid too? She was even about to say this, but knowing that it would hurt Suranjan, she had swallowed her words. She had no intention of hurting him, for it didn't irk her to clean up her son's room; in fact she enjoyed it. Maybe he was a good-for-nothing who hardly earned any money, maybe he had not settled down, but he was still her son, and he loved her. He held her in his arms sometimes and passed on the warmth of his heart to hers; he shared his joys and sorrows with her. Once, she remembered, he had kept his head in her lap and wept for his father after discovering an old photograph – of Sudhamay, Maya and Suranjan in Dhaka – tucked away in a book. The image was still fresh in her mind, as though it was just the other day. Kiranmayee had never seen the normally stone-faced Suranjan so overcome with emotion. This was quite a change from Dhaka, where he used to hurl things to the floor when enraged. He had turned cold now; nothing seemed to make a difference to him any more.

Kiranmayee didn't think Zulekha was very happy with Suranjan either, and worried that the young woman might leave her son. He didn't usually get close to anyone, but when he did, it always stemmed from love. And a betrayal hurt him terribly. On the other hand, he didn't care if he was deceived by someone he didn't consider a close friend. Kiranmayee believed Taslima could do something for Suranjan if she wanted to – she was extremely interested in him, and wanted him to be responsible, prosperous, happy. But no one could make something out of someone as detached as Suranjan. Who would say he was grown-up? He still had the romanticism of a twenty-one-year-old about life. Every time Kiranmayee accused him of making her live in a hovel, Suranjan would laugh. 'You've never lived in a hovel in your entire life, why not try it once? One could consider it romantic if it were a millionaire who wanted to slum it.' But even if Suranjan's and Kiranmayee's incomes were put together and tripled, they would never be able to swap their hovel for a mansion. Taslima had lived abroad for many years; she was a spendthrift. Why couldn't she provide Suranjan the capital to start a business? He could set up a pharmacy … after all, he had had a lifelong association with medicines. If not that, she knew so many important people, surely she could get him a job at a company or a college. But then, reflected Kiranmayee, it might be easy enough to get him a job, but would Suranjan accept it? Would he agree to follow rules? A strange man. It is difficult to give up freedom once you've tasted it. The freedom to not be a householder, to not shoulder responsibility. Kiranmayee wanted to request Taslima to help her son become self-reliant. All this talk about Zulekha and Suranjan being a couple … why would Zulekha want *this*? She was young, educated, had a job of some sort, with a salary of four of five thousand rupees. What did Suranjan have for her to want to marry him? Her own community was certain to abandon her. Would she be happy feeling so unmoored? Would Suranjan be happy if Maya was miserable? His own sister? It was better not to enter into a relationship that gave no comfort to anyone. Suranjan's life with Sudeshna had not been a happy one either. The more Sudeshna had tried to get Suranjan for herself, the more he had cut the bond and tried to slip out. He wasn't one to be tied down. Kiranmayee had hoped the relationship would survive somehow, but Sudeshna did not agree. The marriage had snapped.

Kiranmayee's conjugal life with Sudhamay had been replete with trust, happiness and mutual respect, but neither of their two children had found those things in their marriages. It was probably better sometimes not to be tied down in marriage. Surely, a free Suranjan had a better life than a Maya, who was bound by her marriage and had to suffer every day. But not Suranjan, who was blithely unhampered by the duties and responsibilities that come with being married. And yet Maya couldn't snap her ties. Those who wanted to snap ties and to live unfettered, but couldn't, suffered the most, while those who did it without much thought were probably happier. Kiranmayee felt – actually believed wholeheartedly – that women were far more miserable than men in marriages. Taslima was far better off – no needless trouble in her life, she lived on her own terms. If only Maya could do it too.

Such were Kiranmayee's thoughts as she sat alone at home. She launched the strands on the air currents in the room, and they drifted out with her. In the dank, damp yard outside was a naked baby and a stray dog. She walked past them with a few saris and salwar-kameez sets in a jute bag. A row of jewellery shops stood along the road. Not too long ago, Kiranmayee had sold her gold chain to Jagannath Jewellers. Maya would throw a fit if she found out, so she had told only Suranjan. The money had been put into her business. She displayed her wares to two families whom she knew on Beniapukur Road, and sold two garments. They told her they would pay the coming week. After collecting half her dues from a customer in Park Street, she went to Sealdah station. Belgharia was three stations away on the line to Dum Dum. In her old neighbourhood, she collected payments from those she had sold saris to on credit, and then visited some others, managing to sell three more. Spending some time with her former neighbours, she talked about her hopes and despair with them over cups of tea and then took the train back to Sealdah station, and then a bus followed by a rickshaw back home to Park Circus. On the wall of the house in which she lived was a strip of tin with the word 'Mayabon' on it in red. This was what she had named her invisible sari shop.

Kiranmayee had left in the morning, and it was late afternoon by the time she returned. Not in the mood to cook, she lay down without eating. These days, she didn't feel inclined to cook when Suranjan wasn't home. Making preparations for a meal was tedious. A very poor young woman named Mangala came in every day to swab the floors and wash the clothes. Kiranmayee got her to do the chopping and slicing too. She was getting on in years, and these tasks were no longer pleasant. Even if not visibly, she was definitely ageing inside – these trips to and from Belgharia exhausted her. Would Suranjan ever shoulder the responsibility for these tasks? He would not. Even the house rent had to be paid by Kiranmayee these days. Suranjan had never tried to find out how his mother made the money for all of this. Despite his utter indifference towards any and all household responsibilities, she had a soft corner for her son. But how long could it go on? What if she died suddenly, like Sudhamay? What would happen to Suranjan? Kiranmayee was petrified. Would Zulekha take charge of her son? She thought not. As far as she knew, Zulekha had been abandoned by her husband and also had a son of her own. She was pretty enough to find a kind, rich man. Suranjan was a nobody. Why would a girl stick to him? People talked of love, but Kiranmayee didn't think it existed. She had noticed that Suranjan had made some Muslim friends; she suspected they were from Topsia, a den of terrorists. She worried endlessly for her son, and the anxiety was hers alone, she couldn't even share it with her husband now that he was dead.

Relatives, far-flung though they were, never bothered to enquire after them. Nobody visited them either. Everyone was too busy with their own lives to think of other people. Loneliness gnawed at Kiranmayee; she wanted release from this unbearable life by killing herself one day. Her worries marched over her unfed body like an army of ants. Mangala turned up at one point and fried her an egg along with a couple of rutis. Just as she was about to eat, Suranjan came home, tired after tutoring students. 'Want something to eat?' she asked.

'Yes,' he replied, whereupon she gave him the ruti and egg that Mangala had made.

'No rice?' he asked. 'Why this?'

Kiranmayee did not reply. Suranjan wolfed it down; he'd have eaten more if there was more. Kiranmayee contented herself with some muri and a cup of tea.

'You have to do something, Suranjan. We can't go on like this,' began Kiranmayee.

'What can't go on like this?'

'How can decent people live in this neighbourhood?'

'Where else will you get a house in the centre of the city at this rent? Are you saying human beings don't live here, or don't you consider them human?'

'Your father was a doctor. Do you see any doctors' families here?'

'He's dead. We survive on money from my coaching and your sari business. We can't expect a higher standard of living.'

'Get a proper job, then. You're not even trying.'

'Am I not working? All this tutoring of students, is it nothing? Does it hold no value for you? Is money the only yardstick? These aren't your antiquated two-hundred-rupee things, you can easily make five or even ten thousand a month tutoring. Are you saying making pots of money is the only thing that counts? I'm bringing in some money, am I not? I'm not unemployed, I do earn.'

Kiranmayee flew into a rage now.

'Earn? How much? I have to pay the entire house rent of two thousand. For the last three months. Have you even noticed?'

'What about it? You're running a business, what's wrong with you paying?'

'Running a business! Aren't you ashamed to say that? Have you helped out with the business at all? Look how old I am, and I still have to run around from house to house under the blazing sun, while you live a life of comfort. The oppression of Muslims finished us, your father is dead, Maya doesn't have a moment of peace in her life, she's as good as dead too. And you have no compunctions about doing as you please with a Muslim girl. You took her for a holiday, do you remember the number of times I pleaded with you to take me to Puri? You consider me your mother? Do you even think about how I'm suffering?' Kiranmayee burst into tears.

Suranjan lay on his back for some time before leaving the room, with Kiranmayee still crying. He was extremely unhappy, and didn't know whether to blame himself or his mother for it. He didn't try to meet either Zulekha or any of his friends, nor did he take any of their calls during the evening, and went to a bar on Park Street, to drink alone. After four pegs, he called Sobhaan.

'What's up?'

'Don't ask.'

'How are you? Are you okay?'

'I am. I don't know if I'm okay. How's mashima?'

'Everyone's the same. That's life for you, happiness comes, happiness goes, sorrows come, sorrows go.

'Long time. I can never get you on the phone, it's always switched off.'

'I hate phones.'

Sobhaan laughed.

'I miss you a lot, Sobhaan.'

'Really?'

'Very much.'

'But you never call.'

'Talking on the phone is very superficial. You have to sit face to face, look into the eye, touch.'

'Where are you? I'll come over.'

Sobhaan was in Dharmatala. He decided to meet Suranjan at Park Street instead of going back home to Belgharia. They sat face to face after a long time, yes, a very long time. How long? Two whole months, two months that felt to both like two long years. Sobhaan refused a drink.

'This is the problem with you Muslims. You won't drink, but you'll eat beef. You're killing our goddesses.'

Sobhaan laughed loudly.

'Muslims have destroyed me, Sobhaan. I've lost my own country. I had a life there, a girlfriend, caring friends, I've lost them all. I don't know where I am now, or why. How am I? Can you tell me? This is your country, not mine. You were born here, your ancestors were born here. No one in my family was born here, in this land. You have friends and enemies both in this country, this is your soil. I consider your land my land now. I'm trying to force myself to do it. Muslims have destroyed me. Life and death mean the same to me now, thanks to them. My family has been finished. Finished, do you understand? My father is finished, my sister too, my mother is on her way to be finished. As for me…'

'As for you?' asked Sobhaan.

'I was finished a long time ago. This figure you see sitting opposite you is not me, it's my corpse.'

Suranjan ordered another large Royal Stag. Sobhaan asked for chilled water.

'You see, Sobhaan, sometimes we see news about a man who kills his wife and children and then kills himself, don't we?'

'We do. We don't just see it; we read it too.'

'Yes, read it, of course you'll read it. My escapist father didn't do that, you see. He escaped. Escaped alone. To a place from where

I wish I could drag him back by the collar and deposit him in a blind lane in Park Circus or a slum in Sachin Nagar. Or even in a shanty next to Bridge No. 4. He's escaped. After all these years of preaching secularism communalism socialism existentialism patriotism thisism thatism he's gone. Fucking selfish bastard. My father was both a child and the devil.'

Sobhaan listened, and kept telling Suranjan not to drink any more, to go home. Suranjan declared he wouldn't go home tonight. He hated going back to that house, to Kiranmayee's house. Even his mother couldn't tolerate her useless son any longer. A son who could not contribute to the family budget is no longer a son.

'You see, Sobhaan. If I'd been an engineer like you and earned pots of money, I would have had some status at home. Of course, you have to contribute money for Kartik pujo. Ha ha ha. You know what I'd have done if I were you? I'd have raped one of their sisters. I know how to rape, you see. When I'm angry with someone, I rape their sister or wife. I rape them, you see, Sobhaan. I raped a Muslim girl in Bangladesh. Did you know? You didn't? The whole world knows. The entire world knows a Hindu man raped a Muslim woman for revenge. I'm a rapist. To prove true to my name, I still rape women. What I do with Hindu women is lovemaking, and what I do with Muslim women, that's rape. I have a relationship with a Muslim woman, you know, a relationship…'

Sobhaan nodded. He knew.

'Actually, I'm cheating her. Because I rape her. My relationship with Zulekha is one of a rapist, you see. Nothing more. Even today, I'm angry with Muslims – they killed my father, they ruined my sister's life, even my mother leads a wretched life. Who's responsible? Muslims.'

'Enough, Suranjan,' said Sobhaan without any agitation.

'Why should I stop? Does it upset you? Go on, say it, Suranjan is a Muslim-hater. The whole world knows it. A rapist. A Muslim-hater.

They know I'm a Hindu fundamentalist, don't they? Yes, that's who I am. But still I piss on Achinta's face, you see, Sobhaan, I piss on him.'

'Never mind all that,' said Sobhaan.

'I live in Park Circus. You know how the Muslims live, don't you? Below the poverty line. Like insects, like worms. They run to the mosque for the namaz; that's their only identity. The mosques overflow with them on Fridays; even the pavements can't accommodate them, the roads are blocked off for the poor buggers to chant their Arabic prayers. Do they even know what they say? Not one of the bastards knows. I've socialized with some Muslims, but I'd have preferred to slaughter them. If I'd been a homo, I'd have raped them. Ha ha ha.'

'That's enough, Suranjan, time to leave now.'

'No, I won't leave. I'm going to drink some more. I'm hungry. I want to eat.'

Sobhaan ordered the food. Naan, tandoori chicken.

Suranjan ordered one more drink, brushing aside Sobhaan's objections. 'Don't worry about me. Have you ever seen me drunk? Never. You see, Sobhaan, I had many friends like you back home. I pissed on their faces. You may be my friend today, but if you act smart tomorrow, I won't spare you either.'

'Is that a threat?'

'Yes, it's a threat. No one's afraid of me, but they don't know what I'm capable of. Only Muslims become terrorists. I'm a Hindu, a caste Hindu, all my ancestors are Hindus. I can bomb you out of existence. I'll wipe out Topsia Tiljala Khidirpur Metiabruz Park Circus. Wait and see.'

'Don't drink more, Suranjan, stop now.' Sobhaan tried to take his glass away.

Suranjan gripped his arm firmly with one hand and reached for his glass with the other. 'Many people, you see, Sobhaan, think

I'm an intellectual. Ha ha ha. That's what they think when I spout nonsense. I'm actually an arsehole. I'm dumb, dumb, I don't speak because I'm an arsehole. You know that, don't you? Don't you, Sobhaan?'

The food arrived. Sobhaan served Suranjan with naan and chicken.

'Eat now. Stop drinking, Suranjan, try to give it up.'

'If I told you drinking keeps me alive, I'd sound like Devdas, the romantic young man who philosophizes when drunk. Just like the rich. If I wanted to kill the rich, you'd say I want to exterminate the class enemy. No, Sobhaan, what I want is an outlet for my anger. Why has he made it, why haven't I? That's why. And if I become rich, I'm going to shoot dead beggars like me. Shoot them, get it?'

Suranjan made his hand into a gun and pointed it at Sobhaan's chest. Sobhaan kept eating, and urged his friend to eat too. Suranjan spilt his food, and declared he wanted to drink some more. Sobhaan told the waiters not to serve him any more alcohol. Settling the bill, he wrapped his arm around Suranjan and helped him into a taxi.

'You're going home now, all right?'

'No, I'm not going home.'

'Where will you go, then?'

'Wherever you're going.'

'I'm going home.'

'I'll come with you.'

'Why aren't you going home?'

'I hate my mother.'

'What rubbish. Let me take you home.'

'You don't have to be considerate, Sobhaan. Your friendship is with me, not with my entire family. Take care of me. To hell with my family.'

'Call mashima and tell her you're not going home.'

'No phone at home.'

'She'll worry.'

'Let her. I couldn't care less. Makes no difference to me.'

Sobhaan continued pleading a little longer, but Suranjan was adamant about not going home that night. Sobhaan had no choice but to ask the taxi to take them to Belgharia. The driver refused – he was willing to go only up to Shyambajar. So be it. Another taxi from Shyambajar. Sobhaan held Suranjan's arm to make sure he didn't topple over. He'd always seen Suranjan become incoherent when drunk, but today the profanities had crossed all limits. Suranjan said, 'Listen, Sobhaan, listen to me carefully. I'm going to tell you something. Don't tell anyone. It's a secret. Top secret, all right?'

'All right. What is it?'

'Have you heard of Taslima Nasreen?'

'Of course.'

'She's fallen in love with me.'

'Really?'

'Really. She probably thinks I'm a star of some kind. She has no idea how useless I am. In Dhaka, she wouldn't even give me the time of day, and she wrote a book about me. She's a celebrity now. You know what a celebrity is, right? A big celebrity. But now she's giving me so much attention that I want to run away.'

'How do you know she's fallen in love with you?'

'Suppose someone fell in love with you, Sobhaan. You'd know, wouldn't you? You would. I saw it in her eyes, I saw it in Taslima's eyes. But I don't understand why she likes *me* of all people. Must be a rich woman's fancy. But I don't want to give in so easily. I want to toy with her. She toyed with me in her book. I want to toy with her in real life.'

'How'll you do that?'

'I don't know yet. Give me some advice. I'm not much of a player. No girl in Dhaka wanted me – Hindu or Muslim or Christian. Sudeshna and Madhabi came in and went out of my life almost immediately. Not even the sex-starved MILFs wanted me. I fucked them, that's all, but none of them loved me. Does Zulekha love me? She clings to me because there's no Muslim man anywhere who can make her happy. And no Hindu man will be involved with a Muslim woman. So it's best to stick to a good-for-nothing debauch named Suranjan with no caste or creed. I can do sex well, Sobhaan. I know how to rape. Who gets sex for free these days? The MILFs would at least give me gifts in return.'

Sobhaan shouted at him now. 'That's enough, shut up.'

'Taslima's very lonely. I can tell. There's no way she'd fall in love with someone like me otherwise. What have I got to boast of, tell me? Nothing. All I can do is rape. And she knows that. Who knows it better than her? She wrote about it. One day, you know, Sobhaan, I want to rape her.'

Sobhaan scolded him again. 'Be quiet now.'

'Yes, I want to,' continued Suranjan. 'I want to rape her to make her understand what rape is. And why should I spare someone who made a rapist out of me? Why should I not rape her, tell me? Suppose someone told the whole world that you, Sobhaan, son of Mr So and So, are a great rapist. Are you not going to rape her, are you not going to rape that bitch?'

'But the whole world doesn't know you're the Suranjan of the book,' said Sobhaan.

'Maybe not, but anyone who gets to know me, who gets intimate with me, comes to know. Sudeshna knew. Zulekha knows. I have a world of my own, everyone in it knows. And even if I leave it for another world, everyone there will know too. I have no escape.'

The taxi raced along. Sobhaan couldn't even hear everything Suranjan was saying, but Suranjan grabbed Sobhaan's shoulder and forced him to lean towards himself so that he could hear. 'I can fuck that bitch any time,' he said, snapping his fingers.

'Shut up,' said Sobhaan angrily.

'It's no good trying to shut me up, my friend. I won't let her off the hook. I raped someone, it was my personal affair. Maya was raped, that's her personal affair. Every moment of the day, I feel like a rapist. Every single letter in *Lajja* haunts me, haunts Maya too. She used to hate her body, so she'd sell it. She sold her body at that Dunlop crossing of yours. I saw her standing there waiting for clients. One night, I dragged her home and beat her to a pulp. If you don't respect yourself, you're finished, you understand? Finished.'

Suranjan kept up his filthy rant, and Sobhaan gave up. Taking him to his own house, he helped him into a bed with spotless white sheets in a beautifully done up room. The table lamps set around the bed gave off a gentle glow, and a bunch of red roses stood in the flower vase. The fragrance of night-flowering jasmine – that had bloomed in a pot near the window – spread across the room. It felt like heaven to Suranjan. He asked whether there was any alcohol at home. 'No,' said Sobhaan, and brought him a bottle of chilled water and a glass instead.

'Why are you so angry with everyone?' Sobhaan asked.

Taking off his shirt and flinging it to the floor, Suranjan burst into laughter. Propping a couple of pillows against the headboard, Sobhaan sat back on the bed.

Suranjan lay on his stomach with a pillow beneath his chest. The air conditioner was on. His eyes began to close in this luxury. 'No, I'm not angry with anyone, Sobhaan,' he answered. 'I'm angry with myself. I have no other truth to tell you, nothing more.'

'Sleep now, go to sleep.' Sobhaan ran his fingers through Suranjan's hair. Taking his hand in his own, Suranjan said, 'I wish I knew how to quit you.'

'What did you say?'

'I said I wish I knew how to quit you.'

'Why did you say that? You can quit me easily if you want to, can't you?'

'I can.'

'Then why did you say it?'

Suranjan said hoarsely, 'It's a line from a movie.'

'Oh.'

Sobhaan gazed at Suranjan's sleeping face for a long time before going to bed himself. His wife, child and parents were astonished. Why had he come home with a drunk man at this hour of the night, what was going on? All he told his parents was that it was a friend in trouble. He didn't tell them what kind of friend he was or even his name. Sobhaan lay down on the sofa in the drawing room, while his wife went to bed in another room with their child. The atmosphere was tense.

Twelve

Suranjan got back home in the afternoon to discover that Maya had moved in with both her children, along with two large suitcases. She had declared she wouldn't go back to her in-laws' house, and would stay here with her mother and brother. Her children would go to school as usual, but from here.

Neither Kiranmayee nor Suranjan asked any of the usual questions like why, what happened, or what have they done to you. Suranjan didn't know how they would accommodate five people in two rooms. This wasn't the first time Maya had walked out of her in-laws' house in a huff. Every time, she had said, 'Enough, I can't live there any longer', only to pack her bags and go back to her husband's after a week, reasoning that she had to accept her husband, no matter his inadequacies. Suranjan didn't know who put these ideas in her head, nor did Kiranmayee. None of them had ever told Maya to go back or to adjust with her husband or that her husband was still her husband, even if he was a fool, that one's husband is one's god. Strife takes its toll on the human body, either allowing fat to accumulate, or creating a haggard appearance. Maya's body was like a whip – her plump cheeks were hollowed out, her jet-black hair, which used to fall to her hips, had been cropped short because she couldn't manage it. She wore saris made of synthetic fabrics these days instead of elaborate cotton or linen ones, which allowed her to travel easily on the metro or to run after buses and autorickshaws. Maya was self-reliant; without the two children, she could have been just fine here. Why did women have to sleep with drunkards!

After Maya's arrival, the house burst into life, it was a real family now. But how would they live in these two small rooms? On her part, Maya kept saying, 'The room I used to sleep in with the children is much smaller than this one.' Suranjan bought a camping cot, which could be unfolded for one adult to sleep on, the adult in question being he himself. He gave up his own bed to the children, while Kiranmayee and Maya, mother and daughter, slept on Kiranmayee's bed. Suranjan did not care for commotion and disorder, but strangely, Maya's decision to move in and all of them living together gave him a great deal of peace. It was almost like going back to their earlier life, as though his adolescent days had returned, those days in Tantibajar, all the excitement and exuberance and fun and games of childhood, all those times filled with love. Kiranmayee's life also changed suddenly with her grandchildren around her. But they couldn't possibly live here. They would have to rent a bigger house. And yet Kiranmayee didn't rule in favour of the move, for there was no telling – what if Maya changed her mind, what if her husband or someone from his family came to take her back, or what if she decided to go back on her own? What would Kiranmayee do in that case, with a bigger house?

Maya was unwilling to listen to anyone, however, becoming more and more obstinate by the day. Declaring that she wouldn't live in a dilapidated, dank, damp house in a congested lane, and promising to pay the additional rent herself, she found a much nicer house in Beckbagan with two large rooms, a bigger kitchen, adjacent toilet and bathroom, and even a little veranda, and moved in there.

This area too was dominated by Muslims. But then why would they wrinkle their noses at this, considering they had lived next to Muslims since birth? Even the fact that the servants were Muslim caused no discomfort. The lane in which this house was situated was less mouldy and wider than the previous one, which was why the rent was eight hundred rupees more. Maya had their possessions fetched from Park Circus and set them out here. With her own savings, she bought a steel cupboard, a bed, four wicker chairs, nice curtains for the doors and windows. She did this all on her own, without involving either Kiranmayee or Suranjan, as though it were her own household to which she had admitted her mother and brother. She had got an increment. There was no looking back for Maya now. And yet, she could not break out of conventions entirely – not even her entire reasoning and discernment, all her courage and power, could prove equal to tradition. She may have walked out of her husband's home, because it made no sense to live with such a husband, but she did not shun the accessories of a married woman.

One day, Suranjan laughed at her mockingly: 'Why are you still wearing these when you have no relationship with your husband? So that he comes to no harm, heh?'

Maya remained silent, staring angrily at her brother, her chest heaving with agitation, tears forcing their way out of her eyes. Finally, she exploded: 'Listen, Dada, this world belongs to men. You know that very well. It's your world, it's a world where *you* can do as you please. If I wipe off these signs of being married, brutes like you will chase me. For what? For my body. These signs are just to save myself from men like you, nothing else.'

Holding the morning newspaper in front of his eyes, Suranjan was stunned into silence. He didn't know what to say. All he knew was that he wanted to leave the room. He considered it escapism, this habit of walking out when he didn't like what someone was saying or doing, but he had not been able to give it up. For once, however, he tried not to do it, and fixed his eyes on the newspaper. He was wondering why Maya had used 'you' to refer to men in general. Had she learnt something about the primary basis of his relationship with Zulekha? Considering Maya thought Zulekha to be a thorn in her side, she shouldn't really be defending her. On the contrary, she should be supporting what he was doing with Zulekha. Surely she felt that showing any tenderness towards a Muslim woman was incorrect? 'But brutes like you, people like you ...' What did that mean? That he was a brute, that people like him were thugs who lusted for women and ruined their lives, that women should be protected from people like him? Which woman had he lusted for and ruined? He reflected on his life, trying to look at himself through the eyes of all the women he had known. Was Maya referring to Sudeshna, with whom his relationship had become embittered because he had sided with his sister? He had done nothing underhanded with Sudeshna. Lust wasn't the basis of anything there, and he hadn't ruined her life either. But what Maya had said was applicable in Zulekha's case. She had been the victim of his brutish behaviour, his lust. Still, Maya had no reason to feel compassionate towards Zulekha. Had she fired those arrows at him in self-defence, not knowing that they'd strike home? Maya must have spoken out of great suffering – one that had led to resentment. Usually, it was the bitterness that was visible, not the pain.

For the first time in days, his thoughts turned to Zulekha. He didn't know how she was. He hadn't heard from her either. She used to come over when they hadn't met for a few days, but that had stopped. It was impossible for her to visit him here, nor could he see her at her uncle's house. That left the outdoors, fields, tea shops, pavements, streets. Neither of them seemed to have the urge to meet. Or perhaps one of them did, but was holding back out of a sense of hurt. Suranjan felt that way sometimes, but right now he was overcome by lethargy. He was often overcome by such despair that he didn't feel like getting involved with anything in the world. Zulekha was busy with her job; let her immerse herself in it. Suranjan was of no material use to her. The lack of food, clothing and shelter probably left people uninterested in romance, contrary to what was expected of a sincere lover. He had noticed Zulekha's detachment too: she had become a little more self-reliant, and was considering moving to a boarding house or a hostel for working women. She was too busy now to have time for Suranjan. Was that it, or was it his lack of emotion and his passivity that had put her off? Considering he had no one else to love, why was he shunning Zulekha, especially after they had had such a good time in Rishop? They had woven all those dreams there, but perhaps that was what had hastened this outcome.

Dreams became a heavy burden with the pressure of fulfilment. It was possible to be happy without dreams, without a plan or programme, without promises, without expectations. We'll live together, a house, a yard, some plants, tea together, dinner together, the same bed, back home at night, go to bed, kisses and lovemaking, a child, school, finances, grey hair, retirement, grandchildren, death. A secure life laid out, happy and comforting. It made Suranjan tremble. They had talked about their dreams cuddling together during the icy-cold nights of Rishop. The sky was moonlit. You had to see Kanchenjunga by the light of the moon to believe how exquisitely beautiful it was. His best time with Zulekha had been at Rishop: what else could he have asked for in a lifetime? The memories would bring him great happiness for the rest of his days. Let Zulekha live the way she wished to, in happiness. Being happy was everything; dreams that lay in the future were the best way to be happy, fulfilling them meant destroying them too. Realized happiness was not as pleasant as the yet-to-be-fulfilled dream of happiness. Without this excitement, all there was to do in this cold-as-death life was to wait for the end in the darkness of despair, just as he was doing. Zulekha tried sometimes to trigger a tide of hope in him, which rose briefly, only to subside when she left. Possibly she no longer had any dreams featuring him. Let her not. She had only sent an SMS, 'where?' He had replied, 'home.' That was it, there had been no other exchanges. Suranjan hadn't sent an 'I miss you' message. Was he even missing her? At that time, he had felt he was not. In fact, he had found himself preferring the company of a book to romancing Zulekha. He had found himself preferring a chat with Sobhaan. Even spending time with Maya's children seemed to bring far more joy. His relationship with Zulekha may well have grown out of his loneliness, the void created by the conflict with the bad company he was keeping, some upheavals within himself, moving house, starting afresh, sweeping out an old life to begin a new one. It was this emptiness that had ushered Zulekha in. Atonement? No, that was rubbish, atonement never led to anything, what had happened had happened, the way Zulekha had been abducted and raped could never be wiped out of her past. Even if all her rapists were hanged, the macabre memory would remain alive as long as Zulekha did.

The house looked much nicer than the earlier one – it was turning into Maya's dream home. None of her in-laws had bothered to check on her, and Kiranmayee was very pleased with Maya's decision to free herself from her unbearably agonizing daily life. But would she succeed? Kiranmayee was apprehensive: what if Maya suddenly lost her temper with one of them, or was displeased by their behaviour, and decided to go back home? She didn't know how Suranjan was taking the whole thing. He was withdrawn, spending time with his nephew and niece or reading when at home, and busy with his tutoring. Zulekha was missing. Had there been a tiff, had they broken up? If they had, so be it: what use was it for Kiranmayee to worry about it? Whatever god did was for the best. If

Maya's presence meant Zulekha's absence, then maybe this was best all round. A girlfriend or even a wife could be temporary, a sister was for ever. The Sudeshnas and Zulekhas had come and gone, or would go. Someone who hadn't settled down even at this age wasn't going to do so now. Kiranmayee didn't think Suranjan was young enough to marry any longer, and he didn't seem interested either. Many men spent their life unmarried, and Suranjan appeared to have the same fate. Not that they had the kind of riches that might make them wish for an inheritor. They survived, just about. There was no need to add to the family. None of them made the kind of money that held the promise of a dazzling future. This was how they would have to live always – on earnings from tutoring students, from odd jobs, from peddling a few saris, here in these localities that claimed to be in the heart of the city, in houses in dark, dank lanes, surrounded by Muslims. And they would have to strive for whatever little happiness and comfort was possible amidst all of this. Suranjan may not have had children of his own, but that regret would dissipate if he could bring up his sister's son and daughter well. Maya had the same thought in her head, perhaps Suranjan did too, in his unconscious mind at any rate.

Maya had united the family. They might have lost one member, but had gained two. Zulekha was not part of this family, nor Maya's husband. Suranjan of course had no objection to any unusual arrangement, in fact he enjoyed it. These out-of-the-ordinary things brought some signs of life with them.

Maya decided to celebrate her daughter's birthday, cooking an elaborate meal for everyone. She was in a good mood. Suranjan had said he would invite a friend, at which she had told him: ask a hundred, but no Muslims.

He knew she was thinking of Zulekha.

'Who are you inviting?'

'No one you know.'

'So what? You can tell me the name.'

'Shobhon.' He deliberately replaced Sobhaan with Shobhon.

Suranjan called his friend to invite him to their new home on the ground floor of a three-storeyed building. Giving him the address, Suranjan added, 'Your name is Shobhon as far as people here are concerned.'

'What's that you said?'

'I said your name here will be Shobhon.'

'Is that so?' Sobhaan laughed.

'What are you laughing at?'

'I've had to pretend to be a Hindu before too. And that was the name I used.'

'I know that.'

'I wasn't expecting to have to do it in your home.'

'Nor was I. But there's no other way, not today, at any rate.'

'What's the occasion?'

'Just a little celebration. My niece's birthday.'

'Lots of guests?'

'No, just one from outside the family. You.'

'What are you inviting an outsider for? Keep it a family affair.'

'Why are you talking like this? Because you don't consider us to be close friends?'

'No, it's not that.'

'What is it, then?'

'All that way just to eat? I'm not a food-lover … I'd rather…'

'Can I tell you something?' Suranjan spoke resolutely.

'What is it?'

'I'm longing to see you. That's why the invitation. The meal is not the objective.'

Sobhaan was silent for a while. 'What time should I come?'

'Whenever you like.'

Balloons and streamers with happy-birthday signs had been put up for the party. A cake was cut. By way of food, there were three kinds of fish for grown-ups, along with rice, dal and begunbhaja, and fried rice and chilli chicken for the children. Nothing very special, really, but still, Sobhaan was astonished at the quantity of food. Kiranmayee said, 'We're from East Bengal, Shobhon, everyone eats well there. It's normal to have many courses, to treat guests. Things haven't been the same since Suranjan's father left us, we barely get by, but my daughter wanted to celebrate.'

Suranjan was very happy to have been able to include Sobhaan, who was playing all sorts of new games with the children, in these family festivities. Maya was delighted that her children had discovered a new uncle. Since it was a birthday, Sobhaan had brought colour pencils, a drawing book, books of rhymes, a globe, and a fat illustrated encyclopaedia, all of them in a red backpack. Maya turned over the pages of the book, saying. 'Thank you so much, Shobhon da, it's a wonderful book.'

There was no dining table in this new house either. They ate on the bed, spreading newspapers. Maya took special care of the solitary guest.

'Where do you live, Shobhon da?'

'Belgharia.'

'Where in Belgharia? We used to live there too.'

Suranjan answered, 'On Feeder Road.'

Kiranmayee nodded. That was where well-off people lived. Maya and Kiranmayee took turns to ask Sobhaan the usual questions about his family, his work, business. Maya declared to Kiranmayee that he was the nicest of Suranjan's friends, that he had never made such a nice, polite, amiable friend before. She also said she had no idea why he had maintained a relationship with a good-for-nothing, lazy and hopeless fellow like Suranjan.

The three adjectives Maya had used for Suranjan stayed with him. He knew that much was expected of him because he was a man, but did that mean he would never be spared these barbs? Did he have to be told constantly, till it rang in his ears, that he was useless, for he made a living tutoring students, something that only those far younger than him did, and which brought in very little money?

Money. Suranjan sighed. As a child, he had learnt that in a poor country, the rich were inevitably dishonest. It was possible to live without a great deal of money; the important thing was to be a fine human being. But had he become one? He realized he hadn't. When he thought about it deeply, he knew this only too tell. When he stood next to Sobhaan, he knew this; when he looked into his eyes, he knew this. Deep in his heart, he loved Sobhaan, but he hated him no less. He was delighted when Kiranmayee and Maya praised Sobhaan, because he was his friend, but he felt jealous too. No one had ever lavished such praise on him. Handsome, intelligent, well-educated, sincere, cultured: that was Sobhaan. Why would someone like him even consort with Suranjan, why would he consider him a friend? Suranjan suspected it was because Sobhaan was as lonely as him.

Suranjan told him that all that he had said the other day was under the influence of alcohol, don't mind.

Sobhaan said, 'Would you not say those things if you weren't drunk?'

Suranjan shook his head. He wouldn't.

'Do you drink to be able to say them, or do you say them because you're drunk?' Sobhaan asked with a smile.

'Probably both.' Suranjan smiled back.

'I think so too.'

'Why don't *you* drink?'

'I just don't.'

'Because your religion forbids it?'

'Not at all.'

'Then why?'

'Never got into the habit. And I don't want to be addicted to anything. I don't smoke either.'

'You're like those good boys in school with glasses. Everyone says they're good boys, but it seems no one is as good as you.'

'That cannot go on very long. Maybe they say it because I'm tall, I comb my hair neatly, I wear glasses. I've been no less of a rogue than anyone else in my childhood.'

'What! You know how to be a rogue?'

'Very well indeed.'

'Have you reformed now?'

'No.'

'Why didn't you fight back against Achinta, then?'

'Not going to get my hands dirty with rats.'

Sobhaan smiled as he sipped his tea. Suranjan's skin began to prickle. Was Sobhaan really the paragon of virtue he appeared to be? How easily he had dismissed a virtual gangster as a rat!

Sobhaan had driven to their house in his own car that evening. After he left, Suranjan began to think about him. Why was he interested in Suranjan's company? Was it just friendship or did he have an ulterior motive? A wall of suspicion sprang up.

Thirteen

Zulekha felt that the dreams she had begun to weave with Suranjan in them, after their return from Rishop, were pointless. Whom was she trying to establish a relationship with? A man who had not stood by her side during a time of crisis. What kind of boyfriend was Suranjan anyway? When she had told him that it was impossible to keep staying in her uncle's house, that she had to leave at once, even if it meant sleeping on a park bench, he was unmoved. Zulekha had stared at him in disbelief.

'Aren't you going to say something?'

'What should I say?'

'Do you have nothing to say, Suranjan?'

Suranjan remained silent. He didn't look remotely perturbed. How he could be her boyfriend and still be so detached was beyond Zulekha. His silence dampened her spirits.

Finally, she said, 'Your house? Can't I stay in your house?'

Suranjan remained quiet. Zulekha felt tears of humiliation gather in her eyes. She didn't want tears, but they still came. It wasn't possible to go on arguing very long in a tea shop, nor to keep blinking back tears. Zulekha left. The only thing Suranjan said was that he would find a place for her to stay and call her before evening. Zulekha waited two days. The call never came. Nor did Suranjan take her calls. All she got from him were three SMSs, all of them saying, 'I love you.' These I-love-yous had tried but failed to placate Zulekha. How could she believe he loved her when he had abandoned her during her most difficult time? Why couldn't he have told her, 'Zulekha, I cannot help you in any way. Even if you're homeless and on the streets, there's no room for you in my house.'

The way he had stood by her after the gang rape had made her believe he had a heart, but now she reflected that it hadn't really needed him to have a heart. He had reached out to her only out of a sense of guilt. But then you couldn't have a conscience unless you had a heart. So many heartless people went about killing and harming others without feeling the slightest pang of guilt. Zulekha believed that contrition could free you of guilt, while love needed love to sustain it. But no, Zulekha could not sense Suranjan's love for her. Those three words carried the smell of penitence, not love.

Once she had weathered all the storms, picked a hostel after inspecting four or five of them and moved into it, she gave him the good news over the phone: he needn't worry any more, she didn't need his support, she had overcome her crisis. Suranjan sounded both joyful and busy: 'We're celebrating at home, birthday celebrations.'

'Where?'

'Beckbagan.'

'Whose house is that?'

'Oh, I didn't tell you. We've moved. We're in Beckbagan now.'

'I see. I didn't know.'

'Sorry, I didn't get around to telling you.'

'So, how are you?'

'Fine, I'm very well.' Suranjan's keenness to end the conversation was evident. Suppressing it, he said, 'Oh, by the way, I'm going to introduce you to a real gentleman one of these days.'

'What are you talking about?'

'Shobhon. You must meet Shobhon.'

'What on earth are you saying? Are you very busy?'

'Yes, very.'

'All right, enjoy yourself. I'll go now.'

Zulekha disconnected the call. She didn't want them to, but her tears began to flow, making her eyes smart and her heart heavy. Wiping the tears, she tried to read a magazine, but her eyes wouldn't focus, and the tears came again. She went for a bath, taking her time with it.

How intense those dreams had been. She'd returned from the mountains with a mountain of dreams, and now she had to contend with a Suranjan who had turned cold, who had refused to hold her hand in her hour of need. Would any boyfriend, even the worst kind, do this? He had a house to live in, in it a bed on which he had slept with her many times ... Couldn't he have made room for her, at least for some time? Leave alone a boyfriend, had Suranjan even acted like a friend? How would Zulekha continue her relationship with him? Suranjan's indifference was much more humiliating than Mohabbat's obscenities and inhuman beating.

When the man you love does not stand by you, when he does not respond to your appeal to him, when he does not try to comfort you when you're hurt, when he can sit by dispassionately while you're sinking, what kind of love game can you play with him? Every morning, every afternoon, every evening, every night, she had expected Suranjan to call her, to find out how things were. She had imagined he was busy but would come running to her as soon as he was free. She had built a house on the quicksand of hope. Zulekha's tears flowed with the water from the shower.

No more of the old life, she told herself, she would have to start a completely new one. Getting a place at the BKB Women's Hostel on Hazra Road was like finding a slot in paradise. There was

Giribala Hostel on Lansdowne Road too, but it was full, so there was no choice but BKB. A room for two, which she was sharing with a Muslim woman from Murshidabad with a bank job. With nowhere to stay in Calcutta, no family, she too had had to opt for a room in a hostel. They had chatted a little. An unmarried woman, her name was Mayur. Her name cheered up Zulekha immediately – she had never known someone could be called Mayur. The roommate had asked her whether she was married and had children. 'No,' Zulekha had answered. She used to think of Sohag as her son, but now she had realized that he was actually Mohabbat's child – she had merely given birth to him. She had taken care of the baby after he was born, cleaned his nappies, fed him. But the boy was growing up with his father's mentality; he even resembled him. He had no objection to slowly forgetting his biological mother, since he had been given a replacement. He was probably not missing her, and even if he thought she was better than his current mother, he had realized even at this age that it was wiser to adjust to the new one. Zulekha had no choice but to cut the umbilical cord. She had no friends or family now, no one to call her own. She had been so helpless that she had been compelled to take her rapist as her lover. But even this generosity proved futile, for the man she had mistaken as being her lover, did not love her at all. She knew that she would have to walk away from familiar circles, even if it meant becoming even more lonely than she was, currently. If new friends had to come into this new world, they would, and if they didn't, her life would remain unchanged. Just because there were crises in life, it did not mean she had to wail, beat her breast, or kill herself. Bad people would do bad things, charlatans would go on cheating others and telling lies, why should she waste her life over them? Zulekha wiped her eyes again, this time firmly. She had lost a lot of weight over the past few days, she noticed as she stood in front of the mirror, rubbing cream into her face. Her face looked more attractive now, and the food at BKB would ensure she lost some more weight. She would get bed and board at this women's hostel for twelve hundred rupees a month, and it would be a far better life than at her uncle's house, where the atmosphere was hellish. They weren't so much her relatives as they were bloodsucking leeches. She had stayed on out of desperation, only because it was easier to meet her son there, but when it became absolutely unbearable, and as her ties with her son loosened, she decided to leave. No one enquired after her. Zulekha thought no one on earth could be more bereft. Everyone had someone to check on them once in a while, but not she. Perhaps those who used to know her thought she was dead. This life was now hers alone, even if it was not much of a life. But she didn't want to think of it as a burden any more. She examined herself closely as she rubbed cream into her face. Her body was full of blemishes: marks where there should have been none, no mole where there should have been one. Large eyes, but small lids. Her nose could have been sharper. Her hair was thick, but not silken. Her lips were lovely, Suranjan had kissed those lips many times. Apparently, slim arms were preferable, but it was her arms on which flesh gathered. Today she felt good about this imperfect body, blemishes existed in the mind, not on the body. That was what she thought today. Who was going to tell her how to identify a flaw? As she was standing in front of the mirror, Mayur spoke to her.

'You're very beautiful.'

'Me?'

'Yes, you.'

'Tell me, why is your name Mayur?'

'My sister chose it for me. She had been to Ajmer once, and from there to Jaipur, where she saw peacocks and went crazy. I was born soon after, so she named me Mayur. Don't you like the name?'

'It's a lovely name. I've never known a name so lovely.'

Zulekha guessed that sharing a room with Mayur wouldn't be intolerable. No one wanted to live in a hostel; everyone would prefer a life amongst family and friends. But it was life in a hostel that Zulekha sought. There was no point getting involved with a vacillating coward like Suranjan. She told herself that no man with such a confused personality could hope to lead a healthy life.

Her job was boring, involving her standing behind the counter and talking to customers with a pretty smile when they came up to her. She had to communicate in English or Hindi when required. Knowing three languages had helped her get the job. The salary was five thousand rupees. She had never earned a rupee in her life before. This was her first income, the first time she was taking every decision in her life on her own. The first time she had become self-reliant, not being beaten up by anyone, not being abused, not swallowing contempt and humiliation, not living on alms, not living on someone else's pity. If this was not the best life, what was? True, the job was dull, but it wasn't as though her married life had been a shining one. That was a tedious job too, cleaning the house, cooking, serving the food, and all of this without any pay. She was just an unpaid maid in Mohabbat's house. Suranjan had made her dream, but those dreams were unreal. Zulekha's fate did not hold real love in store for her. It was difficult to accept this truth, but she had no choice. Like her height of five feet four inches, she had to accept this too. She could keep wringing her hands, but that wouldn't add an inch. Many women had not only not found love, but lived with oppression all their lives. Today Zulekha felt grateful for her experiences. Being abducted, then serially raped by her assailants, having sex with Suranjan in her husband's house, being caught by her husband, being beaten up by him, being divorced by him, being at the receiving end of hatred and censure from her family back home, Rabiul and Sultana's contempt, the torment at the hands of her uncle's family, all of these had opened up a new possibility in her life. She would not have been standing where she was now had her life been smooth and uneventful. She would not have found a world of her own, had it not been for people's crassness, cruelty, selfishness and obsession with religion. She had assumed she had no choice to when it came to being vulnerable, fragile, and dependent on others. She would never have known of her own strength and courage had her husband not thrown her out. Zulekha was not thankful to Suranjan for teaching her how to touch a man's body with passion or for the love he had given her, but for having abducted her with the intention of raping her. This one incident had changed her life, and for this, Suranjan had earned her lifelong gratitude. Getting to know the other girls in the hostel after work, learning more about the life here from older residents, watching TV, sleeping – this was the sum total of her days now. Her fingers itched to call Suranjan, but she turned her attention elsewhere to conquer this terrible loneliness. She restrained her fingers, her hands. But it was Suranjan who called one day.

'Come over this evening.'

'Where?'

'Outside Kala Mandir, six-thirty. We'll go off somewhere.'

'Go where?'

'Anywhere.'

'What do you mean, anywhere?'

'Don't you want to?'

'Is there any reason I should?'

'Come and see. I'll show you something new.'

'Something new? What?'

'You'll see. I won't tell you now. It's a surprise.'

The promise of a surprise gave Zulekha palpitations; she couldn't concentrate on work all day. She had been asked to operate the cash machine, but her mind was elsewhere and she kept pressing the wrong keys, mistaking the figures. What could the surprise be?

Would he say let's get married, would he say we'll live together from now on? Would he say these days apart from you have made me realize how deeply I love you, I cannot live without you? What else could he say? Would it be come home with me, Maya no longer has a problem with you, or I've got a good job with a fat salary – twenty thousand a month? Or maybe, you took me to Rishop, let me take you to Shimla. Or, let's go to Mandarmani for a couple of days. Or Andaman. What surprise could Suranjan possibly have in store for her?

He called again two hours later. 'Listen, come to Jimmy's Kitchen instead. It's around the corner from Kala Mandir.'

'All right.'

Another call at six.

'Listen, come to Marco Polo.'

So Zulekha went to Marco Polo on Park Street in the evening. No, she hadn't dressed up specially for the occasion, just a white blouse and an everyday blue cotton sari. No make-up, only her usual cream. Light lipstick. After a gap of a fortnight, she was meeting someone she used to see every day. Far from being calmed, Zulekha's yearning grew further on seeing Suranjan. How handsome he was looking. His blue shirt and slightly dishevelled hair was making him look even better. The mole was in its usual place – how often she had kissed it. She felt an urge to touch it now. Suranjan's eyes smiled when he caught sight of her, his lips too. An intense look, but brief. He shifted his gaze quickly. Zulekha sat opposite him, at a slight distance.

'Wow,' said Suranjan.

'What's that for?'

'Lovely.'

'What is?'

'You are.'

This was where Suranjan differed from other men. They might say, the sari looks lovely on you, but Suranjan would say, you look lovely in this sari.

'You're looking good too.'

'Hmm.'

'Meaning?'

'You've grown confident.'

'I wasn't before?'

'Not as much.'

'That's good, then. I'm improving, not deteriorating.'

'Absolutely. Your self-esteem has always been high, unlike mine.'

'So what made you think of me? If you've forgotten me, why not keep it that way? How come you asked to meet? What surprise?'

'You'll see.'

'I'll see? It's not something you're going to say?'

'You'll see.'

'Show me, then.'

'Wait.'

The conversation continued in the same vein for some time. Suranjan ordered a whisky and Zulekha, a Bloody Mary. She had had her first taste of this cocktail in the mountains thanks to Suranjan. They had barely taken a sip or two of their drinks when Sobhaan arrived.

'This is my friend Shobhon, aka, Sobhaan. Mohammed Sobhaan.'

Zulekha gave him a glance, lowered her eyes, and sipped her drink. Sobhaan sat down next to Suranjan and ordered a Sprite.

'This is Zulekha. She's the one I was telling you about. Wonderful girl. Started from zero, has a job now. You can't imagine how strong she is mentally. It's beyond my reach. And this is Sobhaan, he's fantastic, you could say he's my idol. A mountain of willpower, well-established, too. You two are very alike in personality: ambitious, career-driven. I thought it would be good to get you to know each other.'

After this, Zulekha directed most of her conversation towards Sobhaan. Where he lived, where he was from, his job, his business, whether he owned or rented the flat on Feeder Road. She was startled to hear he owned it.

Suranjan said, laughing, 'You have no idea, he has a car too, he drove here today. Was it easy to get parking?'

Sobhaan nodded. He only answered the questions, without asking any of his own. What Suranjan had told him about Zulekha was enough; he didn't want to know anything else.

Zulekha said, 'I have an insignificant job. I wasn't supposed to have been working at all, I was meant to take care of my husband and child. But a horrible incident changed everything. You know what they say, a friend in need is a friend indeed. To tell you the truth, I don't really have a friend; the only one I had was Suranjan. I live the life of someone who has no one to call her own. But I want to see what lies ahead. I want to take on what life brings, whatever it might be. And you?'

Sobhaan was much better looking than Suranjan. Enlightened, intelligent, well-dressed. It was difficult to say how he had befriended a person who was so unlike him. Zulekha knew that being handsome didn't make a man attractive; what mattered was the heart. She downed two Bloody Marys as she chatted with Sobhaan, and realized that she was enjoying his company, that he was a combination of integrity and good manners. Or so it seemed. The truth would become apparent only in time. But what did it matter how noble Sobhaan was? All that she had discovered was that Suranjan had a good friend. That didn't make him rise in her estimation, one did not become a worthier person simply by virtue of having a friend, one had to do something worthwhile. Zulekha's

eyes began to smart again, but she chased her memories away with
her Bloody Mary.

'You don't speak very much.'

Sobhaan smiled. 'There's not much to say on the first day.'

'Did you fall in love with your wife and marry her?'

Flustered by the question, he took his time to reply.

'Never mind, no need to answer. I think the word "love" makes
you uncomfortable.'

'Doesn't it make *you* uncomfortable?'

'Not in the least. Love came to me only once; I don't know if it'll
come again. To some people, it comes only once.'

'Why do you say that? Have you locked the door to your heart?'

'I haven't yet, but I'm thinking of it. What about yours? Locked?'

Again, Sobhaan smiled shyly. He wasn't used to this sort of
conversation with a woman. He might have been able to talk about
this with Suranjan.

'You're like those good people in films.'

'People say that because I don't talk much.'

'You mean you're not really good? Maybe they say so because you
have money but no arrogance.'

'You're quite like Suranjan.'

'How do you mean? As far as I know, I'm not like him at all.
What do we have in common? That we both drink? This is only the
second time in my life that I'm drinking, though.'

'No, it's not that.'

'What is it, then?'

'Both of you are full of praise for me though you know very little
about me.'

Suranjan was listening closely to the conversation; he was
savouring it. Was Zulekha deliberately trying to ignore his presence,
or had she fallen in love with Sobhaan? He couldn't make out.

Neither politics nor economics, neither society nor caste and creed figured in the exchanges, what did crop up were love and romance, relationships and separation. This was how Suranjan liked it. He got into a bad mood when other subjects came up, especially politics and economics, declaring that these were too difficult for him to understand. What did he enjoy, then? Sports. What about history or geography? History, never, geography is still all right. Family? Huh. Books? Boring. Music? That's fine. Theatre? No, with a sigh. Why not? Why not what? Why such aversion to these things? I don't like them. What do you like, then? To lie on my back, to muse, to do nothing, to sleep. Romance? Not for me. Do you like tutoring students? I do. What do you think about yourself? I don't think about myself. What do you enjoy the most? Joking. With whom? With myself, with others. Suranjan asked and answered himself.

The conversation continued, brilliant in some parts, incoherent in others, sometimes meaningful, meaningless otherwise. The night grew deeper. Sobhaan settled the bill. Suranjan was quite drunk. Zulekha was unaffected.

Sobhaan was a decent man. Not a stain on his milk-white shirt. Perfectly combed hair. Clean-shaven. No pockmarks or pits on his face. Gleaming teeth. Not false, not yellowed. Six feet tall. Not skinny, nor overweight. A few years younger than Suranjan.

A man like this should be desirable, especially to Zulekha. Sobhaan dropped Suranjan in his car at Beckbagan, Zulekha at Hazra. Later in the night, Suranjan called Zulekha. She had just slipped into bed.

'What do you think?'

'Very nice.'

'Wonderful, right?'

'Yes, wonderful.'

'I told you.'

'It's been such a long time since I've had good food. After the inedible stuff at my uncle's and now here at the hostel, it was … delicious.'

'No, I was talking about Sobhaan. Did you like him?'

'Oh, Sobhaan. Yes, why not?'

'Very handsome, isn't he?'

'Yes.' Zulekha proceeded to say what she had been meaning to in the restaurant. 'You said you'd give me a surprise. Why didn't you?'

'But I did.'

'When? All this drinking is killing your brain; you can't remember a thing.'

'My surprise was Sobhaan. Mohammed Sobhaan.' Suranjan's voice suggested he was revealing a great secret.

'Why should he be a surprise, he's just your friend.'

'I introduced him to you.'

'I'm glad. The first time around, it was your rapist friends. I didn't know you had non-rapist friends. For that matter, I don't know that this one isn't a rapist too.'

'What nonsense. I've said sorry to you a thousand times about that first day. Please don't bring it up any more.'

'Then tell me what I should talk about. What sort of discussion would you like?'

'Tell me what you thought of Sobhaan.'

'Why do you want to know what I thought of him?'

'He's a computer engineer with his own business. I think he's planning to set up a company in Salt Lake.'

'Excellent. See if you can get a job there. I'm sure he'll give you one if you ask. He seems very generous, he picked up the bill.'

'Yes, he is. He pays all my bar and restaurant bills.'

'You have no idea, Suranjan, how helpful a good friend can be. We keep talking about family, but it is often a friend who stands by you all your life. When I had to leave my uncle's house, you disappeared after promising to help. It was a girl I knew who let me stay at her house for the next few days. She was merely an acquaintance then, not yet a friend, just a colleague, but still she did me this favour. You couldn't do what a friend should have. So someone you've been friends with a long time needn't necessarily be a true friend. On the other hand, someone can become a real friend in a couple of days.' Zulekha wiped her eyes as she spoke, but didn't allow her tone to waver. Suranjan of all people would never get to hear the tears in her voice.

'See if you can, with Sobhaan…'

'See what?'

'See if you can have a relationship with him…'

'What do you mean?'

'I mean, isn't it better to have a relationship with him than with me?'

'What the hell are you saying? Have you gone mad?'

'No, I'm quite serious.'

'You're not in your senses tonight. I'm ending the call, talk to me tomorrow.'

Suranjan protested vociferously. 'No, talk to me now. I want—'

'What do you want?' Zulekha asked eagerly.

'I want a relationship between Sobhaan and you.'

'Why do you want it?'

'Because I'm not worthy of you. Sobhaan is.'

'Worthy of what? What sort of relationship do you want it to be? It can be of many kinds, friends, brother and sister. Which one?'

'Make him your boyfriend. Marry him.'

'Marry him?'

'Yes, marry him?'

'Weren't you and I talking of getting married?'

'No, that won't be right.'

'Suranjan, you don't have to be my boyfriend if you don't want to. But I didn't ask you to be a matchmaker.'

'You didn't, I took it on myself. It's because I love you that I'm suggesting this. I'm a debauch, a good-for-nothing, a rapist, my life is marked by despair. What we had between us was temporary, I would go back to normal immediately after I left you, every time. I'm lousy. I'm a Hindu.'

'What do you mean? When did you start thinking in terms of Hindu and Muslim? Did you bring Sobhaan to meet me because he's a Muslim?' Zulekha couldn't get over her astonishment.

'You'll get along with him.'

'How do you know? Because he's a Muslim?'

'Yes.'

'For shame, Suranjan. You could have said this if I'd set store by religion, if I had a soft spot for Muslims. I have criticized many things about you – your lethargy, your drinking, the bad company you keep, your indifference, your callousness, your irresponsibility, you're irresponsible through and through, but I've never brought up your religion.'

'Don't keep referring to my religion. I have no religion.'

'If you didn't, would you be trying to hand me over to Sobhaan just because he's Muslim?'

'You'll be happy with him.'

'How do you know?'

'I know. I also know you'll never be happy with me.'

'Are you an astrologer? Who knows, maybe you've been practising astrology. Anyway, why are you so worried about my marriage prospects? Have I said I must marry at once?'

'You need to.'

'That's my business. You're cutting off our relationship. Are you cutting it off?'

'Yes.'

'I see.' Zulekha smiled through her pain. 'Sobhaan is married; he even has a child. Have you forgotten?'

'So what?'

'So what? What are you saying?'

'A man can have four wives among you people.'

'What did you just say? You people? What do you mean "you people"?'

'Among Muslims. As if you don't know.'

'How much lower will you sink, Suranjan?' Zulekha paused, clamping her lips together to prevent her voice from breaking. She must remember that the person talking to her had never loved her; he had only deceived her, from the very first day. This thought would take the agony out of her voice. Allowing it to run through her head for some time, she parted her lips to speak slowly and deliberately.

'I think, Suranjan, my life will be better if my headaches are mine alone. I'm releasing you from your responsibility. Your atonement for having me raped by your friends has ended today. Your god will not punish you now. You're free of all responsibility, of all wrongdoing. So, move on. Find a nice Hindu girl and do what you have to with her. A goddamned Muslim girl will find another goddamned Muslim boy for herself. You needn't work yourself up over it.' Zulekha kept wiping her eyes, overflowing with tears, with her left hand.

'Don't talk that way, Zulekha. I feel like coming and seeing you now. Are you crying?'

'Of course not. Why should I cry? How strange, what's there to cry about? A Hindu and a Muslim getting married will be slaughtered by society. They lose their families, they lose their jobs, their lives are ruined. Everyone condemns them. Who's going to live with such shame? You're advising me like a well-wisher should. There's no reason to cry. I'm thanking you – many thanks. I'll go now. I have to be up early.'

Zulekha disconnected the call and tried to sleep, but she got no sleep all night. She began to scroll through the old SMSs on her phone. Those days were within reach again, but also miles away. So it was true that she had loved the wrong man. Knowing he was a rapist, knowing he was a Hindu, knowing she would be ostracized by her family. By now, Mohabbat must have spread stories about Zulekha among all her relatives and anyone who knew her, in the city and back in the village. She was an outcast now. Much like becoming a prostitute. No one would look for her, just like no one looked for women sold to the brothels of Shonagachhi. She erased the SMSs she had sent to and received from Suranjan. The night went by just pressing the keys. She was about to start the first day of a new life.

Reviewing her life, Zulekha took a decision the next day. She would study, take the MA examination as a private candidate, or attend evening BEd courses at Jogmaya College, just like Mayur. Zulekha looked at herself properly after a very long time. What she realized was that paying attention to her own life, taking care of herself, meant freeing herself from thinking about men.

Fourteen

I hadn't heard from any of them in a long time. Two visits to the Park Circus house yielded no news. I had been looking for them desperately, but Suranjan didn't take my calls. One day, Zulekha called me from an unknown number. I don't usually answer such calls, but then I forget my own rule too.

Zulekha wanted to meet, I couldn't imagine why, though. When I asked about Suranjan, she said he was fine, just fine.

'Just fine?'

'Yes, just fine.' Zulekha's hurt feelings were spilling over in her voice. Mine was calm, curious, with no trace of resentment.

'Why isn't he taking my calls?'

'Because he's thrown his phone away.'

'Thrown it away? Where?'

'Ballygunge Lake, that's where.'

'The lake? In the water?' I muttered to myself, while Zulekha reeled off her story, about her MA, her BEd, her roommate Mayur, Mayur's daily routine, the bittersweet experiences of life in a hostel. I interrupted her to ask about Kiranmayee.

'She's all right.'

'Any news of Maya?'

'No, but she's fine too. They're all living together now.'

Living together. Zulekha had many things to say, a phone call wasn't enough. She said she would visit me and tell me everything in person.

When I told her I needed to talk to Suranjan, she gave me their Beckbagan address, and repeated that she would come to see me soon. I asked her to drop by any afternoon.

Why should I go looking for someone who hadn't bothered to keep in touch? I'd rather meet Kiranmayee one of these days. There was something motherly about her, it was like a magnet.

Zulekha visited on a Sunday, when it was getting on for evening. We sat down amidst the plants in the veranda. Zulekha seemed different from the last time we had met, saying courteously, 'I shouldn't be wasting your time.'

'What'll you have? Some tea?'

'A Bloody Mary would be good.'

I was a little startled. This was what being with an alcoholic had done to Zulekha – she had learnt to drink too. I had some Absolut Vodka, a friend had said it was good with a dash of lemon and chilli.

'I don't have the ingredients for a Bloody Mary, can you make do with this?'

'Aren't you having a drink?'

'I'll have tea.'

'You take one too. You can have tea any time, but have a vodka with me. I don't like drinking alone.'

'I get whisky and vodka for my friends every time I come back from a foreign country. I think everyone in Calcutta drinks. You've seen Suranjan.'

'Not everyone drinks. Sobhaan doesn't.'

Eventually, I did get up to pour myself a vodka. I usually drink only in the company of very good friends, when there's absorbing conversation, delicious food and fine red wine. But I'd hardly be able to explain this to Zulekha, and it would be harsh to tell her that she wasn't one of those close friends, nor was the conversation scintillating. And so I added chilled water generously to a little vodka and took a sip in the pleasant breeze. Zulekha was halfway through her drink already.

'So, how are you?'

'Very well.'

'What did you want to see me about?'

'Nothing in particular. I've been wanting to see you for a while. I felt you might understand what I'm going through right now.'

'Tell me.'

'Suranjan doesn't want to continue our relationship.'

'Why not?'

Zulekha waved her glass in the air, silent. We were sitting on wicker chairs, not exactly face to face, gazing at the sky. Birds were flocking back to their nests; I couldn't take my eyes off them. So many birds, did they share the same home?

'Why should your relationship with Suranjan have to end?'

'He alone knows why. I had nothing to do with it, the decision was entirely his.'

'Why such a decision suddenly? He had told me just the other day – the day you returned from Rishop – that he wanted to live with you.'

'Yes, it was he who had brought up the idea of getting married. It wasn't one-sided, both of us wanted it.'

'And then?'

'And then he suddenly went off me. Wouldn't meet, wouldn't stay in touch. He even changed his phone number. He never wanted to use the phone anyway, apparently his mother had insisted. It's all very strange.'

'But why are you telling me all this? What can I do for you?'

'There's nothing you can do for me. Now he's trying to force a man on me. Says this man is a Muslim and I should marry him.'

This was a huge surprise. I shot out of my rocking chair, spilling some vodka in the process, but I couldn't be bothered, I was focused on what Zulekha was telling me.

'So I'm thinking of having an affair with this Muslim man in full view of Suranjan. I was never what you might call religious, and I thought he wasn't either. He never performed rituals, I never saw him pray or anything. On the contrary, he would criticize Maya for her obsession with temples and deities. But he's actually such a coward, so narrow-minded, I feel bad about it.'

'You're angry now. Maybe you'll think differently once you calm down.'

'Why must I do everything calmly? I'll have the affair since he wants me to.'

'Is love so important? Do you always need to replace one man with another?'

Zulekha was taken aback. Unsure of how to answer, she said, 'No.'

'In that case, you don't have to take a decision at this moment. Take some time to think it over.'

Zulekha laughed. 'Too much thinking complicates matters. I've taken my best decisions on the spur of the moment.'

'Like what? Which were your good decisions and which were the bad ones?'

'I thought a lot about my marriage. It was a bad decision. I thought a lot about entering into a relationship with Suranjan too – obviously wrong. The good ones include getting a job, moving to a hostel, enrolling in college. All taken in a moment.'

'You're very disciplined, Zulekha. Suranjan must be just the opposite.'

'That's how it looks, but actually deep inside he's much more disciplined than I am.'

'Really? Of course, you know him much better than I do.'

'He's not exactly the way you've written about him in *Lajja*. You've written he's obsessed with politics … *I* don't think so.'

'Maybe he isn't now, but he was back then.'

'The whole thing with him happened accidentally. I still have feelings for him, why shouldn't I? But I see no reason to keep them alive.'

'How can you forget someone overnight? You're bound to miss him.' I had to make another drink for Zulekha. Handing it to her, I said, 'But don't you turn into him. Don't drink more.'

'No, bubu, I promise I won't be like Suranjan.'

'Isn't there anything good about him?'

No answer. Zulekha said she wanted to meet Sobhaan, and demanded to be allowed to do it at my place. I didn't know him, I said, and couldn't invite him.

'I'll call him over,' she declared with great enthusiasm.

I was a little surprised: Zulekha's behaviour seemed quite mysterious. Without being given proper permission, she called Sobhaan on the phone and asked him to come over, giving him the address of my flat. I was annoyed: was I going to be saddled with this pest now? I had masses of writing to do, I'd stopped socializing at home for nearly a year now. It was far better to read or even reflect on things instead of wasting time on meaningless conversation. I didn't even have the time to play with Minu, who gazed at me plaintively with the football lying at her feet. She simply refused to play alone these days; I had to join in.

'Sobhaan, please, Sobhaan, please.' Zulekha kept pleading so loudly on the phone in the veranda that it seemed ugly.

I couldn't hold myself back any longer, and said, 'Listen, don't force anyone to come here. Besides, I don't even know him, why are you asking him here? It would be better to…'

'Better to…?'

'Better to meet somewhere else. I have to write. I don't see the point in everyone gathering here. I don't even know who you're inviting, who's this person?'

'A friend of mine.'

'A friend of yours?' I frowned sceptically.

'Yes.'

'Or is he a friend of Suranjan's? Didn't you say he was trying to force someone on you? Is it this man? Seems more like you're trying to force yourself on him.'

Zulekha bowed her head. 'You're misunderstanding me.'

'How should I understand you, then? Here's a man who doesn't want to come here, but you're insisting. Is Suranjan aware of this?'

'This is what he wants.'

'So do you, it appears.'

'Me?'

'Are you trying to tell me you don't?'

With a sigh, Zulekha said, 'I don't care what people say, I don't consider you a man-hater.'

I wondered whether it was a smart comeback or a genuinely intelligent one. Zulekha appeared rude and foolish to me – someone trying to become modern very quickly. Her sari was a loud pink, she was wearing long danglers in her ears, a large teep on her forehead. I was tempted many times to tell her to remove both the danglers and the teep, but I didn't, for the simple reason that if these things were to her taste, who was I to stop her? But I could still express my opinion. To do that – or was it my anger I was venting? – I said, 'You dress up a lot.'

'Dress up?'

'Yes, dress up. Have you noticed how you repeat what I say?'

'Do I?'

'You do. Like Suranjan.'

'Does he do it? I hadn't noticed.'

'He does.'

'He does.'

Suddenly, Zulekha said, 'I need to use the bathroom,' and marched off towards my study. Strangers don't have access beyond the drawing room in my house. I dislike anyone intruding; it's rude. I could have shown her the way to the bathroom myself – there are three in the flat, and guests are forbidden from the one I use. Earlier I used to allow them in, but then found all my bottles of Chanel No. 5 going missing. Even people I considered close had pocketed my perfume without telling me. While it must have been one or two bad people who did this, it made me suspect everyone. So I didn't want anyone to go into my bathroom, not so much to guard my Chanel as to keep my mind free of suspicion.

Back from the bathroom, Zulekha settled down comfortably and proceeded to criticize Maya – Suranjan's wife had left him because of her, and now so had Zulekha. Suranjan would never be at peace as long as his shrew of a sister was around him. I didn't care for what Zulekha was saying. I had never been able to accept her relationship with Suranjan with a liberal mind, I had always felt it wasn't built on a strong foundation. Neither of them had told me what the basis of their relationship was. I was always capable of drawing my own conclusions, but, to be honest, in this case I wasn't interested enough. I even told Zulekha, 'Old relationships end, new ones begin, that doesn't mean you have to say bad things about someone.'

'It's just that I can't be as generous as you.'

'It's not a question of generosity, just a matter of character. Each of us has different characteristics.'

'So you're trying to say it's in my character to criticize others?'

Was Zulekha here with the specific intention of belittling Suranjan? And since she stayed in a hostel, she had nowhere to meet a potential boyfriend except at my house. What other reason could there be? I began to feel sorry for Suranjan. Zulekha must have done things that made it impossible for him to continue his relationship with her.

Perhaps love and romance become secondary in a time of extreme political, social and familial uncertainty. Or is it the other way round?

Zulekha's expression radiated a fervent plea for more vodka. I had the urge to turn her down, to throw out someone as crude and ill-mannered as her, to say, 'Go somewhere else with your new boyfriend. My house is not a public meeting place.'

Of course I couldn't say or do any of these things, but my demeanour signalled clear disinterest.

A handsome man was standing at the door. Sobhaan. He wanted to meet Zulekha. Greeting him, I went into my study, giving them the opportunity to talk in the drawing room. Sujata served tea and biscuits to them. A little later, Zulekha barged into my study: 'Come out, bubu, you didn't even meet him properly.'

'I'm sure you have things to tell each other. Finish your conversation.'

'Nothing important. It can be done on the phone too. He's come a long way ... what will he think if you don't talk to him? You're so famous, this kind of behaviour doesn't suit you.'

'How strange! What behaviour are you talking about? I came away because you wanted privacy with him. And now you're blaming me.'

'I know you don't like me one bit. But...'

'But what?'

'But I love you so much.' She took my hand.

At this moment, she didn't appear fake, so I went out and sat down with them. Muslims don't have free access to my house: you never know what's on their mind. There were two policemen posted outside, and yet a complete stranger, a Muslim man, had walked into my house. Had I even lost the right to decide who could visit me and who couldn't?

'There's no one like Sobhaan, bubu.'

'How do you know? How many times have you met him?'

'Twice.' Zulekha smiled sweetly at Sobhaan. Was it an indulgent smile or a courteous one?

'Suranjan has told me about you,' said Sobhaan.

'How is Suranjan?'

'Very well.'

'What is he doing these days?'

'Tutoring students, which he loves. They are big fans. Two girls had come to his house the other day. Class VI, I think. He was playing chess with them.'

'Is he very moody? I haven't met him in a long time.'

'He was talking about you the other day. We were having dinner at a restaurant on Park Street. He spoke about you for a long time.'

'What did he say?'

'That you're very nice, very generous. He will visit you soon, he said.'

Sobhaan seemed to be making it all up. Clean-shaven, clean-cut, he sipped his tea elegantly. 'He's become addicted to water these days. Goes to the Lakes every evening.'

'Has he started jogging or something?'

'That's not a habit he ever developed. I don't think he's going to start jogging now.'

I was thinking about the Lakes. Why did Suranjan go there?

'Do you know how his father died?' I threw the question abruptly at both of them.

Sobhaan said, 'I believe someone named Shankar Ghosh – a relative, apparently – pushed him into a lake. I heard he had run up a lot of debt.'

'I think it was a different reason,' said Zulekha. 'The family wants to keep it a secret, but as far as I know he committed suicide on a dark night in a lake near their house. Something to do with Maya.'

'What was it?' I was eager to know.

'Suranjan had said, "All of us have had to suffer because of Maya. We had to leave our country and lose our father."'

Zulekha's reminiscence made me reflect deeply. I noticed that no one was as concerned about Sudhamay's death as I was. To them, it was a death like any other; none of them had known him, after all. No one had followed his dreams, no one helped him air his grief. None of those who could have touched the naphthalene-scented days of his childhood and adolescence were here.

'Are you married, Sobhaan?'

Zulekha was sitting intimately close to him. Her instinct was to move away at this question, even if her body did not oblige. Sobhaan nodded. Yes, he was married.

'Children?'

'A daughter.'

'How old is she?'

'Three.'

'What's her name?'

'Mon.'

'Mon? What a lovely name. What's her full name?'

'Dilruba Parveen.'

'Does your wife work?'

Sobhaan smiled sadly. 'No, she doesn't.'

'Why not? Are you in favour of wives not venturing out of home? Isn't she educated?'

'She is. But I don't think she wants to work.'

'You don't *think*?' My voice was laced with sarcasm.

Zulekha felt that Suranjan was forcing Sobhaan and her on each other. The desire for revenge on Suranjan illuminated her path, and her infatuation with Sobhaan provided her the ground beneath her feet. So she was over the moon with delight right now. Extramarital relations are considered quite normal in Bengali society. Even if Muslim, Zulekha and Sobhaan belonged to the same society. Zulekha might not perform Hindu religious rituals or wear the symbols of a Hindu wife, but like everyone else, she too had been born and brought up in a patriarchal society, and that's where her mentality had been nurtured.

All men, I've noticed, introduce their romantic interest as their girlfriend, but after marriage they no longer treat her the same way. 'Now that she's the wife, someone else will be the girlfriend.' I've tried to explain to friends that a woman can be a wife and a girlfriend at the same time, but none of them gets it.

Sobhaan didn't ask me a single question, though he patiently answered all of mine. Wasn't he curious? I trust people even though many people have betrayed me, but I wasn't willing to give Sobhaan full marks right at the outset. For now, I realized, he was basking in the adulation of both men and women, and who doesn't enjoy adulation. But I had no idea how he had become friends with Suranjan. From what I could tell, even if he was a recent friend, they were quite close. Since I had accused Suranjan of being a Hindu fundamentalist, was he trying to prove to me that he could have a Muslim as a close friend too? He was playing games with me, or was it with himself?

Fifteen

One morning I woke up early and drove directly to Beckbagan. It was 6 a.m. The shops were closed; municipality workers were clearing garbage heaps, the disposal truck was parked nearby. A madman was lying on the pavement, filthy and naked. Two men were injecting themselves with heroin. I had to pinch my nose shut with one hand and manage the steering with the other. Zulekha had given me the address. I knocked on the door, and a harsh male voice responded behind it. I wouldn't have known it was Suranjan's if he hadn't opened the door – bare-bodied, dressed in a lungi. It was oppressively hot inside. A fan whirred overhead, a young boy was sleeping on a camping cot. Mosquito nets were draped over both the beds. Suranjan rubbed his eyes and stared at me as though he couldn't recognize me.

'Come on.'

'What do you mean come on?' Suranjan sounded annoyed.

'Put on your clothes.'

'What for?'

'Get dressed and come out, I'll tell you.'

It would have taken me a quarter of the time Suranjan took to get ready. Asking him to get in next to me, I drove past Victoria Memorial and across Vidyasagar Setu, out of the city.

'Where are you going?'

I put on a CD of Roma Mondal, singing Rabindranath's songs without accompaniment. These were supposed to be devotional, but I'd always thought of them as love songs.

In answer to Suranjan's question, I said, 'Wherever the road leads.'

'But I don't want to go wherever the road leads,' he answered.

'If I ask you where you want to go, you'll say nowhere. You just want to stay at home or go somewhere to drink in the evening.'

'Maybe that's what I enjoy.'

'I'm not saying you don't enjoy it. But today what I'll enjoy is my taking you wherever the road leads.'

'Have you gone mad?'

I smiled. 'I was always mad.'

Suranjan was dressed in black trousers and an off-white panjabi. Black sandals. The air conditioner in the car was running. Had he put on a cologne? It didn't seem so. Maybe he had used a perfumed soap, which was what I could smell.

'What else do you want to say?'

'Nothing.'

Laughing, Suranjan said, 'You practically abducted me. So women do it too, it's not just men.'

I laughed too. 'It's not for nothing that I talk of equality.'

Our laughter cleared the air of hostility. Suranjan seemed to breathe freely. It was a glorious morning, beautiful music. I hadn't seen what dawn was like in a long time. I hadn't listened to music in a long time.

'What's wrong with you?'

'I don't know.' Suranjan shrugged.

The next song kept both of us silent for a while: *'Chirosokha he, chhero na.'*

I had dragged Suranjan out of his house for several reasons. I hadn't been at ease ever since I was told that he had been frequenting the Ballygunge Lakes in the evening. Was he about to do something like Sudhamay had? When a young man – deeply in love, having a glorious time with his girlfriend, nurturing dreams of a future together – suddenly breaks off his relationship with complete detachment, he may well be suffering from a mental crisis, some kind of extreme depression that might lead him to suicide any moment, there was no telling. Spending hours on the edge of a lake was not a healthy sign. I had no intention of asking him to continue his relationship with Zulekha; it wasn't as though this would automatically dispel his depression. All I wanted was to give him a respite from his monotonous existence. Was there anyone who didn't want to go away somewhere for a bit? You can't just get rid of depression because someone's telling you to, you need a little sunlight in this cold, damp existence, a little of what the heart desires, some care, someone's selfless love, the absence of pressure, even the pressure of love, all of these. I wanted to give Suranjan a taste of freedom today, a bit of the sky, a bit of wherever the road takes you. I wanted to give him the joy of losing himself, of leaving everything behind, of forgetting everything. Who knows how much of this was my own desire too?

We stopped around eight for some tea by the road. Wide expanses of green farmland lay in front of us. There were plenty of palm trees here, besides coconut trees, of course. I have always been drawn to villages. Every time I am somewhere green and quiet, I vow to go back soon, but don't end up doing it. Doesn't happen, doesn't happen – one has to live with so many doesn't-happens. This is how you have to make it happen: get up and about; go.

Wherever the road takes us. It's been in my blood since childhood. After returning from college, I'd pick Yasmeen up in the rickshaw and set off. 'Where to?' the rickshaw driver would ask. 'Anywhere,' I'd answer. 'Meaning?' he'd ask in surprise. 'Anywhere the road takes us,' I'd explain. He'd start pedalling. Rickshaw drivers liked the idea. They enjoyed taking their favourite routes.

The endless road stretched out in front of us, flanked by green on both sides, while the song '*Biday daao khelar saathi gelo je khela bela*' rang out on the car stereo. Neither of us spoke for a long time. Finally, I told Suranjan, 'Say something.'

'Say what?'

'Anything you like. Whatever's on your mind.'

Suranjan was silent.

'What do you want to talk about? Politics?'

Suranjan burst out laughing. 'No.'

'The economy?'

'No.'

'Majority–minority relations?'

'No.'

'Hindus and Muslims?'

'Absolutely not.' He shook his head vehemently.

'Your parents, your nephew and niece?'

'No.'

'Friends?'

'No.'

'Zulekha?'

Suranjan shook his head. No.

'Your new friend, Sobhaan?'

Suranjan smiled, his eyes crinkling. 'No.'

'Beckbagan? Belgharia? Tutoring? Students?'

'No.'

'Bangladesh?'

'No.'

'Oh, no. So you're not going to speak at all, Suranjan.'

He was averse to talking about any of the things I suggested, but I had to tell him about the seat belt. He didn't want to put it on, but I forced him. And he forced me to stop the car every half an hour, to quench his desire for a cigarette. Smoking was not allowed in the car, so I had to stop.

We had breakfast at a Punjabi dhaba. Lunch near Bardhaman. No, we didn't talk about any of the things I had suggested, only about what we could see, hear or were eating. No past, no future, all we had was the present. Two human beings, born at six this morning. Our lives had begun only at that point. It wasn't just for Suranjan, I needed this escape too. Very much.

Losing our way and then finding it again, we arrived at Santiniketan. A long walk together on the bank of the Kopai. We stopped at the sight of a tree leaning at a steep angle, of the river eroding the bank. We spent a long time watching the sun set. Our hearts were warmed. And then we walked side by side on the trail of red soil, singing all the way – songs that had lain hidden deep within us gushed out like a torrent. We strolled around the Santhal habitation, wandering into their mud houses and witnessing their ways of living. Suranjan had never been to such a place before. He gazed at everything in wonder. Ambling through acacia woods, we talked of everyday things, spending hours walking or sitting or lying on our backs, gazing at the sky without words. Silence could also be beautiful. We listened to the calls of the birds, and slowly, ever so slowly, darkness and light both fell on us. How was this possible? The sky looked down at us with affection, the moon seemed to fill all of it, who knew it was a full-moon night. In the acacia woods, Santhal women were dancing around a fire and drinking their home-brewed liquor. Suranjan drank with them, danced with them too. And then he took my hand and pulled me to the fire: 'You dance too.'

It was the liquor, not Suranjan, that was speaking, for he did not usually address me as 'tumi'.

'How come it's tumi suddenly?'

Dancing in time with the women, he said, 'Why do you address me as tumi?'

'Revenge?'

'Yes, revenge.' Suranjan burst into hearty laughter. Was this the liquor too and not Suranjan? I was convinced it was Suranjan who was laughing without any restraints.

Everything began to feel wonderful, the full moon had lit up the woods like daylight. Gazing at the moon made me feel I was not in this world, that I had had flown to some ethereally beautiful universe on someone's wings. Suranjan was on the ground with a Santhal woman. Was he trying to kiss her? Let him if he wanted to, everything was allowed under this magical moon. The woods emptied out around one in the morning. All of them returned home; Suranjan lay on the white sand, bathed by moonbeams. The moon melted around us, a breeze sprang up. Neither of us mentioned going back home. It was as though we had no life beyond this one.

It was almost dawn when I opened my eyes. I turned on the ignition at once, the trail of red soil on the edge of the acacia woods leading us back to the road to Calcutta. The sun rose as we were driving back, blood oozed over the green with us as witnesses. Suranjan didn't ask even once why I had brought him here. There was nothing important to discuss.

'Let's have some tea.' 'How beautifully green it is there. Let's stop for a bit.' In this way, we escaped the pollution, the congested alleyways, the damp-ridden, dreary, daily existence, to breathe in some fresh air. It did not mean our lives were transformed, just that a breeze had blown into them. One could ask what I had to gain from giving this joy, this respite, to Suranjan. I could ask myself too. Why? But was it really so difficult to answer this? I felt Suranjan was close to me, and why not? He wasn't merely a character I had created, he had an existence of his own. I couldn't control where he went, what he said or what he thought, but still I felt I had a right over him. Perhaps it had been born from the novel I had written. My love, my partiality, my effort to understand him with all my heart, were not to be dismissed.

To return to Calcutta was to enter a cityful of air pollution, sound pollution and obscene traffic. Dropping Suranjan at Beckbagan, I said, 'Listen, you and I will go to the Ballygunge Lakes one of these days, all right?'

'Why to the Lakes suddenly?'

'Why not? Can't we swim there?'

'Swim?'

'Yes, swim.'

Suranjan shook his head, which could mean both yes or no. I didn't try to find out, I drove off.

How beautiful life is, let's keep living. Why does one go to the Lakes ... Is it to die? That won't solve anything. I'd wanted to die too, sometimes; life had become meaningless, I wanted to kill myself. That was when someone, no one very close, had put their arm around me lovingly, affectionately. I was overwhelmed by the gesture. Without that touch, I wouldn't have realized how beautiful life is.

I neither spoke to nor met Suranjan for a few days after this. He no longer used a mobile phone and had given it to Maya, or to Kiranmayee, it wasn't clear, I couldn't tell for sure. How could there be so much slovenliness in one person's life?

One day, when I asked Zulekha about Suranjan, she said he had gone to Bangladesh, by bus. Someone he knew had damaged both their kidneys and was in hospital. Zulekha didn't know how Suranjan had got the news.

My voice shook. 'Who is it, what's their name?'

Suranjan hadn't spoken to Zulekha. She had heard from Sobhaan.

'Who's the friend? Is it Pulak?'

'No.'

'Kajal?'

'No, a different sort of name.'

'Ratna?'

'No.'

'Who, then? Anjan? Subhash?'

Zulekha replied, 'Let me find out from Sobhaan and tell you.' She called back ten minutes later. 'The friend's name is Haider.'

'Haider?'

'Yes, Haider.' Zulekha's voice was calm.

Ending the call, I remained sitting for a long time exactly where I was, in the balcony. Nothing but the huge sky remained.

Sixteen

Sobhaan realized that Suranjan was trying to force him on Zulekha, but was this really possible? He understood Suranjan, but then he couldn't explain his actions sometimes. The more he tried, the more incomprehensible Suranjan's behaviour seemed. And the more mysterious he seemed, the more Sobhaan's attraction towards him grew. When he went to Suranjan's house, he didn't feel like returning home. Go back where, after all. His parents had made him marry his cousin, Naila, who was twenty years younger than him. Not that such an age difference was necessarily a barrier to friendship or love, but in this case, the two of them didn't click, belonging as they did to two distinct worlds. Sobhaan didn't feel this was a barrier to conversation – instead of restricting themselves to their own worlds, they could in fact share their experiences with each other. But with Naila, he had seen, nothing more than trite conversation was possible. It wasn't even as though Naila was cut up about this. She had accepted that her greatest mission in life was to take care of her husband and child and in-laws. Many times, Sobhaan had suggested going to the cinema or eating out, but she had no interest in such activities – these apparently being things only men did. Even when she went out, she liked wearing a burqa.

Sobhaan refused to accompany a woman in a burqa; he found it irksome. He had very little to do when at home. Naila was so busy with their child, she didn't have a moment to spare for him. And what would Sobhaan have done anyway, even if she did? She was obsessed with clothes and cosmetics. Sobhaan would ask her what the point of the saris and jewellery and make-up was, considering she hid them all beneath the burqa. 'I don't do it to show people,' Naila would reply.

'Why do you do it, then?'

'For your eyes alone.'

Sobhaan didn't pay much attention to this. What was the point anyway? How would the sight of a woman all dressed up at home help him? Cuddling the baby and a little banter with Naila was as far as it went, Sobhaan wasn't even excited enough by his business venture to talk about it at home. And so he spent all his time with computers – at work and at home – which was why he responded with alacrity whenever Suranjan said he wanted to meet. Sobhaan didn't have too many friends, but he didn't regret this. He believed that one good friend was preferable to a hundred bad ones, and he considered Suranjan a very good friend.

Sobhaan had always been the good boy of the family. The only thing he had been fascinated with since childhood was books. He was the classic bespectacled front-bencher who never looked at girls, had never had a chance to fall in love, and had graduated from IIT Kharagpur. People outside his family knew him as Shobhon, the lotus that had bloomed in a heap of cow dung.

Sobhaan's maternal grandfather was from Medinipur – he had been forced to leave home for marrying a Hindu woman, and had settled down in Fatullapur in Belgharia. He and his son ran a garments shop, Sobhaan was the only one in his generation to have studied. His siblings were all girls, each one made to get married by the time she was eighteen. Sobhaan had earned a fat salary from his job with a software company in Salt Lake, he had bought a flat on Feeder Road, and had even started a computer shop downstairs. His parents lived with him; the next step would be to start his own company.

It would be accurate to say that Sobhaan too had been forced to get married. Naila had been brought over from Medinipur, made to stay in the house for a few days and then, almost without warning and without ceremony, the wedding was held. Sobhaan had muttered his agreement in desperation: oh all right, just stop bothering me. He had seen Naila all of three times before the wedding and had no idea his parents had been planning all this till a fortnight before. The girl was also practically forced into the alliance. He had heard that she had objected strongly to marrying her cousin, and had kept her eyes closed out of embarrassment during the ceremony. Sobhaan's work kept him busy all day and he had not objected to his parents' wishes. Since marriage was inevitable, and since he was of age, might as well be done with it. And so Sobhaan the workaholic and young Naila Khatoon were married one day. The wedding was done, they spent their nights together in bed, the fragrance of fresh bodies, arms reaching out for each other. Eventually a child was born.

Even if Sobhaan or Shobhon or Shobhon da or Shobhon babu was being forced on Zulekha, he didn't intend to get involved. He felt sympathy for her – from whatever little he had seen of her, she seemed to be brimming with confidence. Sobhaan was keenly aware that it was Suranjan whom Zulekha actually loved, it was him she wanted, so deeply that she couldn't handle the rejection.

The more hurt and angry she was, the less attention Suranjan paid to her. He was made of stone, but he was also a flowing torrent. Sobhaan preferred spending time with Suranjan to going back home early; it was a release from his tedious life. He was learning what freedom was, not having realized that his work was in fact staggeringly boring. Suranjan had strange notions about life, but monotony was part of his existence too, Sobhaan was a source of freedom for him as well. Sobhaan was deeply interested in everything in the world, while Suranjan was extraordinarily indifferent. Sobhaan's personality bloomed by the day, while Suranjan grew increasingly self-centred. It was an unlikely friendship but it had grown, perhaps because they could see each other's pasts. They did not have to open themselves up to outsiders – only to each other.

Sobhaan had not wanted to visit Zulekha at Taslima's house out of shyness and hesitation. He had no idea what Taslima's view of men with Muslim names was. Besides, he had never been in the company of writers. But Zulekha had dispelled his fears – and Taslima hadn't appeared to be an extremist of any kind, she had offered tea and chatted just like any other person. In fact, she had seemed quite sensitive, especially in her questions about Suranjan. Sobhaan felt Suranjan didn't know just how much Taslima cared for him. And idiots always imagined that if someone cared for you, they were in love. Suranjan was an expert at misreading people.

Sobhaan respected young men and women who had to struggle to establish themselves, who were determined to live with dignity and did whatever it took for this. His sisters had been made to marry good-for-nothing men right in front of his eyes; he had not been able to stop them. One of his sisters had had a daughter, for which her husband was blaming her, threatening to marry someone else. Another brother-in-law was saying, get me a fat dowry, your brother is a rich man now. Another one was beaten up by her husband every night. All three of his sisters were dependent on others. Sometimes, Sobhaan would say, let them all move back home, but his parents didn't want any of them to leave their families. Every time he saw Maya, Sobhaan felt his sisters could have walked out of their husbands' homes too. Maya's leaving her in-laws' home was not a cruel act; Maya was not cruel. Whenever Sobhaan went to meet

Suranjan, not an evening had passed when Maya hadn't said, 'You must eat with us, Shobhon da.'

Once, Sobhaan had said, 'I had only heard about the famed gluttony and hospitality of people from Bangladesh, I'm seeing it for myself now. I myself am a victim.'

'Victim?' Maya's brows had shot up in astonishment.

'Forgive me,' Sobhaan had apologized. 'I'd meant to say lucky recipient.'

'That's better.' Maya had laughed.

Maya had cooked often for him, but she still didn't know he was not a Hindu. He had nearly got into trouble once, when Maya said, 'I'll make meat for you next Sunday, Shobhon da, what do you like?' Sobhaan had replied, 'Anything, chicken, mutton, beef...'

'Beef?' Maya had jumped.

Suranjan had butted in quickly, 'Everyone eats beef these days. Do you think people are blinded by religion like you? I eat beef, Baba used to, even *you* ate beef back in Bangladesh. We'd make it at home. Only Ma never ate beef, the rest of us did.'

Maya paused. This was true, it was entirely possible.

Sobhaan knew that being identified as Shobhon made things easier in many places. Shobhon. Shobhon da. Shobhon babu. And yet he couldn't come to terms with having to enter even a close friend's house in the guise of a Hindu. When he suggested revealing his real identity, Suranjan said, 'You won't be able to visit us any more. The doors will be closed for you, Maya will do it. She can't stand Muslims.'

Neither Suranjan nor Sobhaan was in favour of introducing Muslims as Hindus or vice versa. They could meet and chat outside, of course, but it would mean going to a bar or restaurant, and Suranjan could not afford to pay the bills there. He could allow Sobhaan to pay from time to time, but certainly not every day. Whatever rickety principles he was still adhering to would be severely dented.

Suranjan used to ask Sobhaan over earlier, but nowadays he came on his own. Sobhaan had even said he would shift his computer shop from Feeder Road to Park Circus, an idea Suranjan had enthusiastically endorsed.

Naturally, Sobhaan met Suranjan regularly, but he also met Maya, not just at Beckbagan but elsewhere too. Maya had once gone to Salt Lake on work and had called Sobhaan: 'I'm in Salt Lake, Shobhon da, where's your office?'

'Tell me where you are exactly.'

'Outside Rita Skin Foundation. Doctor Subrata Malakar's clinic.'

'Stay there. I'll be there in ten minutes.'

Maya's favourite person turned up as promised, taking her in his car to the City Centre shopping complex, which Maya had heard of but never been to. She was as gleeful as a child. All Maya wanted to do was sit somewhere and chat. They ate at Hang Out and talked for a long time. Though Sobhaan had left unfinished work at the office, he called to say he'd be late.

Everything Maya told him about her life made him sad for her. It was much like his sisters' lives. Maya's husband used to beat her; he would pass out on the streets, drunk; he slept with other women. Sobhaan listened to all the details. Maya had left her in-laws' home, but her so-called husband had never bothered to enquire after her. She had informed him she wouldn't go back to that life.

'Send the children back.'

'I fear they will kill them. I might have sent them back if there had been someone to look after them.'

'Why don't you divorce him? Why hold on to these signs of being a married woman?'

Maya had no answer to this.

'You're so strong, you don't bow to injustice, and yet you're defeated by superstition. What is the point of having such a husband? My sisters are even bigger cowards. I keep telling them to use 498A, but they refuse.'

Maya's eyes were brimming with tears now, which made Sobhaan contrite. Maybe he shouldn't have said all this; he still didn't know what to say and what to hold back. He kept apologizing for anything wrong he might have said.

Sobhaan had never known anyone to speak so gently, so much from the heart. He knew Maya gave the impression of being a surly, bad-tempered, discontented woman, but at night she buried her face in her pillow and wept for her brother, her mother, her wretched children. She had wept enough for herself; that was no longer necessary.

Sobhaan had many questions for Maya: how she got to work every day, what exactly she did there, etc. Not even her brother had bothered to seek these details.

'Ranbaxy, near Bondel Gate. I get off the bus at Ballygunge Phari, take an autorickshaw to Kushtia, and then a regular rickshaw to the office. I'm an assistant depot manager. I manage the godown – stocks in, stocks out. Some marketing responsibilities too.'

'That's a lot of work. Must be quite hard.'

Maya smiled. 'Not really. I wish I had something hard to do.'

'Don't you feel like crying sometimes, all these things you have to manage single-handedly? Do you ever fear you might not be able to do it, that you might slip up? It would have been another matter if it was just you, but you have to take care of two children too. Do you feel like crying, then? Here you are, saddled with the burden of having to earn when you should have been enjoying life, travelling, having fun. Don't you feel like chucking it all?'

Maya gazed at Sobhaan, enchanted. No one had ever asked her these questions.

He asked her as they ate, 'What plans for the Durga pujo celebrations?'

'The usual. Buy the children clothes and shoes.'

'And for yourself?'

'For myself?'

'Yes, for yourself?'

Maya smiled. 'Nothing for myself.'

'Why not? You have to do something for yourself too, Maya.'

Sobhaan sounded so tender that Maya's eyes started brimming again. Wiping her eyes, she said, 'I've forgotten how to think about myself, Shobhon da.'

'Leave the children with their grandmother, let's go to the seaside. Mandarmani is a lovely place, the sky merges into the sea there. It's quite close, we can drive down, takes just three or four hours.'

The doors to Maya's heart were blown wide open, a joyous music began to play in her head. 'Let me tell you, Shobhon da, my own brother – I've been in this house for so many months now – he's never asked me, how are you, Maya? Never wanted to know. I operate like a robot: go to work in the morning, it's late in the evening by the time I get back. Not once has he said, let me take you somewhere. And yet … he used to love me so much when we were younger. Come to think of it, I am no longer sure if he ever did.'

Sobhaan wanted to talk to her about Zulekha but did not. He had heard Maya wasn't fond of her at all. How did such a straightforward, beautiful, sensitive woman turn out to be a Muslim-hater? Why couldn't she understand that everyone in the world was the same, that their likes and dislikes, their joys and sorrows, were all similar? There was no reason not to understand. The trouble was that no one explained this lovingly, it wasn't possible to convince anyone through abuse and violence, through anger and obscenities. Not even the law could be used here. That day at Hang Out, Sobhaan told Maya he wasn't a Hindu, his name wasn't Shobhon Chakraborty, he was Sobhaan, Mohammed Sobhaan.

Seventeen

I'm becoming increasingly exasperated with this city. Getting out of the house means getting stuck in a traffic jam. An hour or two passes negotiating Bridge No. 4 or getting to the bypass. What the city is turning into is beyond my understanding. People are coming into money, and money means cars, which in turn need roads, which Calcutta does not have enough of. It isn't possible for so many cars to move about on so little road space, so everything is at a standstill. Calcutta is full of defects, and yet it is my favourite city. I love this city of pollution the best, I adore this hot and humid city the most. That I can use my own language here is very important to me. People here don't get it. I find it impossible to explain why I have abandoned Europe to rot in Calcutta. They conclude that my situation there must have been terrible. Nobody can grasp the possibility that one may leave a place despite having a perfectly good life there. Most people believe no one is badly off in Europe and America, everyone is rich, everyone is happy.

How am I supposed to stay in that foreign land with no family or people of my own, no language or culture that I can own? Apparently, no one knew that I was so greedy for these things. My greed has made me go down in people's estimation.

In my life, my friends are my family, those who love me are my own people. At that moment, Kiranmayee was like my mother, Suranjan like my friend, and Maya like my sister. Passing my life as I do without relatives, I unconsciously turn those I know into family. The people in question probably have no idea.

Suranjan had felt no need to inform me that he was going to Bangladesh. I couldn't understand how anyone could be so heartless. Where he had gone was his country, yes, but it was my country too. He could go there whenever he wanted, but I couldn't. Even after cutting off his relationship with Bangladesh, after giving up his citizenship and becoming a citizen of India, Suranjan could still go back there, but I, still a citizen of that country, had waited a decade to go back but had not been allowed. Didn't Suranjan feel even slightly sorry for me? Couldn't he at least have told me, if only for the sake of information, that he was going home?

I realized that people might respect me from a distance, but they did not love me. And those who hated me did it from a distance as well as from proximity. I had no chance of finding love, not everyone is meant to get everything in their lives. I had got a good deal of things; love was the only exception. If I'd got love, I'd have known Suranjan was back from Bangladesh. Zulekha gave me this information too. She also told me why he was avoiding me. He suspected I was going to write another novel about him, and that was the reason I kept asking about him, that was why I needed him so urgently.

This hurt me terribly. The portion of sky above the neighbouring houses that I could see through the study window was my space of freedom; in my head, I stood facing the expanse of endless sky and let my insignificant existence sail away like a feather in it, nothing trite could touch me any more. Had I ever written anything nasty about Suranjan? What I had written was with the desire that things would become better for him. Not just for him but for everyone, that humans could consider one another humans, that their identity should be that of a human, not of a Hindu or Muslim, a Buddhist or Christian. All that I had written was for humanity, for human rights. All that I had wanted was to make things better for Suranjan, so that no other Suranjan had to live without security or go insane because of threats, so that no other Suranjan was forced to leave his country. If he understood so many things, why couldn't he understand this. Even if I were to write another novel about him, why should he object? Did I not have the right to make him a character in my novel? Of course, he too had the right to try not to be a character, to forget me.

I did not keep in touch with any of them after this. Could I not be hurt too? I had loved them so much, had any of them given back even an iota of it? Kiranmayee knew where I lived, my phone number, she hadn't tried to find out how I was either. Why was it just *my* responsibility to go knocking on their door to enquire about their well-being? I was mortified when I tried to imagine how they were, I was swept away in tears when I compared their condition to mine. I just naturally assumed they were suffering. But actually they weren't; they could adjust to any situation. Was I suffering too? But I could adjust as well. People commiserated with me when we met: 'Poor you, you must be unhappy all alone in a foreign land', but I was by no means as badly off as they thought I was. I had come to terms with living in grief. When you love, you feel for others. How many people have hearts large enough to suffer with others? If none of you feels the need, why should I go out of my way to find out how you are. With this thought, I passed several months, too hurt to reach out. I made a trip to Europe in between, but many times I trembled with fear at the thought that Suranjan might have jumped into a lake. For some reason, I was convinced that suicide was contagious. I couldn't call Maya, who was using Suranjan's old phone, to find out if he was alive, because she couldn't stand me; so, I called Zulekha. She was very pleased that I had called. She said she was working at the same place, living in the same hostel. Life was much more beautiful now. She was preparing to take her MA exam as a private candidate. What about her son?

'He's with his father, he's fine, that's all I want. If he wants to see his mother when he grows up, he will.'

'And those people?'

'Those people?' Zulekha laughed.

'Suranjan's just the same, in a hopeless situation. I'm in touch with him, like a friend.'

'What happened to all the love? Did it just vaporize?'

Zulekha laughed again. 'What happened was for the best. It wouldn't have worked for me either.'

'Do people these days decide whom to fall in love with based on whether it'll work out or not?' I laughed too as I asked this.

'Actually, that's true of everything. Just that in the case of a relationship, it stays below the surface, but it's very much there.'

'Hmm. And Sobhaan? Are you his girlfriend now?'

Zulekha laughed again. 'He still takes Suranjan and me to restaurants. But he doesn't have time for me. He's busy with Maya.'

'What?' I was astonished.

'Maya and Sobhaan are getting married on the 6th of next month,' said Zulekha.

She told me she met Maya sometimes these days, and that Maya had said she would visit me at home to deliver the wedding invitation.

'What are you saying? Is this true?'

'Of course. Why should I lie to you?' Zulekha's voice was icy.

'How can Maya and Sobhaan get married? Maya is...'

'Maya is what?'

'Maya has changed since she came to India, didn't you know?'

Zulekha said she knew nothing about any change in Maya. She was charmed by the little she had seen of Maya. Cheerful, uncomplicated, generous. Zulekha praised her to the skies. Independent, hard-working, confident, spontaneous.

'Really?'

'Yes.'

'You don't think she's actually quite different deep inside?'

'Different? How?'

'A Muslim-hater…'

'Muslim-hater? The question doesn't arise. Why are you saying such things?'

'Actually she was assaulted…'

'Yes, I know. You've written all this, but you shouldn't have, considering she's a woman.'

'Why not? I didn't make it up.'

'Not all truths are for airing in public.'

'Has she said anything about this?'

'No, she hasn't, but I'm saying it. Suppose you were to write that I was raped by someone, would I like it? I'd feel anyone who looks at me is thinking about nothing else. I wouldn't be left with any identity besides that of being a rape victim.'

'So should I not write the truth?'

'Is our society ready to hear the truth?'

'Should we conform to society or rebuild it?'

'You cannot rebuild society all by yourself. How many people do you have with you anyway? And all this business about rebuilding society, I am sorry to say, is just a romantic notion. There's no such thing in reality.'

I sat in stunned silence as Zulekha argued for Maya, who was about to marry a Muslim. Everything seemed uncertain. Had it all changed, or was I a complete fool?

'I cannot believe they're getting married.'

'Oh yes, they are. It'll be a lavish ceremony. You have to come.'

'Are you telling the truth, Zulekha?'

She laughed loudly. 'Why should I lie?'

This was true, why should Zulekha lie?

'All right, come over one of these days and tell me the whole story.'

'I will.'

'I've got you some vodka from abroad.'

'Really?' Zulekha seemed delighted by my invitation. She said she would certainly come the next day.

But it wasn't as though there would be an and-they-lived-happily-ever-after once Sobhaan and Maya got married. At least I didn't believe that was how it would turn out. Let's say they had fallen in love deeply with each other and decided to get married – they might as well. But what about Sobhaan's wife and child? If Naila had been a self-reliant woman, she could have left her husband thanks to his exploits. But Naila was not Zulekha, not everyone could be Zulekha.

I couldn't concentrate on anything else for the rest of the day. My urge to meet Suranjan grew more intense. You never know when your hurt and anger is swept away. No one had ever insulted me the way he had, no one had displayed the kind of arrogance he had by ignoring me for days on end. Here was a person whom I could not abandon, but in whose company I could not survive long either. Suranjan had changed a lot. His evolution through the changing circumstances was of great interest to me, mainly because, to tell the truth, I had written *Lajja* about him. All of the other characters in the novel could be analysed, but because I'd been unable to do it with Suranjan, my interest in him had not diminished even today. I wasn't sure whether he would spend the rest of his life the same way. I hadn't even imagined that his relationship with Zulekha would not last.

It was a matter of great surprise to me that the Muslim-hating Maya was linking her life to a Muslim. It was as astonishing as a communist turning into a fundamentalist, a leap from one pole to the opposite one. Suranjan did not provide a shock of that kind, however. He crumbled in seclusion. He was the kind of young man who could be described as being neither ordinary nor extraordinary. He was detached, and yet not all that detached, in his day-to-day life. I haven't observed too many people like him. The apprehension that raises its head in my mind every now and then – that he will drown himself in a lake – may well be completely unfounded. Would anyone else die of suicide? Perhaps they would. I've always felt suicide is contagious. Dr Sudhamay Dutta had done it. Was it not possible that one of the witnesses of that suicide might wonder, when loneliness was tearing them apart on an utterly depressing afternoon, whether it was worth living any more? I was still shaken by Sudhamay's death, I was not yet sure why he had killed himself. People said many things, but no one except the person who actually did it could know the reason.

I didn't know how to conquer my desire to see Suranjan. Was it possible for a wish to last forever? One day, I didn't know when, but one day I would no longer have the urge to find out how Suranjan was, whether he was alive or not, whether Maya or Kiranmayee were all right. But I did want them to be happy – no matter what their lives were like, I felt a sense of responsibility for them. And though there was no reason for me to think that way, it did feel as if they were characters I had created. So my Suranjan must not die of drowning. My Kiranmayee should live in peace with her children and grandchildren. And my Maya shouldn't have to suffer any longer. Let them all be happy, wherever they are, in Phoolbagan, Babubagan or Beckbagan, let them be safe.

It was painful to imagine I wouldn't see any of them ever again. But since we lived in the same city, surely we would run into one another somewhere – on the roads, in an alleyway, at the cinema. If nothing else, there would at least be an exchange of pleasantries.

Eighteen

L ife was not limited to people one met or did not meet. It was
much bigger than that, no matter what kind of life it might be.
If life moved to just a single beat, it would have halted well before
coming to an end.

Maya had never had a romance with anyone. She used to be
infatuated with a young man or two in Bangladesh – she had even
wanted to marry one of them – but they had considered her friends.
None of them had wanted a romance. It wasn't as though Hindus
and Muslims didn't marry one another in Bangladesh; it was quite
prevalent, but it hadn't happened in her case. All the friends of
Suranjan's whom Maya had liked were Muslims. In particular, she
liked Haider a great deal, but she hadn't allowed anyone to come
to know of this, not even Haider himself. Haider, however, treated
her as he would a younger sister. Sometimes he would say, 'Why are
you growing up so quickly, kid?' She didn't like this. Hindus, Maya
had seen, were a frightened lot, always anxious. She hadn't found
anyone bold and outspoken among them, no one to be enchanted
by. Of course, it was possible that she had not seen their true selves
in specific moments. She liked Kajal Debnath, but he was married.
Maya had noticed that anyone she liked had some sort of problem

as far as she was concerned – they were married, in a relationship, uneducated or gay. She hadn't met anyone right for her. She didn't believe there could be perfect men anywhere in the world.

That Maya had come to like Sobhaan, without bothering whether he was Shobhon or Sobhaan, was for one reason only: she had realized that this particular distinction was meaningless. One man might be a good person and another, not. This did not depend on their religion. Personally, she followed religious rituals, but Sobhaan had not questioned her about these even once. He didn't appear to be religious. And even if he was, Maya would probably not have objected. That was how she felt now, at least. But if he did actually believe in his faith, she didn't know what her reaction would be. It was not a surprise to her that most Muslims believed in their religion, even if it was unexpected for others. She had grown up amongst Muslims in Bangladesh, where practically every one of her closest friends was religious. Being religious meant new clothes twice a year at Eid, celebrations and festivities, visiting friends, and some symbolic fasting. That was as far as it went. She had never seen any of her friends read the namaz. There was no question of wearing a burqa or even of covering their heads. These little religious acts were all it took for them to say they were Muslims. They were friends equally with Hindus and Muslims and Buddhists and Christians, and Maya was just like them. She had never differentiated between her friends on the basis of religion; she hadn't grown up with such a mentality. The environment at home was always of a kind where religion was irrelevant. The only thing that mattered was to be a fine human being, and that was what Maya had tried to be. But what had she got in return? What had Bablu, Ratan, Badal, Kabir, Suman, Iman, Azad and their gang – those Muslim swine – given her? Maya knew all of them; all neighbourhood boys. She wasn't supposed to have survived – they had done as they pleased with her body. A bunch of hyenas who had found a body stuffed with flesh. Maya had withdrawn into herself with shame and loathing afterwards: why did she have to survive, she had asked herself. But then she had wanted, and still wanted, to kill each of them, individually. Rapes and gang rapes were daily affairs everywhere in the world, just like in Bangladesh, just like in India. Men were evil and powerful, women were innocent and powerless, and this was the main reason for rapes. But Maya's being raped by Muslims was not related to power – it was about her being a Hindu. Even a defenceless Rabeya or Rokeya in her place that day would not have been raped. For they had not raped a woman, they had raped a Hindu. They had carved the word 'Hindu' on her body, a word which had never existed in Maya's dictionary. For her, it was no longer a word; it was resentment, obstinacy, humiliation, shame, hatred, death, rape, blood, misery, grief. Maya used to be a human being. Those Muslim men had converted her into a complete Hindu. Since then, she had accepted everything that had anything to do with Hinduism. Maya was not born a Hindu, she was never a Hindu, but she became one the day she was raped. She was now a Hindu with all her being. She had not hesitated to push away all her memories from childhood and adolescence, all her recollections of her country. She had felt that all her good friends, all those Muslims, were rapists, deceivers, Hindu-haters. What else could she have done anyway, there was no other balm she could apply on her wound, a gash that was not to be healed. There was no treatment in the world for a heart with one hundred per cent burns. The ashes that remained of her heart after it was charred had to be cast to the winds. The ash that had flown in the skies of Bangladesh was not from Maya's body but her heart. She had scattered them over the city of her birth, and vowed never to return to that hell. Her life had been split into two, and she had been reborn that day, desperate to return to the land of Hindus, which she now considered her own. It was like discovering that the person she called mother was not her real mother. And now Maya had to push away everything that was fake so she could return to the arms of her real mother. She had tears of happiness in her eyes when she set foot in India for the first time.

Several years had passed since then. Where was that Maya now? It was Sobhaan who stood in front of her; she hadn't met a better man in India. It wasn't the fault of young Hindu men that she hadn't met them, nor was it hers. No one can be blamed for not meeting their perfect match. Maya didn't believe in destiny, though she sometimes felt that it would have released her from many disappointments if she did – she could have just blamed fate and been relieved. She liked Sobhaan. Had she known from the beginning that Shobhon wasn't really Shobhon, she might not have allowed herself to like him so much. But she didn't know if she would have done herself a favour in that case. What was special about her life anyway? Husband and family were supposed to be the greatest treasures in a woman's life, and she had been compelled to give them up voluntarily – she was no longer interested in them. No one of sound mind could live with these particular treasures; Maya had distanced herself before she could be overcome by mental illness. This was probably the final test she would be confronted by. She had left with her children and her belongings, not to visit her mother for a holiday but permanently, but even if she behaved as though she had the right to stay with her mother and brother as long as she liked, she knew very well that society did not grant her this right; it pointedly reminded her where she should rightfully be, where it was suitable for her to live. No, she wouldn't listen, she was going to ask for a divorce, not because of her relationship with Shobhon or Sobhaan, but so that she didn't have to die a horrific death.

If only she could chant a magic spell to make Sobhaan a Hindu, turn him into Shobhon for real, the resentment seething within her might have subsided a little. Maya didn't know what hole she would fall into if her relationship with him went further. She wished he hadn't been as wonderful as he was. She had humiliated him repeatedly to be free of him, like the other day, for instance.

'You're married. You love your wife, don't you?'

Sobhaan was silent.

'You go back to your wife every night, don't you? What if I said, don't go? Can you do it?'

Silence.

'Forget your wife tonight and stay with me. You say you go mad if you don't see me every day. If you marry me, you'll do the same thing; there'll be someone else who will drive you mad if you don't see her every day.'

Sobhaan listened without demurring.

Maya gave him a shove. 'Your wife is younger than me. Why are you giving up a young woman to go after someone older like me? Men look for young women. More physical pleasure.'

'Enough! Stop.'

'Why should I stop?'

'Because this is rubbish.'

'Rubbish but true.'

'No, it's not true.'

'Then tell me what's true? I'm dying to hear the truth.'

'Why?'

'Because no one tells the truth, I don't hear it anywhere.'

'Do you tell the truth?'

'I do.'

'Such as?'

'You really want to hear?'

'Why shouldn't I?'

'I'm Maya.'

'I know you are.'

'Several Muslim men raped me. Several men of your religion. I would have died; they had thrown me into the lake. I don't know how I survived. Ever since then, I hate every single Muslim in the world. This is the truth.'

'Do you hate me too?' Sobhaan asked quietly.

'Since I heard you're a Muslim, I've tried to hate you. It hasn't worked.'

'Why not?'

'I don't know. There's more. More truths. Listen. Listen if you think the truth is unpleasant. In the house where we lived after moving to India, a man used to assault me every night.'

'Really?'

'Yes. There's more. I didn't stop him.'

'Why not?'

'In fear. I'm a coward, a terrible coward. My heart is broken; my body is damaged. A broken, fragile, vulnerable person cannot stop anyone.'

Sobhaan listened, his head bowed.

'Want to hear more?' Maya was screaming now, her voice wavering, her chest heaving, her eyes streaming with tears. She felt an agony in her breast, one that spread across her body, making her tremble. 'There's more. You know how prostitutes stand on the road, all dolled up? Yes, I did it too. Because if this body is meant for men, for wicked and malevolent men to enjoy, if I don't have the strength to resist, if people do sell their bodies, then why shouldn't I? The family was penniless. My parents were helpless. My brother might as well have not been there – he was useless. And so I was forced to sell my body. Why wouldn't I? Who would I keep it pure for? And what's the definition of pure anyway? You will grab a body and defile it, and then you will want an untouched body, how does that work? What kind of demand is this, Mohammed Sobhaan, do you have an answer?'

Sobhaan sat with his head bowed, bewildered, pressing his temples with his fingertips.

'What is it, darling, got a headache? Your headache has just begun. Stay away from me, or the ache will increase so much, your head will fall off one day. If you want to save yourself, stay away from this raped woman, this whore, this Muslim-hating Hindu fanatic, save yourself. One day I might take revenge on the rapists by killing you. You people have something called a Muslim brotherhood, don't you? Then let one brother face punishment for another brother's sins. The Hindus here demolished the Babri Masjid, and *we* had to atone for this sin in Bangladesh by being raped and killed. We had to run away, we had to escape to survive. How can I call it survival, though? We had to escape to die.'

Maya raised Sobhaan's bowed head with both her hands. Kissing him on the lips, she said, 'You claim you've fallen in love with a Hindu girl. You haven't fallen in love; you're having fun because you've never had the opportunity for such fun in your life. All you've seen are Muslim women in burqas, uneducated, and even if they're educated, they're conservative. So you've used Suranjan to enter Hindu society, and now you see this independent woman – matches men stride for stride, takes her own decisions, she's left her husband at the snap of a finger. She seems magnificent, the company of such a woman is completely different from being with uncouth, awkward Muslim women. And then she doesn't neglect you either, knows how to look after you, she can cook and serve, she can talk about science, knows her history and geography too, isn't that right? You're enjoying yourself, but you don't love her. When it comes to love, it'll be someone from your own religion. Same with me. But then I don't even consider anyone who's not a Hindu a human being. No, that's not right. Do you know why? Because I also hate the bastard I married, hate him the same way I hate those Muslim rapists. But I don't say this, because I'm a Hindu, because I always protect Hindus, I want to protect them.'

Sobhaan's eyes were inflamed, he stared at Maya dumbfounded. Maya continued shouting. 'Why do Muslims live in this country? Why do they live here to make our lives hell? They've been given their own country ... not one but two countries, let all Muslims go and live there. What pleasure do they get living as minorities in a Hindu-majority country? They must be getting some pleasure, or why would they stay here? I cannot stand their pleasure. But the real thing, you know what that is? Men are all the same, Hindus or Muslims. They're swine either way. They will inevitably drive women to despair. Your wife is suffering as a Muslim's wife, I suffered as a Hindu's wife. You're not suffering, my brother isn't suffering. He too left his Hindu wife to fuck around with a Muslim woman. He's having fun too. He's now making a name for himself for being secular. You're making a name for yourself too. These Muslim men pretend to be secular and marry Hindu women. His name is Abdur Rahman, but before he introduces himself, he says my wife's name is Moushumi Mitra. They use their wife's religion to rise in people's estimation. And once they've risen, they behave the same way with their wives as all other men. They're men too, after all. You don't need to rise in anyone's opinion; you're already there, thanks to your education and job and business. Why do you need to marry a Hindu woman? I'm not going to marry a Muslim; I don't want to marry a race of terrorists and die. It's better to become a prostitute, better to kill myself.'

After this, Sobhaan jumped to his feet and strode away. Seeing him leave from her window, Kiranmayee came up to Maya. 'Why did Shobhon leave without even having a cup of tea?'

'He left.'

'You could have given him a cup of tea.'

'No need. He doesn't have to be given anything here. This is the last time he's visiting this house. He won't be coming again.'

'Why not?'

'Don't ask so many questions.'

Maya shouted Kiranmayee down. At thirteen past two in the morning, she woke up to the sound of an SMS arriving on the mobile next to her pillow and read it. It was from Sobhaan. I love you I love you I love you. Maya put the phone on her breast and shut her eyes. Tears rolled down her cheeks.

Nineteen

Why this talk of marriage? Zulekha hadn't brought it up, she was quite happy the way she was. Why did Maya have to get married either? Who was it who actually wanted to get married: Sobhaan or Maya?

I was talking to Suranjan as, once again, we drove out of the city. 'Maya,' answered Suranjan.

'What are you saying? Maya can't stand Muslims.'

'Rubbish. She's just like me, all her anger is on the surface.'

'Really?' I stopped the car abruptly and looked Suranjan in the eye. 'Did you say it's all on the surface for you too?'

I simply had to stop again at the junction of the river and the sea. We leant against the car, drinking tea with milk and sugar in small earthen pots from a roadside shop. I wasn't supposed to have milk or sugar, but I didn't make a fuss. The sunlight glinted on the water. The sight of the shimmering silvery surface of the river improved my mood tremendously, I felt very close to Suranjan. He had admitted that his resentment was only on the surface; deep within, he was a humanist.

Still some doubts remained, to dispel which I asked, 'Why did you break up with Zulekha, then?'

'Not for reasons of communalism.'

'What reasons, then?'

'The reason two people cannot get along.'

'That's not the truth.'

Suranjan was silent.

'You had no problem with Zulekha that warranted ending the relationship.'

'I'm not worthy of her.'

'Nonsense. That's not what you really think.'

'Tell me what I really think.'

'That's for you to say. I can only tell what you don't think.'

'If you knew that, you'd also know what I think.'

'There's no such rule.'

'There is. Zulekha or Julia or Jaya, any relationship with any woman can break. And why just women, with men too. My friends from Belgharia are no longer my friends now.'

'You went on a holiday together…'

'Yes, we did. So?'

'What was it that made you break off the relationship?'

'It's personal.'

'Of course it's personal. But I really want to know.'

'Uff.'

We ordered more tea after the 'uff', still leaning against the car and talking as the silver water flowed in front of us. Even if it was a heated conversation, it was with Suranjan, whom at this moment I considered myself close to. He too probably thought of himself as closer to me than before. He had certainly become more informal in his speech.

'Your love for Muslims is excessive.'

I was startled. 'What do you mean?'

'You know perfectly well what I mean.'

'No, I don't.'

'You do, but you want to know what I'm thinking. I'm thinking that your love for Muslims has become excessive after moving to India.'

I looked at him in utter astonishment. 'Love for Muslims? What kind of a term is that? Are you trying to say my love for Hindus was greater before moving to India?'

'Yes, that's what I'm trying to say.'

'Why? Because I wrote *Lajja*?'

'Yes, exactly.'

'Et tu, Suranjan?' After a pause, I sighed and continued. 'You know what I think? You're deliberately saying things to needle me. You get pleasure out of annoying me.'

'That's not true.'

'It's true. You insult me constantly.'

'Insult you?'

'Yes, you do. Are you saying you don't? You keep cutting me off completely. Why? It keeps happening. You want to convey to me that you don't care. You want to tell the person who cares for you, who's waiting for you to call, that you don't give a damn about her, that it makes no difference to you. You're a sadist; you like making people suffer.'

'I like making people suffer?' Suranjan laughed. Loudly. I looked at him laughing in this peculiar way. He said, 'You suffer too?'

'What do you think, am I not human?'

'Not even Zulekha is drawn to me as much as you are.'

'Go on, spell it out. Say I'm so deeply in love with you that if I don't get you, I might kill myself here right now in these waters.'

Suranjan rolled his eyes. 'You're perfectly capable of doing that. Don't laugh.'

'Suppose I wanted to have a romance with you. Would you say no?'

Suranjan shook his head. He would say no.

'Why? Because of your pride? What have you got that you can afford to turn me down?'

'I'll turn you down because I have nothing.'

'What do you consider something or nothing anyway?'

'Only a person who has nothing knows what it means. Someone who's got everything will never know.'

'You're obsessed. The same obsession with money. Cash. Riches. Do you not think of anything else, Suranjan? It's unbelievable how fond you are of wealth.'

'I wasn't talking about money.'

'Then what are you hinting at? What is it that I have that you don't?'

'A heart.'

'You don't have one?'

Suranjan shook his head and sighed. Gazing at the waters stretching to the horizon, he said, 'I cannot love Zulekha the way she loves me. And my relationship with her, I've noticed, seems to be becoming just a physical one. The heart is distancing itself.'

'Your heart or hers?'

'Both of ours, or perhaps only mine.'

'Have you found someone, then, from whom your heart will not be distanced?'

'I'm not looking.'

'Why not?'

'Why do I always have to be part of a couple? Isn't it possible to live without love and sex? I'm fine, I don't feel bored. You don't have either of these in your life right now, do you?'

I shook my head. No.

'Are you dying of grief because of it? You don't lack for emotion, but you're not dying.'

'We need a lot of things to live, but we survive without a lot of things too.'

'Actually, we need nothing but food. Not even clothes and shelter. Without food, we'll die; so, to survive, we have to eat. We won't die in this hot country if we don't wear clothes. A fire is good enough to ward off the cold in winter. And one can live happily beneath the open sky, a dwelling isn't really necessary.'

'You can survive on fruits too; why even bother to cook?'

Suranjan looked at me through narrowed eyes to gauge whether I was mocking him.

'So we can wear bark and go back to prehistoric times, live like apes on trees. Right?'

Finally, Suranjan realized that I wasn't supporting him.

'Go on with what you were saying. I have emotions, and yet I can survive without romance. Since you don't have any, you should be even more at ease with life.'

'Right.'

'Right.'

Both of us got into the car. Instead of going farther along the same road, we turned towards Raichak. We were going to eat at the Radisson Hotel restaurant there – at least tea and snacks, if not an elaborate meal. When we got out of the car at the Radisson, Suranjan said, 'You're addicted to spending. Drop it.'

'I get emotional when I'm with someone I like; money becomes irrelevant then. I just want to spend some time with you in a nice place. So what if it's expensive, we'll have a good time at least.'

'This is rich-people talk. They want to use their money to buy the right setting.'

'No, it's got nothing to do with being rich; it's about love.'

'If it was just love, a tea shop on a pavement would work just as well. You don't have to spend money to explain to me you love me or care for me. If I want to understand it, I will anyway.'

'So what have you understood?'

'That you love me very much.'

Something went cold in my heart at once. Was Suranjan going to repeat the same thing: 'Not even Zulekha is drawn to me as much as you are.'

'That's not right. Listen, Zulekha misses you very much, I want your relationship to be the way it was.'

'I'm asking you to drop your love for Muslims.'

'Stop this nonsense. You can call it my love for human beings. I don't distinguish between Hindus and Muslims. I'm above religion, I'm completely free of it. Fatwas are being issued against me, there is no love lost between Muslims and me. And you've just issued a reverse fatwa. I only think of women, Suranjan. Zulekha is an oppressed woman, just like Maya. Do you think I differentiate between them? I can't even imagine doing it, but you can, so you do. Ninety-nine per cent of people have no idea what it means not to have a religion. Every time I think you don't have one, you prove me wrong.'

'There are enough atheists in this city, go and spend time with them. Why me? Why this pleasure trip? Why the company of someone as rotten and unworthy as me?'

'You're right, Suranjan. I wonder about that as well, sometimes. Why do I do it? Possibly because it does not follow that I will like everything about a person who has broken free of religion. Even those who have no religion can be horribly patriarchal, you know that.'

'As am I. I'm tremendously patriarchal.'

'Yes, you are. But I still like your company.'

Gazing across the Ganges as he sipped his tea, Suranjan said, 'You like my company because you can lecture me to your heart's content. You wouldn't have been able to do it if our philosophies matched perfectly.'

'Maybe *you* would have lectured *me* in that case, and it would have hurt my ego. I don't have the generosity to accept anyone else's guidance.'

'Right.'

'Right.'

Both of us laughed. I looked into Suranjan's dancing eyes, but before my admiration for him could become evident, he said, 'Be careful now, don't fall in love.'

Laughing loudly, I asked, 'What if I do?'

'You can do it on your own. I'm not falling in love with you.'

'Why? Because you're unworthy?'

'That was just modesty.'

'What's the reason, then?'

'You were so pretty when you lived in Bangladesh. Not only a doctor but also a popular writer, and a beautiful woman on top of that. All the men would gape at you; you were the empress of their dreams. But how grotesque you are now! Feminists don't care for their looks, and when women aren't beautiful, when men don't look at them, they turn into even bigger feminists.'

'You're a misogynist. I haven't met anyone who hates women as much as you do. The reason you have decided not to keep in touch with me is that you are communal. Even I have considered not keeping in touch with you because you are communal.'

'Why do you call me communal? Which community do you belong to?'

'You belong to the Hindu community, I do know that.'

'And you?'

'Maybe you think I consider myself part of the Muslim community. Not at all. Mine is the community of secular humanists. There's room there for humanity sans religious affiliation.'

Suranjan nodded. I wasn't sure he understood.

Astonishing me, he said, 'Let's spend the night in this hotel. The rooms seem quite good.'

'I have a car; we can go back quite easily. We aren't marooned in a jungle that we can't leave at night.'

'Can't we have a good time here as friends? We'll drink vodka in the balcony and chat all night.'

'Excellent proposal.'

'Then let's do it.' Suranjan's eyes were glinting.

'No.'

'Why not?'

'Learn to respect women first. Then we can spend as many nights as you want.'

'I do respect women. I respect my mother, don't I?'

'Only you know whether you do, and how much. But you have no respect for me. Nor for Zulekha. Probably not for too many other women either.'

'Why should I respect you? Just because you're older?'

'Age is not the factor. What you don't have is the respect for women that comes from considering them as human beings. You don't have it, nor do other men like you. That is the biggest problem. Do you have the slightest respect for Zulekha? You don't.'

'Why should I have to respect her? She's my girlfriend, I love her.'

'There can be nothing without respect. That's why the love didn't last – because there was no respect. It's the foundation on which you build love; in its absence, everything is temporary, artificial.'

I rushed Suranjan back into the car. As we drove off, I said, 'So, Maya's getting married to Sobhaan. Unbelievable.'

'I don't know how it will turn out. But Maya probably needs this marriage; she's slowly going mad, and needs emotional support. Considering everything she's been through, she'll probably find it difficult to go on without someone at her side. And she's gone and had two children. Now should she take care of them or make something of her own life?'

'Will Sobhaan make this mistake knowingly?'

'Sobhaan is trapped.' Suranjan laughed.

'What's your view as a friend? What advice would you give Sobhaan?'

'I'd tell him not to marry her.'

'Really? But it's your sister.'

'Should I want someone's life to be ruined just because my sister is involved?'

'You're such a misogynist.'

'Sobhaan's life will be over. He will neither be able to live with his family, nor manage to live with Maya. She will always put her children's interest ahead of everything else. She only wants Sobhaan because of his money. I don't think there's anything else to it.'

'No love or anything?'

'There's love. On Sobhaan's side. He's probably fallen in love for the first time in his life. I wanted him to have a relationship with Zulekha.'

'Why? Because both of them are Muslims?'

'Yes.'

'When will you grow up, Suranjan?'

He rolled the window down to gaze at the river in the distance. The wind blew in furiously, making his hair fly. His words flew out on the same wind: 'I'll probably never grow up in this lifetime.'

'You're suffering from an inferiority complex. Don't go and kill yourself suddenly.'

'I might, actually.'

'When relationships hold no value for someone, they may kill others or kill themselves.'

Suranjan smiled sweetly. 'I'll never kill you, my darling. If I can, I'll kill myself.'

'Don't do that.'

'What's your problem? Who are you to stop me?'

'I'm very important,' I said emphatically. 'Get rid of these complexes and frustrations, Suranjan, or you'll be in trouble.'

'Don't worry so much about me, please,' said Suranjan. 'Who am I anyway? No one. Nothing. My life has no value. Even an ordinary man is not so bloody ordinary as I am. You are the extraordinary one, you're the celebrity. You're just wasting your time worrying about me. That's why I don't want to meet you any more.'

Negotiating our way through the crowds, garbage and poverty, I said, 'Is that why you keep disappearing repeatedly?'

'Damn, I don't feel like going home right now.'

'Where do you want to go?'

'Let's go to the Sundarbans.'

'I don't know the way.'

'I'll guide you.'

'I don't feel like going there.'

'You of course are a slave to your desires.'

I couldn't help but smile at this.

'Listen, it's better to be a slave to one's own desire than to someone else's.'

'If this car were mine, if I were the one driving, you'd have been a slave to my desire.'

'What would you have done?'

'I would have taken you to a forest with tigers in the Sundarbans and we'd lie down there.'

'What if a tiger came?'

'I know you'd stay put, I'd just climb a tree.'

Suranjan didn't laugh. I did, and said, 'That's probably exactly what you're like.'

'You're right, that is indeed what I'm like. Would I have dumped Zulekha otherwise? Nor would I have tried to push you away. I wouldn't be able to dump you; my heart wouldn't take it. This is far better: meeting two or three times a year, each of us a slave only to our own desires and nobody else's.'

'That's it, no more contact from tomorrow.'

'Right.'

'Right.'

The subject of Maya's marriage came up again on the way back. Suranjan said he would try to prevent it. He felt Maya was showing signs of mental problems, and that she should see a psychiatrist. She had become desperate for conjugal pleasure, and wanted a predictable, orderly life at any cost. She was trying to fulfil the dream of her adolescence and using it to camouflage her resentment. But could anyone guarantee it wouldn't burst out of her one day?

'Sobhaan didn't rape Maya in Bangladesh, or did he?'

'He didn't.'

'So then?'

'Just like Hindus tend to lump all Muslims together, Muslims too do the same thing with Hindus.'

'Those who generalize—'

'Are fools, right? We are fools.'

'Oh no, you're no fool.'

'Then the conclusion is that intelligent people are communal.'

I was silent. It was difficult to keep track of Suranjan's thoughts; they changed direction without warning. Sometimes I felt I knew him well, and the very next moment I wouldn't know him at all. I had realized that he had no clear idea about my ideology or beliefs. He had said that he hadn't liked the couple of other books of mine besides *Lajja* that he had read. I told him I speak up for Muslims in Gujarat and Palestine, in Afghanistan and Iraq, for Hindus in Bangladesh, for Christians in Pakistan, for Jews in Europe, whenever they're oppressed for their religious affiliations, I stand by them. I believe that religion is no one's identity; your only identity is that you're a human being.

Still, Suranjan remained unmoved, refusing to change his opinion about me. He felt that I oversimplified things, like in a morality lesson: be on the side of the oppressed, defeat the oppressor.

'There are good people and bad people. There are distinctions between fundamentalists too: Hindus and Christians cannot be as hardcore as Muslims.'

'Is that so?'

Suranjan was insistent. 'Yes, it is. Don't imagine this is some silent love for Hindus inside me that's speaking. This is a fact. The monotheistic religions are more violent than the polytheistic ones. So, viewing all religions the same way, lumping all religious fanatics in the same bracket, may be good for your humanist politics, but not for history. You'll score a zero there.'

Suranjan's demeanour was quite different these days – he spoke with more confidence, he talked to me freely, as though we had known each other a long time.

'I have a couple of friends in Diamond Harbour. Want to visit them, Suranjan?'

'Who are they?'

'Shaqueel and Ahmed.'

'Muslims?'

'Shut up.'

'Hindus?'

'Shut up.'

'Don't keep shutting me up. Don't get worked up about Hindus and Muslims; don't work me up either. Let's talk about something else, let's talk about love.'

'Love is all I talk about all the time. It's because of love that I think of humans as humans, nothing else.'

'Huh!'

'Why huh? You know what, Suranjan? I let you get away with so much, I forgive you so easily, that you think you can do whatever you like with me, say anything you want to, that you can confidently claim that what is wrong is actually right.'

'Yes, I can. Don't let me get away with it, then. Stop me. That's all there is to it.'

I stopped the car outside a house in Diamond Harbour.

'Whose house is this?'

'A human being's.'

'It's obvious you aren't visiting a wolf or a vulture.'

The way Suranjan was shrugging annoyed me greatly. He was not as innocent as he looked. Zulekha had probably seen through him too, even if not in exactly my way.

Mahua Chaudhuri came out of the house as soon as I called her. Tall, young, just twenty-two or twenty-three, she was the kind of young woman whom people unanimously labelled beautiful. She was dressed in jeans and an abbreviated white top. Coming to the car, she tried to practically drag me into the house. I got out and stood on the pavement talking to her. It wasn't much of a conversation: I'm not going in, tell me how you are, what are you doing these days, come inside, if any of them find out you're here all of them will come running, come in for five minutes, I haven't seen you in a long time, I was passing this way, I thought I'd stop by and say hello, this is Suranjan my friend, the elocution is going well, I have a programme coming up, Bratati will teach at home, you can go to her house in Golf Green. As people started to gather, I hugged the exuberant young woman who belonged to an elocution band in Diamond Harbour and took my leave.

'Where'd you get hold of this one?'

'This one?'

'The chick.'

'Why are you talking about her like that?'

'I could have done worse, I could have called her a piece of ass, I could have said where did you pick up this fine piece of ass, I could have but I didn't.'

'You're a saviour. The girl's been saved because you didn't say it.'

Suranjan began to chuckle. I felt like slapping him. Turning up the music, I began to drive at breakneck speed. I had no wish to talk to him. Five minutes passed. Lowering the volume of the music, he said, 'Calm down. I'm not a bad person. I was just winding you up...'

'Why were you? What good does it do you? How did it even occur to you to do it?'

'Unless you're angry, you behave like a lover. When you're angry you become a feminist.'

The words 'fuck you' rose to my throat. I had the urge to shove him out of the car on the dark road and drive away. I knew he would laugh if I called him a male chauvinist pig, so I didn't.

'Give me her phone number.'

'Why, do you want a romance with her?'

'Yes.'

'But how? She's a Muslim.'

'A Muslim?'

'Yes.'

'But didn't you say her name is Mahua Chaudhuri?'

'Yes. Muslims have such names too, don't you know? You used to live in Bangladesh. Do you know any young women to be named Khadija or Rahima or Ayesha nowadays?'

Suranjan nodded. This was true, Mahua Chaudhuri could easily be a Muslim's name. Not just Chaudhuri, he had known surnames like Biswas, Majumdar, Tarafdar, Sarkar or Mandal to belong to Muslims too.

'Children are given Bengali names these days instead of Arabic ones. If anyone thinks Hindus have a birthright to Bengali names, they're mistaken.'

'Sometimes you behave exactly like Muslims.'

Hindus and Muslims cropped up so often in my conversations with Suranjan that I feared I would have to stop breathing freely and gasp for air for the rest of my life.

'I behave like a secularist. Like a pure atheist. But you haven't met many people like me, so you can only see Hindus or Muslims. The eye you could have used is blinded by a communal cataract.' I continued speaking: 'The partition of India could have been avoided, but not enough effort was made to prevent it. There was no need for the Partition. All these riots and communalism make me wonder, if they did split the country on religious lines, why didn't they do it properly? All Muslims must go to Pakistan, all Hindus must pack up and come to India. That was what it was about. If it had been made compulsory, there wouldn't have been so much discord today. Instead, there would have been caste riots here, and Muslims would fight one another there – Shia Sunni Ahmadi Qadiani there's no lack of sects among Muslims – each is an enemy of the others. After millions of deaths, the survivors in the two countries might have become friends. But this was foiled.'

Suranjan spoke softly. 'You're not speaking from your heart. You don't believe in borders and boundaries and religions, why should you be interested in the Partition? I read somewhere you believe humans are the children of the earth, let everyone live wherever they want. The earth belongs to everyone.'

Suranjan demanded some weed to smoke. I had no idea where to get it, I told him I couldn't help him. He mentioned a lane in Park Circus where it was available. It was impossible, I had given my security guards the slip and come out, I couldn't wander around Park Circus all alone. Suranjan's next demand was to have dinner at my place. I didn't have much food at home. By the time I dropped him home after a meal at a restaurant on Middleton Street and came back, it was twelve-thirty at night.

Twenty

Finally, Maya confronted Zulekha, demanding that she shouldn't trouble Sobhaan, that she not even think of him as a close friend. If Zulekha released Sobhaan, Maya would not object to her relationship with Suranjan.

Zulekha took Maya to her hostel room. She fried up some muri right there, and made tea for the two of them. After hearing out Maya's complaints and requests, Zulekha told her, 'Maya, listen. Both you and I have been through a great deal in our lives. I think we have more important things to do than fight over men. I'm not thinking of either Suranjan or Sobhaan at this point. I'm busy finding some ground beneath my feet, I'm not going to allow this to be obstructed for the sake of a man. And as for love and romance, with all those poems and songs and plays about them, they're nothing but short-lived. I had never thought my relationship with Suranjan would break; the strangest thing is that it ended for no obvious reason, it snapped just as our love for each other was at its peak. That's why the best players like to retire when they're still at the top of their game.'

'You left Suranjan so that you could get Sobhaan. I've seen plenty of opportunistic women like you, lousy women all of them. You think you'll find another person as honest as my brother in this day and age? As soon as Sobhaan appeared on the scene, you tried to grab him. How greedy.'

'I'm not greedy, you are. You could never stand the fact that Suranjan and I were in a relationship. Why have you changed your view now? Because you need Sobhaan. You no longer care what your brother is up to with someone from a different religion.'

'Don't you dare say bad things about my brother.'

Zulekha flew into a rage. 'I clung to that rapist brother of yours because I felt that I was damaged goods, I had no value for society, I was dead, I was a worm in a drain, I was a heap of garbage. Why else should I want to link my life with your brother's? Who is he? What is he? Does being raped mean the end of one's life? I hooked up with Suranjan out of hatred for myself. I had no such thing as self-esteem. But I don't hate myself any more. Your brother's a chameleon: a rapist today, a feminist tomorrow. Ask him to see a psychiatrist.'

Maya sat in stunned silence. She didn't want to know why Zulekha was referring to Suranjan as a rapist. From what she had heard from Kiranmayee about their relationship, there was no coercion. When people get furious, their diatribes become a mixture of truth and lies, she reflected. Surely Zulekha would no longer utter the word 'rapist' once she had cooled down.

Maya surmised that Zulekha was trying to move away from her past. Zulekha told Maya clearly that Sobhaan was hers to do anything with, she herself couldn't care less.

Zulekha was not in touch with Suranjan, for all intents and purposes. Suranjan no longer used his mobile phone, or they might have spoken on the phone sometimes. The truth was that there was nothing left in the relationship to rebuild.

Maya usually felt bad when a relationship ended, whether there was a good reason or not. The fact that she had left her husband also made her unhappy at times.

Zulekha was busy with her work and studies. She would look for a better job after her MA examinations. Her friendship with Mayur and other women like her had deepened. She had set up an organization named Bold Girls in the hostel; leaflets were being distributed asking the other inmates to join. The Bold Girls met every night, their membership growing by the day. They encouraged their members to pool their strength so that each of them could lend support if one was in trouble, so that each of them could stand up in protest if one was humiliated. Female unity – without this, nothing mattered. Once this was in place, the women who were forced to be subservient, who had no choice but to depend on others, who had lost their identity, would no longer feel isolated, they would know the others were with them, they had many shoulders to lean on, many hands to lift them up from the dust. If the boss made a proposition in the workplace, Bold Girls would send a warning letter to the company, and even file a case if need be – three of the members were lawyers. If any of the women couldn't afford to pay her examination fees, contributions were raised. There were four doctors too, who provided free treatment if anyone fell ill. The organization was started by Zulekha and Mrittika Guha, a lawyer at the Alipore court. After this, every new member had come up with new proposals. There were women of Mayur's age as well as of Zulekha's. The meetings that began at eight in the evening were originally held in Mrittika's room or Zulekha's, but now, with increased numbers, they had moved to the dining room.

Maya listened to Zulekha's account of the Bold Girls with close attention. Zulekha was no longer interested in Suranjan or Sobhaan, she didn't talk about them either.

'What are your plans in life?' Maya asked.

Zulekha said she wanted to make Bold Girls an even bigger organization, to take it beyond the hostel. They had already spoken to another organization named Maitree, two of whose members would be attending the next meeting. The other organizations in the city were not every active because their members were busy with their husbands and children and families, but Bold Girls didn't have that problem, so they were taking the initiative to ensure no one remained passive. They would hit the streets with their issues, and Maitree would join them, that was the idea.

'What's the use of all this?'

'I'm a woman, I know what a woman's life is like. I had a wonderful boyfriend, I had a friend in him too. But as soon as I needed a place to stay, my boyfriend went underground.' Zulekha burst into laughter. 'If your boyfriend runs away even when you're deeply in love, out of fear that he'll have to take responsibility, whom will you trust? I've seen my husband too. I don't consider these people human beings at all. To tell the truth, I don't trust any man on the planet. If a man wants to be my friend, no problem, I'll have a good time with him, we'll go out and party, but that's it, nothing more. I was *this* close to making the mistake of trying to cement a relationship. Never again.'

'And what about Sobhaan?' Maya waited anxiously for her answer.

Zulekha went to make some fresh tea.

'The fact is I didn't spend a great deal of time with Sobhaan. I can't say much about him. Suranjan had wanted a relationship to develop between us – so strange, can something like this happen so easily? Can you force anyone to enter into a relationship? How stupid do you have to be to demand such a thing! In fact, you have to be a fiend to say this to your girlfriend. Apparently, Sobhaan and I would make a fine couple, while he would be Devdas. For heaven's sake, can two people have an affair just because they're both Muslims? My husband was a Muslim too, so what? Men are men, Maya, whether they're Hindus or Muslims or Christians or Jews or Buddhists, they are men. And men live in a patriarchal society with all its benefits. Is there room for women in this society? You have no idea what I've had to go through just to be where I am today.'

Maya had visited Zulekha with great trepidation. She had expected Zulekha to curse her and throw her out. But here she was, welcoming her warmly with a cup of tea. Maya found it unbelievable that men played no part in all the stories Zulekha was telling her – they were all about women, what the women at the hostel were like, how many members Bold Girls had, what each of them did.

'Do you have an opinion on the fact that I want to marry Sobhaan? Any objections?'

Zulekha smiled. 'Why should I have any objections? Who am I to Sobhaan? You can check with his wife. But then what if she has objections? It won't come in the way of your marrying him. Muslims can have up to four wives.' Laughing loudly, Zulekha said, 'Disgusting!'

Then she continued, 'A fourteen-hundred-year-old practice still continues, and people shout from the rooftops what a noble religion Islam is. Muslims are shouting, of course, but so are Hindus, in case they're not considered secular. I'm sick of it all.'

'You talk a lot like Taslima Nasreen.'

'How do you mean?'

'Patriarchy, secular—'

'Yes, I'm a great fan of hers. I talk to her quite regularly,' Zulekha said.

'I believe she spends a lot of time with my brother.'

'Why not? She's probably writing a novel. Haven't you met her?'

'No, but I'm thinking of inviting her to the wedding.'

'I'm also thinking of getting her to inaugurate the first Bold Girls event.'

'That's nice.'

'But it won't be easy. Some of the Muslim women here can't stand her.'

'What, you mean even a *Muslim* cannot stand another one sometimes?'

Zulekha stared at Maya in surprise. 'Which world do you live in anyway?'

Maya was taken aback.

Zulekha said, 'Muslims are issuing fatwas. She's a writer; she couldn't live in her own country. Even Indian Muslims have put a bounty of five lakhs on her head.'

Maya shrugged. 'I don't understand Muslims.'

'It's not that you don't understand, you don't try to understand. Or you pretend not to.'

Maya's face turned cloudy. Zulekha continued, 'There are separate laws for Hindus and Muslims. Muslims still follow the religious code, which does not give equal rights to women. Should this be allowed in a civilized country? Shouldn't the same law be followed by everyone?'

'Why are you opposing the laws of Muslims? You're a Muslim.'

'So what? You don't have to be a Hindu or a Muslim to protest against injustice; you just have to have common sense.'

'I've heard it's the Muslims who don't want the law to be changed.'

'Make that "the fundamentalists don't want the law changed". The Hindus here cannot distinguish between ordinary Muslims and Muslim fundamentalists; they refer to all of them as Muslims. Fundamentalist Hindus are labelled communal, but fundamentalist Muslims are considered to represent all Muslims. This is how people push Muslims deeper into the darkness and turn more of them into fundamentalists.'

Maya gazed at Zulekha's fury in wonder – eyes lined with kohl, pencil-thin eyebrows, she looked beautiful.

Suddenly, Zulekha jumped to her feet, tucking the end of her sari around her waist. 'Why do you still wear those markers of marriage? Aren't you divorced?'

'Not yet. It'll be a while before I get the papers.'

'You've decided to get married again, but here you are with the signs of your previous marriage…'

'I'm thinking of keeping these even after marrying Sobhaan.'

Zulekha collapsed on a chair. 'Why on earth?'

'I've got used to them.'

Zulekha sighed. 'When Suranjan spoke about you, I pictured a spirited woman, courageous and rational. But I haven't seen a woman as fearful and weak as you.'

Maya's eyes brimmed over with tears.

Zulekha continued, 'You can't leave one man before you get another, can you? Women like you cannot do without men. It's weak women who need men, just like weak people who need religion. Same thing.'

Wiping her tears, Maya said, 'I'm scared to remove these. Sobhaan says he has no objection.'

Zulekha said, without any context, 'I earn less than you, Maya. I know how much you earn, Suranjan told me. I earn much less.'

Tightening her jaws, Maya retorted, 'You don't have children.'

Zulekha spoke through clenched teeth. 'I do. I've dutifully extended the family line. Who says I don't have a child? I do.'

'Oh, so you're having a great time here without your child, doing your Bold Girls? Are you even a mother? How can you live away from your child?'

'This is much more important than tending to a child.'

'What is more important? Your Bold Girls?'

'That, of course. But what is more important to me is to live without being a burden on a man, without depending on one.'

'I certainly couldn't leave my children behind.'

'Which is why you need a surrogate father. And Sobhaan is a good one. That's why you're trying to snare him. What have you done together so far, have you slept with him yet?'

'Chhih!'

'Why? How will you know whether he can have sex unless you sleep with him, whether he has erectile dysfunction or not? You'll be in trouble afterwards. Then you'll have to leave him too, and look for someone without that problem. You can't live alone; you'll always need someone.'

'How do you manage to stay alone? I'm sure you have someone too, someone you'll marry.'

'Marry? Not in this lifetime. I don't believe in rebirth, or else I'd have said, not in the next lifetime either.'

Maya said she would leave now, her children were waiting for her. Zulekha walked her to the gate. Maya asked eagerly, 'Is Sobhaan a good man?'

'Yes, he is; quite nice as a friend.'

'What'll he be like as a husband?'

Laughing, Zulekha said, 'I can't tell you that, he was never my husband. But you could ask his wife.'

Maya looked grim.

Back home, she found Suranjan tutoring his students. Still she told him that she had met Zulekha.

'Really?' Suranjan shot to his feet in excitement and took her into the next room. 'Tell me. Did she talk about me?'

'Not at all.'

'How is she?'

'She's a bitch. A total bitch.'

'Is that what you thought?' Suranjan seemed deflated.

Suppressing her anger, Maya said, 'She doesn't want me to marry Sobhaan; she wants to marry him herself.'

'She said that?'

'She's got objections to my marriage.'

Maya started sobbing. Drawing her head down to his chest, Suranjan said, 'Don't cry. Who's she, why do you have to cry because of her objection? If you want to marry Sobhaan, you will. How does it matter if anyone says anything?'

'How could you be seeing that bitch, Dada? She must have made you suffer a lot.'

'I'd told you not to meet her, you insisted. Never mind now, Sobhaan's coming at eight, he's planning to take you to the movies, go and have a good time.'

Wiping her eyes, Maya went into the bathroom. Kiranmayee had taken the children to the park; she'd bring them back after their playtime. Whether she wanted it or not, her life revolved around her grandchildren, and the more this took root, the easier it became for Maya to step into the world outside. Her life earlier was limited to her office and her home, but there was so much more in it now. Maya was thinking of Zulekha, that smart bitch. Her head reeling from humiliation, she let the shower soothe the sting all over her body and wash away her tears. Why so many tears? But let them flow, Maya thought – like many other decisions in her life, this too was a mistake, meeting Zulekha. Why did she have to sit there listening to Zulekha's nasty, cruel words? Had she not faced ignominy already? Would she have to face more? Sobhaan Sobhaan Sobhaan. Maya couldn't remove thoughts of him from her head. How close he held her to himself; when he touched her hand with his warm one, there were so many caresses in that touch, so much heart. Maya, a raped woman, Maya, who had almost died, held her head high today on the strength of her own confidence; she had found some ground beneath her feet on her own effort, no one had helped her. And yet she had had to hear today that she was weak, that she was a coward, that she was dependent on men. How was she to explain to Zulekha that this one observation at any rate was not correct? Zulekha knew nothing about Maya; she had no idea about her dark past; she was clueless about Maya's demolished, lacerated life. Even after this, she had found a job, kept it while bringing up her children and giving them a good education, left her husband and found space for not one person but three in the household of her good-for-nothing brother and her son-obsessed mother. Would Zulekha have been able to do all this? Maya knew she wouldn't have. Zulekha had had it easy. She had an affair without her husband's knowledge, when he found out he threw her out, she lived with a relative first and then found a trouble-free job, and was now living in the safety of a hostel, having a lovely time with her girlfriends. Her life was a thousand times easier than Maya's.

Let her come and see what Maya's life was like, the turmoil she had to face. Maya loved Sobhaan, but she hadn't been able to convey this to Zulekha, to whom the word was unknown now. She had forgotten that people could love one another, that love could make them dream of being together. She had learnt that men were the oppressors and women were the oppressed. Maya wasn't denying this, but not all men were like that, some of them could still be lovers, some men even killed themselves out of their love for women. Men and women were not separate races, both belonged to the human race, among whom were the good and the bad. Sobhaan was one of the good ones. When he kissed Maya, when he kissed her all over her body, they were kisses Maya had never got in her entire life. She didn't know lovemaking could be like this. Sobhaan had told her he had no physical or emotional relationship with any other woman. Sobhaan had told her he loved her, that this was the first time he had fallen in love with a woman, the woman was Maya. Sobhaan had told her he didn't care for caste or creed, he only cared for the person, and he had not met a woman as magical as Maya. He didn't care what the world would think of him, whether society would ostracize him, he wanted Maya to be with him all their lives, as a friend, as his constant companion, as the mother of his children, as his lover, as his wife. No one had loved Maya this way before. Her lifelong thirst for love had been quenched by Sobhaan. He had a wife, but then Maya had, or used to have, a husband too. Those relationships were meaningless now; they had both been forced to marry the wrong person. Once you've found the right person and understood your mistake, the sooner you can get out of it, the better. Maya realized that living would be unbearable without Sobhaan; he was the one who had brought dreams and comfort and happiness into her bleak life. She might survive if he left her, but there would be no joy in that existence; she would live for the sake of being alive; gaze into a void with empty eyes, watching the sunset, waiting for death. Besides, at this age, as the mother of two children, which man's selfless, untainted, heartfelt love could she expect? Sobhaan was a boon from the gods for her. No, Maya didn't consider him a Muslim, she considered him a man among men, just the kind of lover she had prayed for.

When she came out of the bathroom, she found Sobhaan sitting in Suranjan's room, while Suranjan was getting dressed to go out. Where was he going? Apparently, he had something to attend to. Maya had noticed that, of late, Suranjan went out when Sobhaan came over. Clearly, he wanted to leave the room free for them, so that she could lock the door and make love to Sobhaan in peace. She spent hours with Sobhaan in the room, with the door shut or even open. In fact, she had locked the door only four times. On two of those occasions, Kiranmayee had said after Maya came out: 'Seems to be a good boy. Get married quickly if you plan to marry him; we'll be in trouble if people get to know, they won't spare us.' The other two times she had said nothing, only keeping the children busy elsewhere, so that they didn't hammer on Suranjan's door in search of their mother.

Maya's hair was wound in a towel; she was dressed in a nightie, water streaming down the strands of her black hair near her chin, her eyebrows glistening. Sobhaan gazed at her, mesmerized. Drawing her closer, he kissed her lips, eyelids, eyebrows, chin.

Maya locked the door leading to Kiranmayee's room. Sobhaan jumped back.

'Why did you do that?'

'I've done it before too.'

'What will your mother think?'

'She knows we're getting married soon.'

'Still.'

'Still what, darling? Don't you want to?'

'Of course I do.'

'Then why all this hush-hush?'

Maya drew Sobhaan down to the bed. He was dressed in a white t-shirt and blue jeans; his shampooed hair was flying in the breeze from the fan. Oh, the pleasure of flinging oneself on someone so beautiful! Maya lay on him, kissing him. Sobhaan's eyes closed with passion, he held her tight and said, 'I can't live without you, Maya.'

Squeezing the tip of his nose, she said, 'Of course you can.'

Sobhaan touched her nose too, saying, 'Only you can make me live, only you can make me die, it's all in your hands.'

Maya felt an indescribable pleasure. Zulekha would be so jealous if she could see them. Was there anyone who didn't want love? Could Zulekha deny that she wanted it too? Maya didn't think so. She had seen the flames of envy in Zulekha's eyes earlier today. No one embraced an ascetic life by choice, only if there was no option. If Zulekha had someone like Sobhaan, she would have been madly in love too.

Resting her head on Sobhaan's chest and gazing at the white walls, Maya found her eyes brimming with tears again. She was recalling all the things Zulekha had said.

'What's the matter, baby, why are you quiet?' Sobhaan asked Maya, caressing her arm.

'I met Zulekha today.'

'Where?'

'I went to her hostel.'

'What did she say?'

'She doesn't want us to get married.'

'Why not?'

'I think she's jealous.'

'Jealous?'

'Her own relationship has ended. Those who aren't happy themselves can't stand it when others are happy, you know.'

'But isn't she busy with her work and studies? She's very ambitious.'

'She's formed a women's organization; she's become quite the feminist. Taslima's influence.'

'Hmm.'

'Tell me something, did you have anything with her?'

'Naah. It was just an ordinary friendship. You know how it is, you meet someone three times and they're a friend. You think it's easy to be a real friend?'

'Do you have any real friends?'

'I do. Suranjan.'

'I don't understand how he can be anyone's friend. No integrity.'

'He may be callous, he may be careless, but he's got integrity.'

Neither of them realized when the time for the film and for dinner had passed. They jerked upright in bed when Suranjan rang the doorbell.

Twenty-one

Calcutta has a smell of its own. I get it whenever I land at the airport upon my return from Europe. A hot and humid wind that sticks to the body. My love for the Bangla language and culture had made me wind up my sojourn in Europe and move to Calcutta, but the initial enthusiasm among my friends had waned considerably by the time I started living here. Vowing not to live in a hotel any more, I had initially rented a furnished flat on Purna Das Road. It was a nightmare. Burglaries, the loss of the gold necklace inherited from my mother, a cut-throat landlord. I spent one lakh rupees in the very first month. But still, the one bright spot amidst all this was the company of friends – the drawing room would overflow with them every evening. The next time I came to Calcutta, I rented an empty flat rather than a furnished one, indefinitely. When I landed at the airport, I had no idea where I was going to stay; my suitcases were in the trunk of the taxi. Looking up To-Let ads, I finalized the terms with the first landlord I called, without even looking at the house or negotiating the rent. That's the flat I'm still living in. There was a mountain of dust inside it on the day I entered. What I liked most was the dimensions of the rooms, the unbarred windows, with not a sign of iron even in the balcony. It was open on all sides, so open that it seemed the sky had entered and taken up a place in my armchair. In the room I had identified instantly as my study, the window offered a view of the sky, rows of coconut and betel nut trees, and an old building with the kind of slatted doors that our house had in my childhood. I was always drawn to old architecture and the memories it held. So the rent didn't matter. I stayed on. At first I had thought I couldn't afford it, that I'd move to a cheaper place in a month or two, but a year passed and then two. I was in Bengal, I could speak and hear Bangla, every morning I sat down by the window with my tea and a pile of Bangla newspapers. The breeze played with me, the birds sang for me, my heart was at peace. Where would I go if I forsook Bengal? Why would I go?

I came out of my love for Bengal, for Bengalis, but where are all the people who used to throng my flat? I haven't seen any of them in the past year. They've vanished, leaving me so very lonely. I feel bereft now. I reflect on the number of not-friends whom I call friends all the time. I say I have lots of friends, I say I am not alone, I never was. I stay two thousand miles away from loneliness out of fear, or is it shame. What if someone were to think it's my fault that I don't have friends, that it's a flaw in my personality? Wherever in the world I go, I have many, many friends who make my life worth living, I console myself. I meet someone, and without knowing whether I'll meet them ever again or even tomorrow, I add them to my list of friends to make it longer. I even consider many of my enemies my friends, to derive what joy I can, to stir a wave in the dead water, how else am I to live in exile? Friends are the only people I can call my own, whom I can think of as my homeland. Friends are always at hand, in good times and in bad, offering love and affection, putting an anxious palm on my brow when I've got a fever; they are my father and my mother, they are my sister, they are family. And so I think of so many not-friends as friends, for I have no choice, I cannot live otherwise. I am lonely – frighteningly lonely, actually. I have no one I can call a friend, but this is an ugly truth I reject with all my heart. I lie, I say I am surrounded by countless friends, I am very happy. This is the one lie I have to repeat endlessly, I am ashamed to fool myself, but still I have to do it.

I am forced to meet people whose views I do not agree with. But what's the alternative, for who can survive without people? My life is such that I have to be imprisoned in my house. When I go out, the police go with me. Often I hoodwink them and disappear. I had taken Suranjan out this way twice, in two different directions. I wondered later why I did it, and the answer I arrived at was that because I wrote a novel about Suranjan, because he was the protagonist of my novel *Lajja*, I felt a responsibility towards him or a right over him. Afterwards, when I reflected calmly, without being clouded by emotion, Suranjan appeared to be just like everyone else: a combination of progressiveness and conservatism, detachment and selfishness, generosity and meanness. I had taken him far away from Calcutta not because of his desire but thanks to mine. At least I had the consolation of doing whatever I did, right or wrong, of my own volition.

Had Suranjan not come to meet me, I would never have felt the urge to know how he was after moving to Calcutta, how his parents and sisters were faring after leaving their homeland. I pursue some of my characters till the thick smoke hanging over them lifts. What I had heard about Maya or seen of Kiranmayee had not appeared mysterious in any way. Although they did not act as though they were my own people, there was another reason for me to think of them that way – they were from my country, the only people in this city whom I used to know when I lived in Bangladesh. It was a spontaneous feeling and not some intricate planning that made me consider them family. There were plenty of people all over the city who were originally from East Bengal, but none of them was like

Suranjan and his family. Suranjan had left Bangladesh a year before I did. It would be truer to say I was forced to leave. But I'm not capable of spending too much time in the company of complicated people; they make me feel quite stupid. To tell the truth, every time I felt I had finally understood Suranjan, it turned out soon afterwards that I had not.

Kiranmayee's affection for me also seemed to have ebbed after Maya's advent. She was busier at home now; besides, Maya couldn't stand me. It wasn't possible for Kiranmayee to stay in touch. Keeping my hurt feelings in check, I tried to look at them from their own perspective. This usually makes my resentment vanish, after all, everyone follows a certain logic of their own. I have even tried to put myself in the shoes of fundamentalists to try to understand their mentality, why they wanted to attack me. They must have their own rationale too.

Kiranmayee no longer sent food to my house, or called me, or asked me over, or came over herself without warning and said she had been missing me. Perhaps Maya had filled the space in Kiranmayee's heart in which she had accommodated me. I should have been angry with Maya, but I couldn't bring myself to be upset with her. Putting myself in her place, I realized that if I'd been her, I'd have been angry with me too, I'd never have forgiven me. And then when I argued on my own behalf, I concluded that I'd done nothing wrong either. If Maya had put herself in my shoes, I don't think she would have blamed me. This is what is missing in our lives, this effort to see the situation through the other person's eyes. We see the world only through our own eyes, our own and nobody else's. Sometimes, when I gaze at the sea or a dense forest, I see them through my mother's eyes. She longed to go to the seaside and to visit the mountains and forests, but she wasn't fortunate enough to travel. Whenever I visit one of the spots she dreamt of, I see it with my own eyes and then through hers. In the first case,

I am entranced, but also detached, but in the second, my eyes fill with tears.

Calcutta is gradually turning into a desert for me. There is no opportunity to meet the poets and writers I knew, whom I thought I would become friends with. None of them keeps in touch with me. Many of them tried to have my book *Dwikhondito* banned. Many well-known writers and intellectuals wrote long pieces denouncing me, mocking me, and proposing a ban on my book. I read them. The more I read, the less could I believe my eyes. Half of West Bengal's intellectuals were ranged against me after *Lajja* was published, and they were joined by the other half after *Dwikhondito*. Writers joining hands to demand a government ban on another writer's book – I do not know of a similar incident anywhere in the world.

Loneliness has been sinking its teeth into me like a fierce predator for a long time now. It has vowed not to spare me. I wander around the city aimlessly, going to films and plays and concerts and dance recitals in a frenzy. I splurge on eating out. I do not know what or whom I want; my only thought, as Rabindranath put it, is: not here, not there, somewhere else. But is there another city besides Calcutta where I can find peace? I don't think so. A city or a country does not have a distinctive character of its own; it is its people who lend it character. How long can I continue to love a city where I don't have a single friend? I am bound to gasp for breath sooner or later.

Suranjan had withdrawn into his cave as usual. Now I found it exhausting to drag him out of it: let him live in it the way he liked. Let him go and sit on the edge of the lake, let him nurture the wish to jump in, let him do what he wanted with his life. I grew desperate to focus on my own reading and writing. I wasn't getting many invitations from foreign countries these days, and even when I was invited to attend human rights or women's rights conferences, the thought of spending such long hours inside a plane was terrifying. I hate flying in any case. I have spent a part of my life almost entirely in planes, my legs swelling from long hours in low-pressure environments. Sometimes I threw the invitations away. I never charged for these. All I did was give my time and effort. It was time to stop doing things for others and take care of my own needs. I would stay in this country, reading and writing, immerse myself in these activities. Loneliness wouldn't be able to sink its teeth into me if I kept myself busy. If anything could save me, it was activity. I couldn't go on searching for people like a madwoman. If I wasn't fated to live amidst people, so be it. If genuine human beings had disappeared among the masses, it was not in my power to find them.

It had been six months since I had last met Suranjan, but not once had he tried to get in touch. I had no idea how his family was, or even whether they were alive or dead. For now, I was blocking my urge to find out. And then I met someone, not a member of Suranjan's family but someone who could have been one.

Climbing down the stairs after watching a film at Forum on Elgin Road, I discovered Zulekha next to me. Done with work for the day, she was going home. Zulekha was thrilled to see me, and insisted on taking me to her hostel. Her request was sincere, and in such cases I can never say no, I drop all important work to rush where the heart takes me. Nothing is more important to me in this world than the heart. I had never liked Zulekha very much, and if someone's personality doesn't appeal to me, I find it difficult to get along with them, I just detach myself gently.

Zulekha used to call me regularly at one time and keep me informed about Suranjan and his family, but she had not been in touch for some time. I ushered her into my car to go to the hostel. 'You haven't called in a long time,' I told her. She replied, 'I gave up because the responsibility of keeping in touch seems to be mine alone. How many times did you call me? I used to call you almost every day, but you never called even once. No relationship can be one-sided. I love you a great deal, I've read all your books in the meantime, and my love has deepened.'

I had no real answer. 'I don't call anyone, really,' I offered.

'That can't be right,' said Zulekha. 'I'm sure you call some people. You call those whom you consider your friends. If Suranjan had a phone, I don't think you'd wait for him to call, you'd call him on your own.'

I was silent. I felt Zulekha was both right and wrong.

'So how are they?'

'How are they how are they how are they! How's Suranjan how's mashima what's Maya up to! That's it. Bubu, you've never wanted to know how I am. Have you ever appreciated the enormous struggle I'm putting into my life? Have you ever felt the need to inspire me? But then I got what I needed from your books, if not from you.'

Zulekha kept talking, and I trained my discomfited gaze out the window. Glittering shopping centres had sprung up, interleaved with shabby shopfronts. I haven't seen wealth and poverty living in each other's arms this way in any other country. Skyscrapers cheek by jowl with slums. The funniest thing is that even those who live in those slums say they're fine and ask not to be evicted. Bringing her lips close to my ears, Zulekha whispered, 'What you have said about Islam is absolutely right.'

I was startled. Why did she have to whisper this to me? She could have said it the same way she had said everything else. She was probably being careful; she was afraid something might happen, something bad.

'Islam is not the subject of my writings,' I told Zulekha. 'It crops up in the context of what I write about women's rights or human rights. Just like other religions and regressive practices make an appearance. I have kept my distance from blind faith and religious beliefs practically since my birth. These things have never attracted me. The question that has haunted me ever since I learnt to think was why women don't have freedom. Why are women not treated as human beings?'

Using English words when I speak, as I had just done, makes me angry with myself: I feel uneducated. Was this the influence of Calcutta? Educated people here cannot speak in Bangla without peppering it with English, and I've picked up the habit. My ardent wish is to speak either in pure English or in pure Bangla, and not mix them up. I've spent nearly twelve years in European countries, none of whose language is English. There's no denying that English and French are the two main international languages today, the languages of these two colonizers are used for global communication. I've noticed that even people who know English will not use a single word of the language when speaking in their mother tongue, be it Italian or German, Spanish or Danish. They stick to one language; they don't use a cocktail. Bengalis may not be too familiar with cocktails, but they use their language the same way. This is probably the outcome of the evolution of the language. My musings on languages were interrupted by Zulekha, who said, 'Suranjan is quite well. He's making a documentary for an NGO.'

'Has he ever made films?'

'A short one, but he's got this assignment nevertheless. Apparently, a friend of his is working with him. He's been in Andaman for a month, shooting the indigenous people there.'

I was very pleased to hear that Suranjan was doing something exciting somewhere other than at home. There's nothing more boring than teaching students. What better news could there be than that Suranjan had shaken off his hopelessness and was actually involved in something! Of course, he would probably say, 'Who says teaching students is boring? It's film-making that's boring.'

Zulekha talked non-stop about Suranjan, with the objective of giving me information. For some reason, I don't know what, she thinks I have the right to know every last thing about

Suranjan, and that no one should deny me this right, not even Suranjan himself.

She was dressed in a sky-blue georgette sari, with no make-up on, and no jewellery either. I remembered how gaudily she used to do up her face earlier. Women become so susceptible to dolling themselves up when they're in love that I feel real pity for them. They're prisoners to dressing up at that time.

I'd seen it in my own life. As soon as I fell in love, I began to spend hours in front of the mirror, looking at myself from every angle, not through my own eyes, but through those of my lover's. I was no longer me, I was my lover, my detractor, my sharpest critic. I didn't know how to love myself then – in fact I hated myself, every part of my body, each one of my gestures. And I wasted my time trying to improve myself, to be beautiful, to appear attractive to my lover. How busy women get with their bodies to ensure that their boyfriends love them, that they do not leave them! And men savour this vulnerability.

Wasn't Suranjan tutoring students any more?

'He doesn't have the time. Mister is tremendously busy. Apparently, he will also make documentaries for government offices. He's earning quite well.'

'Already?'

'Yes, it seems he has made a name for himself with a documentary on the Santhals. I've seen it. He shot it at the Santhal habitation in Santiniketan. The dance he shot in the acacia woods on a full-moon night was magnificent.'

'Really?' I was both astonished and electrified.

'Yes.'

'The acacia woods on a full-moon night?'

'Yes.'

The night swam up in front of my eyes. It seemed to have been just the other day, though I calculated I would probably find that a year had passed. But I hate calculations, especially of time.

'How did you get to watch this film? Where is it running, in Nandan or somewhere else?'

'I don't think so. Maya let me see it.'

'Maya? Which Maya is that?'

'Suranjan's sister.'

I was so startled that I almost stopped the car. 'Maya and you...?'

'Yes, bubu, there's a lot between Maya and me.' Zulekha laughed.

'What does she do now? She can't stand Muslims, but then she's married Sobhaan, a Muslim. I was really surprised to hear that. She must have changed a lot.'

Zulekha's eyes were on the road. She was guiding the driver to her hostel. Turning to me, she said, 'Don't you know anything of what's been happening? I thought you'd know this at least.'

'Know what?'

'Maya and Sobhaan didn't get married.'

'What do you mean?'

'Maya has decided not to marry. She's moved into my hostel.'

'What are you saying?'

Zulekha laughed out loud.

'Tell me the truth.'

'This is the truth.'

'Maya stays at your hostel?'

'She not only stays there, she's also joined our organization.'

'Your organization?'

'Yes. Bold Girls. It's only for girls, girls for girls, that's the ideology. I know you'll like it. I had thought of giving you a surprise at the hostel, but the cat's out of the bag.'

'Why didn't Maya get married? I had heard she was desperate to marry.'

'Yes, she was.'

'Did Suranjan stop her? He didn't want them to get married?'

'No, not at all. Suranjan had agreed, but Maya refused. She wouldn't get married under any circumstances. She told me,

Sobhaan is a fine man, but after the wedding he'll become my husband, and then he'll do all the things that men do when they become husbands. If I marry him, I'll have to go through the same pain that his wife does now.'

'But he loved her...'

'Eventually, Maya didn't feel it was love. She felt it was a transaction. These are the things you will give me, and these are the things I will give you in return.'

'There are always expectations, that doesn't make them preconditions.'

'Maybe there were other reasons too...'

'What reasons? That Sobhaan is a Muslim?'

Zulekha shook her head vehemently. 'That wasn't a factor at all. She *pretended* to be a Muslim-hater. Actually, she views everyone equally.'

'How strange.'

'Why should it be strange?'

I didn't answer. Zulekha took me to her hostel room, it was small, but she had done it up according to her taste. There were two flowerpots on the windowsill, some posters on the wall, a bedspread from Santiniketan.

'Lovely, quite the woman's world.'

'Yes, isn't it?'

Photographs of the members of Bold Girls were stuck on the walls, some large, some small. Zulekha pointed out the photograph of her roommate Mayur. Maya's too. Maya with the large eyes, the sweetest of smiles, you wanted to love her right away.

'Why has Maya moved to the hostel?' I was curious. 'She has a home to stay in, her mother's. And the children, where are they?'

Zulekha said Maya went to see her mother at least once a week. Her children were in boarding school; she visited them there from time to time. She had wanted their father to look after them, but he had refused. She considered herself much more independent now that she was living in the hostel.

'But how much longer will she stay here?'

'If her salary goes up, she might move into a flat. There was some problem in her office when she took a few days off to settle the children in their boarding school. Apparently, the company made deductions from her salary. Bold Girls has sent them a letter, we informed the media too. Things are quiet now.'

Zulekha was speaking animatedly. She was looking beautiful without the make-up. There was a time when I didn't use make-up either, I had given it all up. I began doing up my face when I fell in love, but once I gave it up, I couldn't stand a trace of it on myself. I felt it commodified women. But even an uncompromising rationalist like me does some illogical things. I like using a light lipstick and wearing a necklace – not for men, but because I like it. There are so many things to wear, people use natural objects like flowers to dress up in many parts of the world, why should I accept it if patriarchal society tries to suppress women by dictating how they will dress?

Zulekha was talking. Some people can talk continuously, it's a skill. If I'm asked to speak, I dry up after two lines. Zulekha was telling me about the other achievements of Bold Girls.

'Why Bold Girls, why not Bold People?' I asked without context.

Zulekha was flustered. After some thought, she said, 'Is it a bad name? Should we change it?'

'No, it's fine, what's in a name? You're doing great work, that's what matters.'

Now, Zulekha made her proposal. 'Bubu, we've decided you will act as adviser.'

'But why? What advice can I give you? What you're doing yourselves is fantastic, in fact I have a great deal to learn from you. I'll attend your meetings now and then, to listen to you. These experiences must be shared. Please don't create a hierarchy here, don't let anyone be superior or inferior. Give everyone the same opportunity, the same importance.'

Zulekha was fired by enthusiasm. This wasn't the Zulekha I had known, she was much more spontaneous, much less complicated, beautiful. There was great determination in the way she walked and spoke. Where did a woman find so much strength in this city? Zulekha was a complete wonder to me. Suddenly, I wanted to know the truth of Zulekha's rape, had it really happened?

Zulekha smiled. 'That's a surprise. You've resurrected the rape like a dead man from a grave. I don't think about it, bubu. I used to be raped every day after getting married. One man used to rape me every day, many men raped me one day. What's the difference, tell me?'

'Why didn't you file a case?'

'Against whom, my husband?' Zulekha was laughing. 'You're surprised. What's the point of filing a case? There's no use filing a case against those other rapists either. They would have been exonerated, and the lawyer would have taken both my money and my body. That's how it goes. You're young, you've been raped, is there a lawyer who won't try something with you?'

I sat there dumbfounded, unsure of what I should say. Zulekha continued as spiritedly as before, 'Your social stratum is quite high. You have no idea how we have to live on the lower levels. Your reality and our reality are different.'

'You think they're so very different?'

'I do.'

'Who were they? Who are the people who raped you?'

This time, Zulekha laughed even louder. 'Why do you want to know? What good will it do you to know? What will you do once you know?'

'Nothing.'

'What's the point of knowing if you won't do anything?'

'Not everything has to have a point. One can be curious about some things. I just want to know. Who raped you?'

'No one you know.'

'Was Suranjan involved?'

'He says he was. So far as I know, he wasn't.'

'Are you telling the truth or shielding him?'

'Why should I try to shield him?'

'Because you have feelings for him.'

'Do I really?'

'I think you do. But ask yourself.'

Zulekha laughed again. This only increased my curiosity. 'Who were they?'

'A man named Amjad. My husband had borrowed two lakh rupees from him and hadn't returned it. It was probably revenge.'

'Don't be mysterious. Was Suranjan there?'

'Amjad was a friend of his. Who knows, maybe he was there.'

'Why can't you be clear, what do you mean "maybe"? Either he was or he wasn't. Simple enough.'

'Can it really be so simple?'

'Speak clearly, Zulekha.'

'I'm not being unclear. It's not important who they were. Those who had the opportunity were there, those who didn't, weren't. Anyone who had the opportunity would have raped me.'

'Was it Hindus who raped you? Because you're a Muslim?'

'They raped me because I'm a woman. If Hindus could take revenge for Mohabbat's sins, so could Muslims. Neither Muslims nor Hindus would hold back from raping Mohabbat's wife to extract revenge. The clash is between men; but for vengeance they use women. It's true not just in India, it happens everywhere in the world.'

'Why were you silent?'

'Who says I was silent? I had a roaring affair with one of the rapists.'

'So you're saying Suranjan raped you, but you're also saying it wasn't him, it was Amjad and his companions.'

'I'm saying it because he says he was part of that group.'

'Why should you believe him? There's no proof.'

'Why does he say it then?'

'I don't know. To shield Amjad, perhaps.'

'I don't know whom he wants to shield. And besides…'

'Besides?'

'He can be called a rapist even if he didn't rape me.'

'Why? Why should he be branded a criminal without committing a crime?'

'Why should he not be a rapist? You wrote in *Lajja* he raped a woman named Shamima.'

I lapsed into silence, not knowing how to respond to this.

'When a prostitute is raped, no one calls it a rape. Just as no one calls it a rape when a husband rapes his wife. These two forms of rape are not counted as rape. You counted it. That's why I salute you.'

I wasn't expecting this. She continued, 'You asked why I was silent, why I didn't file a case against the rapists, why I didn't have them jailed. You might be wondering why I indulged them, especially Suranjan, by letting them go free. Yes, I did. Because Suranjan was the best of the lot. He said he protected me from getting raped further. He showed a lot of sympathy because he was repentant. Men do not usually have any sympathy for women.'

'Is this sympathy worth anything at all?'

'It appears not to have any value now because the relationship has ended; it would have been different otherwise. But I am grateful to whoever those people were who raped me, because without that rape, I would not have found release from my rotten marriage.'

'Somehow I cannot believe Suranjan could have done something like this.' I sighed.

'I cannot believe it either. I was blindfolded. Leave alone Suranjan, I didn't see any of them. Suranjan says he was there, I don't know why he says so, I don't know whom he's trying to protect, whose crime he is claiming as his own. I only know about Amjad, I heard his voice myself. But whether it was Amjad and his friends or Suranjan and his friends, the fact is that it happened. Still, it's in the past now, and I don't care. I will never want to know who they were, I will never go to court against them. Mohabbat had enough money to fight a case, but he didn't care either. Perhaps he thought to himself, she's been raped, so what, rape her ten times more now.'

'If educated women like you don't protest, who will?'

'Never mind all that. The rape came as a huge boon. My life wouldn't have been turned upside down without it. You cannot do whatever you want to until society has put you down as tainted in its books. No one lets you do as you please otherwise. I could sleep with Suranjan so easily in his house, he himself wouldn't have accepted it if not for the gang rape incident. But then because I got raped, I got into the relationship with Suranjan and came to know what lovemaking is, or else I'd never have found out.'

I had spoken to many women, but none of them had said something so horrifying as freely as Zulekha had.

'I don't quite understand Suranjan. I had heard he was going to the Ballygunge Lakes regularly. I used to worry he'd kill himself.'

'Why on earth will he kill himself? Suranjan loves life; he enjoys this uncertain, chaotic existence. What a wonderful reason he gave for dumping me – that he was not worthy of me.'

'But that means he respects you.'

'It means he respects himself. He feels like a noble person, a great soul, someone making sacrifices for others. It's nothing but acting.'

I couldn't quite understand how something like a gang rape could take place in this city without anyone coming to know or talking about it, without it appearing in the media, without anyone going to court, without anyone knowing who the culprits were, without a word from those who knew what had happened. I was startled by what Zulekha had said and the way she had said it, I admired it too. Her determination was strong now, but she had scaled such a high peak that I was worried she could be blown off it by a mere gust of wind. If Zulekha was where she was today because of her anger against a particular individual or group of people, it would only need the anger to evaporate for her to melt. She would no longer be the woman of steel she was now. You had to be tempered endlessly by fire to become steel. But I could not accept her view of Suranjan. If he had owned up to the rape, it was to shield Amjad and his friends. I had no independence to mould Suranjan's character the way I wanted to; he was the creator of his own character. For some reason, I began to think that the entire incident of the gang rape was made up, nothing like that had actually taken place, only Suranjan and Zulekha had told each other that it had happened. In course of thinking about it, making up the details, and talking about them, they had both begun to believe it was real. And then again, it occurred to me that only those with psychological problems had such delusions, but I would certainly not place Suranjan and Zulekha in this category. Was the whole thing a mistake? Whose mistake? I was lost in a fog of confusion.

'The Maya I knew,' Zulekha said, 'has changed completely. But I would be wrong if I imagined she has forgiven her Muslim fundamentalist rapists from Dhaka. She is against all rapists and all misogynists, irrespective of religion. But then,' she continued with a smile, 'she also believes all men of all religions are the same.'

'How did she come to this realization so quickly? Just the other day, she was desperate to get married.'

'The madder they are, the quicker they come to their senses.'

'Is that so?'

'Absolutely.'

'I don't think so. Those who have blind faith don't see reason easily. If you're blind, you can't see things clearly. Those who are besotted by the idea of marriage and family are unlikely to lose their infatuation unless they get a severe shock of some kind.'

'Maya's had plenty of shocks, bubu. She told me the story of her life, night after night, you don't know most of it. I'm thinking of making her my roommate once Mayur leaves.'

'Aren't any of you going to get married?'

'You live alone yourself. Why are you advising others to get married, why don't you tell us to be single too?'

'You can manage on your salary as long as you're in a hostel. But can you afford your own place?'

Zulekha made tea for both of us. She had all the arrangements in her room. 'In that case, we'll live together.'

'What do you mean?'

'I mean we'll take a flat together, some of us.'

'Like the communes of the sixties?'

'What's that?'

'In the age of the hippies, men and women would live in communes in Europe and America. They'd rent a house or flat together. Something like that?'

'No, not like that.' Stirring sugar into her tea, Zulekha handed me biscuits from a jar.

'No biscuits for me.'

Zulekha took a bite of her own biscuit. 'No men in our commune.'

My tea spilled as I laughed. 'Are you a man-hater?'

'What's this you're saying? If we allow a man to live with us, he will fuck all of us.'

'The opposite could also happen.'

'What do you mean?'

'All of you can fuck him.'

Zulekha rolled over laughing. 'We'll fuck him to death.'

'Everyone will say you're shameless.'

'Let them.'

I was supposed to have had a cup of tea with Zulekha. I stayed for four cups. I met Maya too. I held her tight in my arms. From her, I got the warmth I had wanted from Suranjan and Kiranmayee. I couldn't stay long enough for their 8 p.m. meeting, but promised to be there the following week. Maya and Zulekha would come to my house soon. I was thinking of taking them to Digha – I hadn't been somewhere far away in a long time. I think my body was overgrown with fungus.

Taslima Nasreen is a secular humanist, a human rights activist, and a prolific and bestselling author, who has faced multiple fatwas calling for her death. She was forced to leave Bangladesh by the government in the mid-1990s and has lived in exile since then. She now lives in New Delhi.

Taslima is the author of over forty works of fiction and non-fiction in Bengali, which have been published in over thirty languages worldwide.

Arunava Sinha translates classic, modern and contemporary Bengali fiction, non-fiction and poetry from India and Bangladesh into English. More than fifty of his translations have been published so far in India, ten in the UK, and six in the US. He teaches translation and creative writing at Ashoka University in India, and edits the Library of Bangladesh series of translated books from Bangladesh. He has won several translation awards.